The shela directive

by Les W Kuzyk

Our Near Future
https://0urnearfuture.wordpress.com/

Other Novels

Pinatubo II
The Sandbox Theory

Climate Fiction Anthology

Climate Spirit

The shela directive

Les W Kuzyk

For my daughter's future

I want to thank my wife Dragana for her direct insights and experience growing up in Yugoslavia as the country transformed into Serbia and my daughter Lana's feedback on character names. Also, for their combined patience during the writing process. I also want to pay tribute to the IFWA and Salty Quills aspiring and accomplished writers for their support and reviews. I would specifically like to express my appreciation for those pursuing avenues of social justice and want to thank any decision making system promoting female participation and appreciation for the feminine.

But the anima has a positive aspect as well. It is she who communicates the images of the unconscious to the conscious mind, and that is what I chiefly valued her for. For decades I always turned to the anima when I felt that my emotional behavior was disturbed, and that something had been constellated in the unconscious. I would then ask the anima: "Now what are you up to? What do you see? I should like to know." After some resistance she regularly produced an image. As soon as the image was there, the unrest or the sense of oppression vanished. The whole energy of these emotions was transformed into interest in and curiosity about the image. I would speak with the anima about the images she communicated to me, for I had to try to understand them as best I could...

Carl Jung,
Memories, Dreams and Reflections

Evening, June 27
to
Morning, July 11
2029

The shela directive

Chapter 1

Monday Evening, July 2—late shift

The infrared screen beeps a possible anomaly.

Jeira falls back behind the Bullet as it picks up speed, glancing at her flight plan, then scanning the incidents list. The tracks are bare, the midnight train now arching its back as the ramp touches ground. Zoomed imagery reveals one—no several yellow blips down on a dead-end street. She runs a quick location analysis with a recent persons count. There's been some congregating, though sporadic. Something else catches her eye, two yellows at an odd angle. Maybe that's the situation auto-inspect noticed.

She banks away from the tracks and circles for a new perspective. Two figures appear to be climbing the ramp framework; they have somehow gotten past the barricades, and they must be fifty feet up.

"Ground, hey Martine, you copy?"

"Copy that, Jeira. What's up?"

"We have a couple subjects way up the structural grid on the Bullet line west."

"Okay Jeira…yeah, I see them. Wow, they are playing with danger."

"Any suggestions?"

"Well, technically it's public right-of-way property, but they are putting themselves at risk. Warn them off. Politely."

"Okay, Marti."

She switches on the left floodlight, rotating the beam to illuminate the pair.

"This is the Urban Police Air Surveillance. Proceed back down to the ground immediately." She watches the camera screen, catching glimpses of them in the lattice shadows, one with a flickering flashlight. A glint flashes off the other's face, maybe from glasses, and he raises a single finger salute her way. "I repeat, make your way down. Now!" She hears her own deep authoritative tones reverberating back from the metal beams. Politely…oh well. They start to descend, and she dims the left flood, spreading it out to help them see their way down.

The fanned light beam illuminates the larger gathering at the street end. The others, who maybe dared these two to first go up and then spurred them on. Looks like a street party, or maybe those who live every night out around the burning barrels. The pair drops off the last steel beam, met with high-fives from their companions. She adjusts the scan camera for a better view. Is Joshua down there, could he be learning something? Could this be more than just socializing?

One group gathers around what looks like remote control gadgets—antennas sticking out everywhere. Models, too tiny to show any infrared heat signal.

"Marti, what do you make of this?"

"I checked. We have no vandalism reports on these ramps, other than graffiti. Minus explosives, they can't actually damage concrete and steel—they can only express whatever they have on their minds."

"So, maybe a party, but I am not so sure. Like some young energy out mingling with the city men. What do you say, Marti, do we call in a ground unit?"

"I dunno, Jeira, I'm checking priorities." A second of silence. "So no ground, record an incident, code Open."

A buzzing noise builds; penetrating Jeira's ear through the helihover glass, and then her eye catches movement. A tiny night-blue Firefly comes zipping across the front of her bubble-shield. She stares—it's almost a reflection of her unit set to miniature looking out from a plasma mirror. Looking back to screen, she zooms in down on the ground, and she finds a thin teenage figure, control box in hand, antennae pointing up at her. Maximum zoom brings in jiggling images of a grin, an up-from-the-streets laugh of challenge at authority. She backs away, hovering higher.

The tiny Firefly has banked straight away from her bubble, now weaving a flight line through the steel girders to disappear behind the ramp. Certainly her helihover couldn't follow. The sign of a good pilot; that is some impressive flying. The tiny craft appears as a dot on the other side, ascending straight up.

She looks for the street name, frowning as nothing shows. She gazes back down. Talent amidst the anonymous crowd. *You just have to find it and help it blossom,* Josh always says. Maybe he is down there; she fine adjusts resolution enhancement, thinking scan face to face, but they are too distant now. Her brother's kind of classroom, nevertheless, where the lessons never end.

A flash startles her, and she focuses close again. The shock shifts her vision to slow motion…and she watches as the little Firefly nose impacts her bubble. The miniature splinters into a myriad of night-blue plexon pieces, exploding off in all directions. The tiny heavier electromag drive penetrates the shatter, then rebounds straight back to puncture through a soft capsule. Her eyes widen as the capsule implodes into a grasping splatter, dripping an oozing purple liquid across the plexon. She feels her heart pound, then her throat constrict—the choking gloved hands—she struggles to restrain blind panic, all in a split second. She takes a deep breath, forcing her mind to focus on procedure: recall standard surface-to-air response. The scene comes back to real time speed and she becomes aware of Martine's voice speaking loudly through her com-phone.

"Jeira. Jeira! What's your status? Talk to me girl."

"That little shit...Marti; you're not going to believe this!"

"Is your helihover stable?"

"Minimal damage, Marti. No explosives. Just my visual field is restricted."

"Status report, girl. Give it to me."

Martine lists off the mandatory checks as Jeira answers. They are not yet finished, when Jeira's eyes ascertain more.

"Wait, Marti. That liquid, it's expanding."

"What?"

"Sort of turning to a froth."

"Return to base, Jeira. We finish the damage report on the way."

Jeira glowers, staring hard at the nameless street below. She swoops down and zooms in close. The young man may be in trouble with his companions, but at the same time, he is laughing wildly.

She fingers her control stick and selects evacuate-home.

As they continue with the damage report, Jeira becomes aware of a slight odor in the cockpit. What now? She accelerates, but no matter what the flight speed, the smell does not dissipate, instead building in pungency. She picks evacuate-emergency—to maximize speed. By the time she locks into traction, she is breathing through her sleeve, arm wrapped over her nose. A slight throat irritation has set in, and then building, transformed to a harsh cough.

Tear gas similar, what else can she guess? Inhaling, she holds her breath while she dons the emergency oxygen mask. With sleeve over face, she docks the helihover half blind. As the cockpit opens, she pushes upward but by the time she has squeezed under the edge of the rising bubble and scrambled out to stumble down the stairs, her eyes are a streaming veil of tears.

Chapter 2

Five Days Earlier

Wednesday Evening, June 27

The two make their way softly around the corner, looking as far as they can both ways up and down the shadowy street. Across and to the left, a brick warehouse stands tall beside a parking lot, occupied only by two bent, rusted SUVs tilted away from each other; smashed glass headlights staring blindly outward.

"Check that out." Josh points. The local spray-can artist has decorated the warehouse wall in huge black lettering edged with dark-neon rainbow. The curvy-sharp script reads *Wire the Wealthy*, like a graphic artist's advert.

Krino nods.

A well-lit door like a clubhouse entrance stands out from the dimness. The illusion of distance almost says another painting on the red brick background, this one at street level. But there are people moving.

"Looks like the place," Josh says as they pause for a moment. "We are now eight hundred and twelve feet and closing on the coordinates she gave. Random location H7."

"Grio's Grab, the sign say," his companion shrugs, cocking his jaw sideways. "We could be there, man."

They turn down the sidewalk towards the door, a canine whining softly and looking back to check that they follow. Under a flickering streetlight, they pass an electrobike chained to a rusty post alongside an old ICE bike on its lockdown plate. The motorbike starts, the lockdown flips up and a middle-aged man in black leather, a headband above dark-colored glasses and a white ponytail, walks up beside the cracked leather seat. He swings his leg over in front to mount and motors the bike off down the street, leaving a broken trail of blue-tinged exhaust and staccato crackling thunder as he shifts through the gears.

"He be one genuine hippy angel from hell, man—a real throw back. Like a recessionary gene. You know what those hippies from way back then was sayin'…make some love, not any war."

"Yeah, I've heard that flower child phrase—make love, not war, wasn't it?" Josh glances sideways at Krino. "That does sound like an expression someone like you would notice."

"Makes some perfect sense, my man. Like Pan panicus, who go by the common talk name of bonobo."

"Bonobo? Is that another wild animal from one of your bio classes? Or are you just creating this one in your mind?"

"There may be some version of a Creator, but I personally am not capable of creating any life form. The bonobo is an ape species, very close to Pan Troglodytes, everyday talk name of common chimpanzee. Biology may not be on your interests list, my friend, but you *have* heard of the chimpanzee. Those bonobos, first known as pygmy chimps, were mistaken for common chimps in the early times."

"So I know of the chimpanzee. And?"

"That's what they do, bonobos. They make love, not war. Clear alternative biological evidence of what humans could be doing. Humans, you hear me? Now I know that species interests you. We are of the same biological family as bonobos; that being Hominidae. So we need to be learning from these bio brothers of ours, dude. But we tend to pattern our behavior much more like the common chimpanzee. Much more aggressive, much more military."

"Now you're really full of it. Monkeys do not go to war."

"Sure as shit do! And I told you apes, not monkeys." Krino looks around. "But chimp conflict is one long story and we almost there. We gotta talk on this one some other time."

"Yeah, right. Hey, are we still on Red Blades' turf, Krino?"

"Naw. Here neutral, dawg. She smart to pick this place. We come outta Blades turf a ways back."

"This location was randomly selected from a group of over a hundred possibilities," Josh says. "She stays on top of things, doesn't she? Neutral and fairly obscure. I have a feeling this one's gonna be more than just another lame get together." He glances at his companion. "What's with the brothers talk? You trying to be black tonight or something?"

"Hey, Josh, I'm nervous. You say random location, well that means I did not know some of the streets we was on, shit, look at Zaca. See those long back-of-the-neck hairs. Fur's still up. That is one clear sign of survival instinct stimulation. A mammalian high alert response."

"She was sensing something for sure…but what could we do? We had to just keep going. Anyway, we're here."

They step from the curb to cross the street.

"Hey, I got me some colored blood."

"Right, you're what ten percent Afro? One of your grandparents was half black. Three days in the sun gets me as dark as you."

"Eleven point six percent on my genetics card…and check the gist of this dreadlock curl, dawg. I got plenty more color than your pure white ass."

"All color, all culture, all cool." Josh recalls one of Asha's flash posters. "Anyways, back on Blades' turf, we weren't a challenge. We have no gang affiliation. We're all cool, so we should be fine going back, too."

"No way, man. We gonna find us a different way back, that is one thing for sure." He swats the dog's curled tail from behind, poofing the hanging hair. "Hey, Zaca. We coming, girl."

As they approach the stairs under an awning, a slim woman with rippling ebony hair steps from a ZipCab. Krino swings the heavy door opened for her and Joshua. "Thank you so much, sir." Her luminous eyes sparkle under dark lashes, and fuchsia streaks flow through her curls piled high. From the left, the early beat of Grio's nightclub booms out a greeting to the coming evening.

Joshua glances at his tc mini screen. "This way," he heads to the right. The woman seems to be tagging along, her dangling earrings glittering.

"We being followed, man." Krino winks, glancing back. "Nice."

"One of these doors…directions make it this one." Joshua stops at the third entrance, a solid metal door set deep in the wall.

Krino grabs the doorknob, stepping back and holding it opened again for the woman. “Beauty before the sub-species,” he beams. Her smile radiates with her eyes. They enter a large room, chairs set in rows around in almost a full circle facing the centre, and the faded smell of industry. Another music, not at all that of Grio’s, taps out a distinct beat. People sit around waiting, some talking in subdued tones.

“This is one fine place…and not the only nice thing here.” Krino glances towards the woman again. “Man, I was hearing these very same tunes earlier today. You know those are U2 vibes from way back.”

“Welcome, gentlemen,” the woman faces them. “I suspect you are in the correct location. If you recognize the music, that would be a positive indicator.”

“Yes, positively,” Krino winks. Then, feigning serious, he asks, “But how do we know who all is in this room? We was walking through one bad hood.”

“Oh, on top of the random location selection, we’re utilizing numerous layers of security, I can assure you of that,” she says with slightly creased brows. “My name is Lana. I’m helping coordinate this event. If you can seat yourselves,” she says, giving them her own wink along with a mysterious smile. “We will begin shortly.”

“Now I’m extra glad we come,” Krino says. He follows Lana’s figure from behind, as she walks over to an Asian woman.

“I know her from somewhere,” says Joshua, stirred by the long forgotten. More than just the eyes or the smile…was it something she had said? He pushes the thought to back of mind, as he usually does with such things.

“Well, tell me all about that place, brother,” says Krino, grinning. “’Cause I wants to know all about her.”

“Yeah,” he says slowly. “Sure.”

They wander around the outside edge of the chair circle, as more and more people file in. Finding seats on the far side, they sit to wait. Zaca curls up patiently under Krino’s seat, her tail hair covering her nose. As they settle in, they notice most swaying with the beat.

“You heard these tunes today?”

"Yeah, those songs was coming in on my tc."

"Interesting. Mine, too."

"Hey, Josh, that's Eli just walked in."

"Looks a lot more brother than you," says Joshua. "You know him?"

"He was banging with the Blades when he was younger. But I hear he got wired in with the Angeles now. You know, Los Angeles del la Calle."

"Right…they do gang intervention and things like that," says Joshua. "You ever face-to-face shake hands with Eli, or you just know him online?"

"I know the man. He come to college one year…I knew him then. When I start my third year Biology, he starts first year in I don't know what…then the chop backs. You know, back then."

"That's a few years ago. Anything more recent?"

"I don't know, yeah," Krino thinks. "Some shela group, I would say."

Joshua glances around the room, up at the partly finished brick walls and the high windows on one side. Many pairs of shoes point this way and that on at the broken linoleum floor; flavors of footwear speaking of owners. His mind wanders, and that woman's voice from the past now speaks somehow familiar. Could Lana be someone from Virtual, one of his own shela groups or even a real encounter? Something about her stirs a memory…somehow maybe connected with his hunch about this gathering. This one's going to have some real consequence. He gets distracted by another face.

"Hey, Krino, there's what's-his-name—John something. You remember him?"

"The old guy? Yeah, dude, just a couple months back. When shela had us over in the good old Flats, on friendly turf. Zaca was not so nervous taking us to that one."

"He actually has a regular job, remember? For the City. He talked about lifestyle analysis or something like that—he's an analyst, or no, not that, he does analysis messaging, that's it. He was pretty frustrated with a few things…hey, are they starting?" The crowd murmur quiets with the music. They look towards the middle.

Lana has moved with her Asian associate to the circle centre. The Asian woman carries a portable Virtual and some kind of device carrier. She sets the Virtual on the floor, sitting cross-legged beside. She pulls out her tc, expanding a Liquid Crystal screen to full and begins giving gesture commands.

Lana turns to face the crowd and the music fades to a whisper. Most notice and hush down even more.

"So welcome to everyone who made the effort to attend this evening's event; I realize it was something of a short notice call. I believe it is safe to presume most of you have been present at one or two of our previous sessions."

She holds her hand up and many in the audience respond in common.

"It would also be reasonable to assume your expectation of further disclosure tonight. You all know shela in some form or other. She has organized this event, and she's decided at this point to offer an action proposal. For those of you who qualify, of course. With this in mind, Xia here will be setting us up for shela in Virtual."

The lights dim as Lana speaks. Xia focuses on screen, gesturing with one hand and the other on a warm-touch pad. A three dimensional scene forms as a soft glow, and a woman gradually takes shape, slowly raising her head to look up at everyone. She appears average to Joshua…extraordinarily average. He stares, and realizes she has appeared as many women at the same time, a shifting pattern, an endless series of female forms and faces.

"Mother7," says Joshua softly. "So shela's going to speak through her."

"Say what?" says Krino.

"She's the latest Wise Feminine avatar…just appeared as an upgrade a few months ago. Still developing in Virtual. As part of the Mother voice series, she speaks for a lot of women…what they each can't say on their own."

"Females. Yeah, man. They are the nicer side of the human species. Like I was telling you, we got bonobos for comparable species evidence."

"Yeah, you gotta tell me more on that…later."

"Good evening," the glowing female image speaks in a multidimensional voice. "We have invited each of you here tonight for a special reason. We know all of you to some degree, and we will know more about each of you in a very short time. Welcome. As you are here, you may well fit in as an active participant with this proposal."

She looks around the room, directly into the eyes of each one there. Joshua can feel her penetrating gaze as her eyes shift from the darkest chocolate through hazel to ocean-green, then a mountain-river-blue, all in a glance, like they can probe his inner channels. Or those of anyone. Zaca whines softly under Krino's chair.

"A special greeting to start. If anyone here has infiltration in mind, we want to welcome you, too. We love you all as our children. Congratulations on getting this far. Even if your intent is mischief, we encourage you to check within—seek the truth. Open up. You may yet be helpful to us and us to you."

Her look exudes earthly warmth, her smile universal.

"Tonight we wish to speak to a scene recorded live yesterday. And we want to log your reactions." She pauses for a moment. "So to assist with our picking up your inner perceptions, we will ask each of you, before we start, to switch your telecell to VirtuALL. We are going to ask you for a reverse feed. We will simply be recording your standard emotional and cognitive tracks to enhance our profiles on each of you. This will help us to best fit you to tasks we will be assigning. If you are walking free tonight, Xia is now handing out a box of wrist pickups. So a few moments to set up."

The Asian woman walks about with the device carrier. Krino watches as a woman rises, checking the time, making comment to those beside her and finds her way to the door. One guy from the other side and two more close to Josh and Krino also rise and quickly follow. Many look around at each other, as they watch the door close behind the ones leaving.

Back in the centre, another three-dimensional scene begins to glow softly as the Mother7 avatar shimmers over to one side and fades to half brightness. A Limousine Hummer V Patriot first forms in the new scene, the vehicle parked in front of the steps of a large downtown hotel. A chauffeur in dark uniform sits waiting in the driver's seat while the dimmer image of another man can be made out sitting in the backseat obscured by dark glass windows. After the scene forms, it stands in a frozen gleam as the crowd finishes connecting to their devices. At the moment when Xia gives a thumbs up signal on the links, Mother7 brightens again and goes on.

"We want you to look for and contemplate on some of the options you will see now in this situation with distinct social action potential. To keep things straightforward, we are asking you to please try to notice three alternative responses used by those challenging the social status quo."

Mother 7 fades, while the dark Hummer in front of the hotel again becomes the highlight. The scene rolls in real time as an attendant in a gold trimmed uniform opens the back door of the Patriot. A man walks briskly down the steps of the hotel towards the opened door, ready to step in to join the other backseat passenger. His dark tailor-made suit, bulging slightly at the seams, sharply highlights his white hair and flushed face. A City News interviewer dogs him with a sound device and a persistent look.

"Mr. Knomley, could we have just another moment of your time, sir?"

"If you could be brief," he turns back to face the newsman, glancing at his wrist. "I do have another pressing appointment."

Behind the black Patriot, several city men can be noticed emerging into the picture, edging their way closer to the vehicle. Clearly men who live around burning barrels, and up against razor wire fences. Neither his driver, the other man in the backseat nor Mr. Knomley seem to be aware.

"Mr. Knomley, a question about your FFT standing. If you are aware, sir, you were profiled on Fortune Five Thousand webshow last night and FFT has now placed you in the highest wealth and income cohort. For the entire country, sir, you rate right in with the top twenty. Do you have any comments on your recent gains, sir?"

"Yes, well, corporate reports do look good this quarter. Demand is up and we are meeting that demand. Our conglomerations help people get the lifestyle choices and financial services they need, and we do proclaim good asset management."

"Mr. Knomley, are you familiar with the FFT slogan? Sharing is Daring, and Daring is Us. The FFT Mag and webcast are both focusing on your Daring Profile, compared with the other nineteen in your bracket. They say your Daring Profile is not keeping pace with your personal and family wealth and income gains. Do you. Mr. Knomley, consider yourself to be a Daring man?"

"I do appreciate your candor. Now, in whatever context you prefer to define philanthropy, I can assure you my family contributes handsomely. To our church, to our community, and please don't forget, our corporations create employment for many, many people; something the media enterprises you are referring to do not take into account."

As the interview goes on, the city men have been circling around behind the Patriot. The driver, sitting patiently, suddenly notices them in a rear-view mirror, his eyes widen with concern and his head swivels over his shoulder to look back.

"Sir, our sources inform us the Crystal Church responds almost entirely to the needs of the Citadel Hill community, such as the maintenance and security budgets of the church. Does your family or your church ever consider the greater community, or the greater city or the idea of society as a whole?"

Mr. Knomley gestures upward with one hand, his attaché case hanging in the other. "Every Sunday as a Christian I put a considerable contribution in the collection, I can assure you of that. Our church has its own board of directors who are responsible for the church budget. I could mention one or two major benevolent activities we are involved in…"

One of the city men standing on a brick ledge beside the Patriot has reached down, and staring with a burning look of loathing, silently begun urinating on the vehicle hood. Another man half-lifts a brick patterned like the hotel flowerbeds, while an arm behind holds the brick hand back. A third walks resolutely around the others, hand reaching deep within the front side of this long coat. As Knomley continues his self-appraisal, two more step up on the ledge to form a group urination, the shiny waxed Patriot shedding the yellow fluid from its black paint as it would spring rain.

The driver sitting in the front seat is now desperately trying to attract his boss's attention.

As the yellow liquid splatters off the front of the Patriot to form expanding dark puddles on the stone drive, the city man with his hand still deep inside his coat has pushed his way around the others; intent it seems on adding red to the color. As he is about to reach his target, the brick smashes into the windshield. Knomley turns abruptly to take it all in, his eyes narrowing as his face twists into a scowl. He pushes his way through, quickly sliding in beside the other man in the backseat, slamming shut the back door of the Patriot. The chauffeur accelerates rapidly from the hotel front entrance drive.

Editors cut the video clip from the hotel and switch back to commentators in the studio. A panel of pundits are gathered around, one sitting in person at a table and two more appearing on wall screens.

The City News anchor speaks directly to the FFT rep on one wall screen. The rep points with a laser light at an image of an entitled Mr. Patrick Wayne Knomley, profiling on a graph his historical wealth and income, both recent and long term.

"FFT, can you describe for us what we are looking at?"

"Well, if you follow the red line on our recent history graph, it shows a definite boon exceeding Patrick Knomley's regular gains over the last two years including gains in his personal assets. Then, looking here over the last few months, an even further increase moves him up into the top twenty."

"Can you describe what the green line indicates for us?"

"Here at FFT, the green line is the Daring line, where sharing anything counts. For Mr. Knomley, we do see a slight increase coinciding with his boon. Now Green includes any giving, including to one's own family."

"And the yellow line along the bottom?"

"That is Mr. Knomley's Golden Glow line. Our FFT sources analyze charitable causes for their benefit to society as a whole, to all of us, according to our classification index of *meaningful* causes. Sharing is Daring, but some Daring shines like Gold."

"And Mr. Knomley's Golden Glow line appears to run almost straight across."

"Yes, what FFT refers to as a flat line. Pretty much Daring dead."

"Thank you, FFT."

The large Virtual scene freezes again, then dims out while Mother7 moves back to the centre and brightens. "So…what we are proposing tonight is action—action directed towards this iconic social situation and what it represents. We believe we the people, not just the city men from this video clip, are increasingly dissatisfied with the status quo. The popularity of FFT has risen, especially recently. So we propose a focus of that popularity into an action plan."

"Yeah, I wouldn't mind pissing all over Knomley's Hummer," says Krino, his chuckle mixed with distain. "Or maybe all over his nicely suited leg. That's how canines mark territory and I wouldn't mind marking off a little of his turf. We used to have public transit. Now I buy my KnomCor tickets to get on his KnomCor train."

"Yes," Joshua muses. "KnomCor, and all their latest tax exemptions." He feels his fingers twitch when he thinks of the brick, not just that, but even more when he imagines the hidden weapon never completely revealed.

"Who was that dude in the backseat?"

Joshua shrugs. "Not sure…"

"Now," Mother7 goes on. "We know most of you have been accessing our databases at your own levels of interest…we have been tracking your activity. We know each of you has special interests and special talents, all lending a hand to our common advantage. So in our action plans list, we want to include each of you in ways that best fit."

She gazes around, into the back corners of the room, of each mind.

"As you likely know, education can be a key factor, both for the *toorich* as well as for us. So, we propose an exchange, a barter offer. We hope they see their own advantage in what we offer, although that is yet to be seen. We propose they finance our formal educational programs in a trade for our informal education of them. Our question to all of you is: what educational materials and, much more importantly, what real life learning experiences will we be offering them?" She looks around the room.

"Would me pissing on Knomley's leg teach him anything?"

"That would be lesson two after pissing on his car," Joshua looks at Krino, calming his clenched fingers as much as he can.

"I would just have to get up close enough."

"Listen, she's talking again."

"...creation of awareness has always brought about the greatest progress. And it is deeply held traditional beliefs that we see as the greatest barrier to re-educate. Three methods here should have caught your attention."

She raises three fingers.

"Personal violence, destruction of property and then there is social shaming. Humanity has a long track record on the first two, but this last method remains somewhat lost in the shuffle, usually associated with simpler cultures. We want to modify our cultural beliefs, to shoot for a reformed basis of understanding. So our task at this time will be to decide on a method. Through consensus, if possible."

"What? We gonna vote now?"

"Women have a more cooperative way," Joshua says. "They have the ability to talk it through until they all agree. Consensus, man."

"You need to hear me talk more on bonobos...and you know, I got this other source too, this study named *The Hominid Within*. A little further along the evolutionary track than apes."

"Hey, the more human the better, but listen..."

"So please consider these options mentally as well as in your hearts; that is emotionally and cognitively. We thank you so much for coming tonight." Mother7 starts to slow, then fades into a woman who is all women, patiently waiting.

Lana moves back to centre. "Okay, people, thank you for your inner track feeds; we'll use this data to update your profiles. Each of you will be given access to a secure com channel, and many of you will be assigned a task or two over the next few days. Then those of us who continue to fit in suitably will reconvene. We'll contact you. Thank you for coming, thank you for participating."

The lights gradually come back to full brightness flooding the room and the U2 tunes increase in volume to fill in the audio background.

"Now I know where she's from," says Joshua.

"Who, shela? Mother7?" Krino frowns.

"Yes, kind of, no…Lana. She colored her hair or something, but those eyes, anyway she gave a one-night lecture in this eight-week crash course I took; The History of Revolution. She's one of the originals; she had an online site going way back when. You remember, the Asha #tags and pages that were around, how they came together to form Shared Holistic Equity Leveraging Alliance. You know, SHELA...shela."

"No shit. She's got brains," Krino says, scratching the dog's ears. "Just like you, Zaca."

The crowd is rising, looking around at each other, cautiously. People start filtering out the back door and the front.

"We gotta find another way home," Krino reminds Joshua.

"Yes sir, let's have a look."

Josh uncrumples his full LC screen, gesturing out a city streets map. Their location shows as a calmly flashing glow. He touches their home neighborhood and a shortest distance possible route appears. He sketches in a rough no go boundary with his finger, looking to Krino to confirm, and the route adjusts to avoid the area.

"Hey, I got a message here. Looks like I have my task already." Josh reads for a moment. "I have to look up a couple guys downtown, go have a talk with them. Kind of like interviews."

"Now that's something on your interests list."

"Yes, so cool. Looks like they're both older fellows and this is some sort of a wisdom search…I'm to gather information about their earlier life experiences and find out what we can add to our database. You should check yours."

Krino reads his own tc on mini screen. "Flowers? I check out seasonal availability, growing conditions for these certain species. Aristolochia, some Stapelias…there's a list." He shakes his head. "Man, what is this about?"

"There has to be a rational reason." Josh grins. "Shela may be warm and fuzzy in some ways, but she can also be very efficient, very effective."

"True. It just don't seem all that obvious at this particular moment what that rational reason might be."

They find their way out the front door, backtracking along the hallway and then down the front steps. Joshua starts to whistle as they follow the dog down the street. A shimmer of excitement inside of him won't stop growing. Maybe this time they'll reach something like the proverbial critical mass, or at least some kind of real step in that direction. When he listened to Knomley, he did feel his fingers clench. But when the city men pissed all over the Patriot, like a team acting in unison, he not only heard a euphoric internal giggle, he really did feel like breaking out into a loud hands-over-the-head cheer.

Chapter 3

Early Thursday Morning, June 28

His eyes shoot open, his body trembling in a cold, sticky sweat. As always. His blurry eyes strain for a view of the promised above, yet instead come to focus on the reality of painted steel pipes snaking across the high ceiling. Just as his own disjointed fibers of conscience intertwine to weave the fabric of his reneged existence. The submissive, the rageful, the apathetic.

"Oh God, please help me." He barely hears his own voice, a voice that veers sharply back on itself, transforming into a snarl…"You bastard Creator. Why me? You lame fuck!"

Oh, whatever. Who cares, who gives the slightest shit. "I should have taken myself out," he growls. "If I only had the courage," he whispers.

The threads of his being now separate from the cloth, winding tightly around themselves into blocks of clay as on a weathered embankment, tumbling broken away from their once higher position, each struggling for new identity among those in the fallen heap. Yet how can a lump of wet earth in such a mound realize the slightest aspect of itself?

He wants to scream for as long as he can, as he has in the past, to be lost and yet somehow free in extreme decibels.

But his ears perk and he listens instead.

The building creaks a hollow groan, reverberating murmurs sidling up the elevator shaft from the corners of lower floors. Creaks coming in with signals of a storyline outside his own, perhaps of the greater plan. The grand plan that makes sense to someone or something out there in the great universe.

He doesn't move, counting his breaths as they ever so gradually slow to an almost normal pace. Disgust wracks his being. Find a clock; *what time is it,* his subconscious habit demands. For what purpose, he argues back. He can sense, as has been the case for such a long time now, that it's the night's hollow middle, when any half normal person would be in their deeper moments of peaceful slumber.

He slowly rolls over in the cot, feeling for the edges of his small world. He eases himself up to a sitting position with his arms behind for support and then, bit by bit, swings his legs over the side. Now squeezing his eyes tightly closed, he reaches up to pull away the little crystals of half-dried tears coating his lashes. Behind closed eyelids he hides for a second, but then forces them open just a slit to peek out. Through the blur over on the table, the bottle looms, waiting patiently alongside the flask of water and the loaf of bread. He carefully wipes his arm across his forehead, then across his eyes, and he stops, holding it there. He can picture the layout and he takes a bottomless breath.

Then from deep down in the morass, the rage springs forth to engulf him, driving him to lunge for the liquor. Clenching the bottle around the neck, he violently twists the cap off, whipping it back behind him. Shivers wrack him as a smile creeps onto his face. But, as he draws the welcoming release to his lips, the other side of his mind screams an unbelievably even louder warning, and he groans. Wrath now surges out from his being's center in all directions with full force and he hurtles the bottle in a first-born's angry howling fit up against the brick wall. He watches in slow motion as the vessel shatters into a million shards, leaving behind a dripping splatter and the endless sonatas of tinkling glass.

The scream tucks tail in retreat to its more familiar lair, underground and deep inside, reverberating back and forth in the confines of his hollow heart until numbness settles in. For who would hear him anyway, he laughs. Who ever has? His head tumbles in slow motion down into his hands to come to a final rest in a deep quivering sigh.

After a moment he peeks again through his fingers and his mind gradually remembers. His hand trembles as he cautiously reaches out to grasp the cross, pressing it softly to his lips, then crushing it in fervor to his chest. *I'm so sorry, please forgive me.* He rocks himself, the infant within, humming, embracing his being into a mantric rhythm. Righteous thoughts, breath in, all fear, breath out. The pace takes him over, encouraging the moment once again to pass. Acceptance. The four noble truths. The way.

A rat scurries in the corner. Rank bitterness in his mouth dissipates at a snail's pace, making its way from under his tongue and dissolving off into nothingness.

The rhythmic breathing, the focus, gradually they gather up tiny pieces of serenity. Respite, always temporary, never to be trusted to stay. He rises. Trapped, caged, like a bird that has never flown free, yet instinctively longing for the rush of air beneath its wings. Agonizing for release. He walks resolutely over to the window, lifting the pane, seeking a breath of the dreamed of fresh outside. The air is foul, but at least cool. Now with the window open, the disturbing music from across the way forces an entrance. He glances down. A group of the intoxicated shout at each other far below, staggering about in an unsteady cadence with and against the beat.

A more familiar thought comes flashing to mind. Maybe, just maybe, now he can step right out, right now and crash down through their laughter to end it all on the broken concrete. Creation of a blood stain on the street, a final mark. There is creation and then there are adjustments along the way; de-creation if you like, the elimination of elements that didn't work out so well in their design. If, well, if only…he sighs. That oh so foolish promise, that antiquated code of honor.

He thinks back to that time earlier in the evening. How easy it was to find the place. How strange, after living in this very spot for six weary months, there it was directly across the dark street. He gazes down at the electrobikes parked around the entrance. The last stragglers to leave Grio's Grab. They will stay later tomorrow with the weekend's arrival. Oh, that he could be one of them. Footloose and at least some version of free.

He shakes his head. Back to his own reality. His VirtuALL feed track would have been such a ridiculous mess. They'll see right through him, of course, but that is why shela took the reading. That is her security measure. He pictures the man outside the Patriot and the other one inside, the ones she used to illustrate, and shudders at the turmoil they would have read in his track at that moment. The man who sat at the head of the dinner table, on those odd occasions when he ate at home, the man who had such influence or lack thereof on his formative years. The stories of struggle, out there in the competitive world of business, the methods necessary to bring nuclear source power to the heroic top, what it took to bring the misguided solar companies, the devious wind co-ops, the misdirected geothermal plants to their knees. The long drawn out war of competition. His progenitor, his father.

He had tried to please his father. He had tried to think and act like him, to be a good son in his father's eyes. But once in a while, he had seen the depths of nervousness and even fear in those eyes, and in those moments he just wanted to reach out to put his hand on his father's shoulder, to comfort him in his fear and weakness. At other times he suspected his father was simply putting on an act, an ages-worn stage show to please those in his own past. That deep within him there was another father, a kind and gentle soul. But those moments were always fleeting, for the drive to compete, the ingrained need to win had long ago covered that other insider option. The well-dressed businessman, quite adept at facing the questioning people with answers, persecuted by those left behind, but well protected on his own forward-looking path. If only…but neither could he be his father nor ever would his father be the one he may have been. All this together and its lifelong influence added to the confusion of the tumultuous pattern that shela would now be trying to interpret.

They'll never pick me…I'll be weeded out right off the top. Why does it have to bother me anyway? Why couldn't I be more like Paul? Paul who stayed safely in the backseat while the city men pissed on and then smashed the Patriot.

There had been some good times between him and his brother, that was true. Removing speed controls from carts at the golf course, careening in and out of the trees to harass the gentlemen players, and of course his own ventures down by the river where Paul would never go. Later, he made an honest effort to be just like his brother, picking out a sports car, and following him to the neighborhood gel tub parties. Then that damn on-the-road-to-Damascus moment. Why him? Why couldn't the redirecting epiphany have happened to his brother who has the name and disposition to match the miracle of that other long ago Paul? He pestered his brother time after time; didn't you ever feel like this? What? Like what? You're on something, you little shit.

The closest his brother Paul ever came to Damascus was sneaking into the Crystal Church to pilfer from the collection—just for fun he said as he surely didn't need the money. Even more fun was sneaking girls in through the back, and hearing their wine giggles under the nighttime altar. One screamed, he boasted once, like she was being touched down on by the All-powerful. Perhaps more truthfully by the weight of Paul on her no longer consenting body.

His eyes fog over and he shudders.

Okay. Think. When shela showed the city men, he did truly feel compassion for them, he could recognize their plight. But his father's tone immediately cut in with its calm logical edge. His father's voice simply stepped past them, they with their hands out, they are, after all, simply beggars. *For Christ's sakes.* Look, my policy is to supply anyone with a job, get yourself a good education and come see one of my managers. That is what I can give you. Opportunity, in this land of the same. In the Crystal Church the minister's approval lay with the blessed, and those who have, certainly have been blessed. We have our status because it is the will of God; we are the ones He smiles upon. Like the Jewish tradition backed Jesus, so the Hindu tradition backed Buddha and in Buddha's old testament, the city men have bad Karma, they are paying for their past. But Buddha walked away from the blessing of wealth and sat under a tree for four years. Shit. His VirtuALL track would be nothing but a jumble. Like his life.

He clutches the crucifix, staring through its crystal facets at the yin yang symbol floating at the crux. Jesus and Buddha joined; east and west bound forever together, heaven and nirvana as one. As they talked about in the SonofmaNirvana gatherings, the best of both can be had. Bringing completion through double closure. They would meet in the Christian church basement, three times a week. Paul came once, and left halfway through with an excuse of a remembered need, never to return. Paul fit in so much better with the regular Sunday morning services, where he could smile unruffled, perhaps recalling his own middle of the night attendance. Forgiven.

For some reason Staphan has been chosen to pay their common brotherly debt. Why no longer matters. To sleep in peace again someday has such appeal. There must be a way to bypass the suffering, certainly that is what Buddha teaches, and Jesus in his own way too. The will of God, known through meditation, to accept circumstances as they are, yet do what He requests. Crucifixion just does not have that much appeal. All that blood, and hanging up in the air in excruciating pain—waiting to die with nothing to do but pray. Now that carries shela's shaming method a little too far. Hopefully, something like that won't be necessary. But whatever can be done about Paul? With that question he definitely needs help.

Oh, that shela would invite him to the next meeting. She just has to. He'll do whatever it takes. He presses the cross to his lips again. If they give him a cross to bear, well, he can carry it…for a while. Up the hill at least, but not the hanging from nails thing with crows eating out his eyes. *God.* To find release from the wrack of guilt, to someday hear the inner bell ring the tones of tranquility.

Easing the window down, he turns back to the cot and table. He spots his cushion and settles himself to sit. Folding his legs carefully into lotus position, he breaths in, breaths out, gradually starting to hum the Ohum mantra. For as long as it takes.

Chapter 4

Early Friday Morning, June 29

He feels the insistent pull of the EyeD, and turns his eyes submissively towards the glow hole. A KnomCor rep speaks directly to Joshua, addressing him by name from a wall screen, assuring him with a persuasive voice how high tech ID scanners, newly available in economy Bullet Train stations, add a layer of security for his personal benefit. He grimaces. Those ahead shuffle forward through the last turnstile, then carefully spread out on the station platform to await their designated portion of the train. The only way he can pass through Citadel Hill is in economy fair, in the back section.

Josh glances about at these people of the city scattered across the concrete floor. A heart-felt vision settles in, one that comes over him from time to time, and he becomes a shepherd out in a grassy pasture looking over his flock. The fierce sheep dog instinct, one he bounces around in his mind never having decided whether it comes as his blessing or his curse; a drive that at times has him gnashing his teeth, having yet to sink them deep in the wolf's throat. And the other feelings, they surely have nothing to do with a dog's instinct, maybe some other predisposition, maybe what he was born to know. He feels the slight tremble in his lip as his fingers twitch. He focuses, on the floor and his tasks for the day.

This time of morning, the people look like those on their way to work—and by their dress, at whatever menial jobs remain in the inner city. As regular commuters, they would have monthly train access passes—regular contributions to KnomCor's ledgers from their meagre incomes. Last night, he had filled out his online special pass application. Shela forwarded the street addresses of his interview clients, older fellows with experiential data still missing from the databases. He truthfully selected *Project Research* as his reason for travel, less truthfully a destination of downtown library. He received initial clearance—pending EyeD confirmation of entry within forty-eight hours. With his clean record he did gain access. He heaves a troubled sigh of contentment, rubbing a finger over the imagined worn handle of his staff, waiting patiently with his flock.

The Bullet glides in to the station, decelerating rapidly, silently, most window shields blackened on the front section as it passes. But not all. One car offers a clear view of the more adventurous, a diner car with a waiter in proper attire serving elegant tables with some chic morning fare. Executive officers, administrators in formal dress, maybe from another walled hill or perhaps a country estate. Joshua's eyes narrow. The rear cars' doors open and he resolutely falls in behind his crowd. The seats fill fast, and he grabs the overhead rail. A young man smiles and gestures as he stands to give up his seat for an elder. Once in a while there are encouraging signs.

Last night's meeting song begins resonating in his head—*one love*—and a string of other tunes crowd in, tapping out their beat. Like back in the trailer; Mom had that album on DVD, and for her it was classic. While he and his sister played, his mother filled the trailer with the beat of that old rock and roll rhythm. And her other songs too. *All the world may live as one,* didn't those lyrics lose their spot as her fave that year? To the songs of *One.* After she found out Bono had been 2005 Time person of the year, she wouldn't stop telling him that was the same year he was born. I know that, Mom. And then the same guy caught media attention on a Time person anniversary, the year Mom first saw him perform on stage. That concert somehow brushed her heart with even more of a secret stroke than the old Lennon songs. The year Senator Asha started appearing at the Dome, buying tickets for anyone who couldn't from a fund source that had the corporations fuming.

"How was the concert, mom?" Jiera had asked one of her mature questions the next day. Must have been a Saturday, 'cause they were all at home.

"Really great." Mom became excited. "Fantastic, actually. They've posted all the songs, so I'll burn discs and you kids can listen."

"Hey Mom, I wouldn't mind going some time." Joshua recalls his quivering voice, struggling to mimic his sister. "Sounds like a place for really cool people." He thought a little and gathered courage. "So what kind of liberal politics does Senator Asha follow?"

And when mom took the time to explain to Josh what the song lyrics were actually saying, that's when his first reaction came. At first his lower lip would tremble, uncontrollably, especially when he was alone, often late at night. He has better control now. At other times his fists clenched so tightly he would later see finger nail marks deep in his palms. Those reactions had followed along with him, ever since.

At times his mother would kneel to give him a hug, helping diffuse the burning within. "Be patient, Josh. When you get older you can do what you need to." She showed him some times how to beat his fists into a pillow, to let it all out. A way of expressing anger, from one of her self-help books. When he finished beating the pillow, exhausted and crying, she would hold him in her arms for a while, stroking his hair and talking about what else she found out specifically about him. Extra sensitive children, the character traits they tend to have, how he matched quite closely, how it was all okay to be that way, in fact, quite important to be so.

Those concert discs took over the trailer for more than a year, and *imagine* lyrics dropped back to once in a while. Gradually, the 'do it' zest of her new stage heroes won out completely. And the concerts melded into part of the campaign the next spring when Senator Asha was winning primaries and caucuses. During those months, mom became almost ecstatic, her life seemed filled with meaning like her dream come true. Bono's rifts on making poverty history, not only overseas as before, but right here and now at home, took a sky-high ride on the back of Asha's gaining popularity. The Senator's campaign promised to bring the ideals to political truth. *When it's one need in the night,* he listens to the memories, glancing around the train car. *Sisters, brothers,* he hums, keeping his lip at a slight tremble, his fingers though tense, never allowed to clench.

Reality hits hard as the Bullet Train's mag-field reverses to clear the wall. The scan tube does a complete warm body count;

this one double checked he knows by human eyes at consoles with special attention paid to the rear cars. Inside the wall, there isn't a single piece of litter blowing in the streets of Citadel. Like being transported into a whole new but untouchable world. Joshua looks out the window at the fine trimmed lawns, the manicured gardens, the pristine streetscapes. Just hard to see Asha or Bono's *one* spanning the two sides of this wall, let alone anybody *carrying each other*.

The Bullet mag-locks at Citadel Station, across from the Crystal Cross that pokes skyward. A few in the car sleep now, some listen to morning music through earphones, others engage their worlds through telecell screens while others connect via voice. Joshua pulls his own tc, selecting Krino.

"Wat'sup."

"Hey Krino, you sure do look like a man with a focus." Joshua views his friend's face on mini screen. "We're stopped right now on the hill." He searches to have an effect on the expression he sees. "And hey, I was thinking about stepping off to grab a cup of java."

"Yeah, you just do that man." His friend looks up. "Like you gonna blast the door off with your belt pack full of plastic boom boom."

"Hey, don't talk that way. Humor or not, that's trouble."

"Yeah."

"So how's your task coming along—you finding anything out about those flowers?"

"You never get a bouquet of these from any regular flower place. Even a plant and garden store only carries one or two of these species. Take this bloom, listen, common name of Carrion Flower. That's one for sure you'd never send for Mother's day. They got some real babes working in the flower shops, but they sure don't get turned on when I bring up this shit."

"You have women imprinted across your mind."

"Ha, ha. Hey, like I say women are some nice people. More docile, nicer than the male gender. That's the general trend in most species. I was telling you about bonobos."

"Right. And monkeys that go to war—like give me a break."

"Not monkeys, dude, apes. Listen up. Chimpanzees live in social groups called troops and each of those troops has a territory. Now the common chimpanzees are also patriarchal, you know, male dominated. So a few male chimps in one troop will get themselves some sticks and head off into another troop's turf looking for the owners. When they find them, they sneak up on them, and if they can, they single out and corner a male. Then they beat him to death and claim a piece of the new turf for their own. That's their way of expanding territory. That don't sound like war to you?"

"Yeah, okay." Josh sighs. "I have to admit, that does sound like a military campaign."

"Now take the pygmy chimps, the bonobos. They also live in troops. They also have territory of their own bordering on the next troop's turf. But there is one big difference between them and common chimps. They are not patriarchal, in fact, they may even be matriarchal. Female bonobos form serious bonds and stick together so as not to allow males to dominate. So the nicer gender for sure has a louder voice, at least an equal voice. And, they do not go to war like common chimps and one could easily argue that comes about as a result of their gender equality. Just so happens, they also have one of the highest rates of sexual activity of any mammal. So you tell me that doesn't translate into make love not war."

"I think you took biology just to analyze your over extended sex drive."

"Look man, females are nicer creatures. Nicer that you or me."

"Right," Josh says. He'd had a fling or two, but never for long. "So how about those flowers? Like what's next?"

"Ongoing research as we speak, Josh. Looks like I gotta go alternative source to find out more. Doesn't really make sense, man, I don't know yet."

"Be careful, bud."

Josh stuffs his tc back in his pocket.

He watches those in the front getting off for a casual break on the Hill. Getting off is not an option for this back section; the doors remain sealed. Except through the transition car, and who would want all that special clearance hassle for a coffee. He glances out the plexon at the extensive platform, the uni-directional view keeping the insides conveniently out of sight for those out there. He notices two uniformed men leaning on their cyan motorbikes, Citadel Security emblazoned on machine and shoulder.

Then his eye catches a young man dressed in unique black and white, maybe his age, making his way through the crowd with symbols on a shirt clashing. A black Christian half-cross on the white side opposes an identical white half-cross on the black side. Some interesting thought group he supposes. Then in that distant face, Josh senses a glimmer of recognition. He stares, tracking the guy's movement, watching as the fellow joins the only other one entering the transition car. He can't see him well, but there's something about that face, maybe the way he walks…why does his sister come to mind, maybe back a few years, could it be?

He'll have to talk to Jeira, ask her, and catch up on how she's doing. He keeps forgetting.

The mag-track charges, locks release and the train pulls ahead towards the bridge. Joshua anticipates the city core, a place where the mix of faces turns into a flock of multi wool tinges. On these streets, the crash of Asha's programs leaps out like night and day. Cultural walls, like the physical one around the hill, glare out on a micro scale, standing rock solid and stretched up to the sky between two people standing on the same sidewalk. *Not the same* those lyrics so pronounced, with inches between. The train slips across the bridge built for a larger river, high above the trickle of flowing surface water, and glides into the underground station—South Downtown. The car opens, and he follows the designated exit path, seeing front section people through steel bars as they mount a separate set of stairs to surface.

Leaving an EyeD record at his exit point, he follows the crowd up a staircase to their street access. He finds a nutritional vendor's stall and orders a Pro-Tein Burger with a bonus NewsClip chip. Click releasing his earphone from his telecell, his slips it behind his ear and clips the news chip into the tc. He selects people highlights, searching for the latest FFT report. As he listens in, he bites deep into the burger, glancing at street signs to get oriented. He knows it's a few blocks to the old residential tower he needs to visit first.

He walks by a scattering of men lying up against a brick wall, some lucky enough to have thermal sheets to keep out the morning cold. The well-dressed walk briskly by, making their way to whatever positions they hold in the office towers. He passes by a concrete wall, reading the graffiti. A list of names like the Veterans Memorial in DC; those killed not overseas but right here in neighborhood skirmishes.

Getting close, he stops to sit at a bench and uncrumples, checking coordinates on the screen map. Up the street, then a left turn. Not far now. Salvo, that's the guy's name. An older fellow, one who's never walked connected so he can't give him a call. He wonders how shela makes contact with these people walking free. If the guy's not at home, he'll just have to ask around.

At the building he pushes the ring button. Somewhat surprised, he gets buzzed in right away without a voice response. Like the guy doesn't care who enters or not. Or maybe he is expecting Joshua. Could shela be that well connected he wonders in the elevator up.

"Hallo," a smiling little old man unchains the apartment door.

"Good morning sir, my name is Joshua. If there is any chance you have a minute, I was hoping we could chat…that I could ask you a few questions. Shela sent me."

"*Si*, yes, of course. *Entre*, please come in. I am Salvo." He grasps Josh's hand for an extended firm handshake, looking directly into his eyes. "She told me you would come visit today. Please, please, have a seat."

His hand released, Josh walks into the place, decorated simply and with a trace in the air of an adobe hut somewhere in Latin America's past. A baby cries behind a makeshift wooden door, and cotton clothing hangs drying on lines strung wall to wall. The old fellow invites him to a wooden chair in what could be a kitchen, a room closed in by hanging sheets.

"Coffee?"

"Yeah, sure."

The old fellow pours a cup from a strong smelling pot.

"I am guessing you speak Spanish." Josh sips at the coffee. "Can I ask you where you are from?"

"Yes, I am from the south. I live here with my daughter now from time to time. My name is Salvo Jesus Artavia. I was born in El Salvador; but I live for some years now in Cuba." He grins broadly, bowing. "At your service."

Josh holds up his tc, setting to record audio. Salvo meets his eye, nodding.

"Ah, this makes sense. I am to ask you as much as you are willing to tell about adjustments among people in the past. What you may have experienced...there were lots of disruptions in El Salvador over the years. Am I right? Were you involved?"

"I live in Salvador for many years. What would you like to know?"

Josh looks into the weathered eyes, sensing a trust. "Well, okay, say any kind of social change that makes life better for people. How about you talk and I listen."

"In Salvador, ah, we struggle for such a long time. Social can be political, no? The struggle for power. From before my time, and unfortunately still today."

"My one professor—she gave us a lecture on the revolutions in Central America in the twentieth century. Quite a struggle…"

Josh sets his coffee cup on the table.

"In Salvador, for sure yes, there were many revolutions. First independence, then the Fourteen Families—the ones who owned the *fincas*, then the army and the death squads." Salvo shakes his head. "Farabundo Marti led the *campesinos* in La Matanza, the massacre of one hundred years ago. Much later, when I was a young man, my brother died in El Mozote massacre and I joined the group with Marti's name, the FMLN. We led our own assault on *la capital,* that was 1989. Then the army killed the priests. So much killing, so much blood."

"History shows a lot, teaches lessons."

"*Quizas*, perhaps," the old guy says, glancing at Josh. "For those who are willing to learn."

"Things improved in El Salvador, did they not? I mean eventually."

Josh sips his coffee, watching the air blow the sheets.

Salvo smiles wistfully. "*Los ricos*, they do not want to let go. They want to stay rich…they want to keep all. You have to take from them; they never want to give. For every family to have land, the big owners have to give up some. Mostly, it never happened. Mostly, the *campesinos* move to the city. A new struggle begins there." He sighs. "Today, Salvador can still only attain associate membership in the ULA, *la Union de Latino America*."

Josh nods. "Any stories stand out on the best way to make change?" He needs focus on topic. "Anything you think most important to tell me."

"You have a little Marti in your eyes." Josh feels Salvo's penetrating look. "Yes, I can tell stories. Myself, I attended special school at that time. In Bogotá for six months. The top school; they teach on conversion by any means available. The biggest lesson was, if you want to influence *los ricos*, you have to control something important to them. You have to make them notice. When we came out of the mountains in 1989, we shoot and kill many—they notice that. Their lives are very important to them. But they react too, they shoot back. They struggle hard to keep their riches. They taught us one special lesson in Bogotá, how to make trade with them for their children. We borrow their children, and we return them for a share of their wealth. Again, they react. Guards, razor wire fences around schools. Many guns."

Josh pushes his tc closer to Salvo.

"Nothing works better? Is there always violence?"

"You know what, there is one story I like to tell to those who might understand." The old man speaks softly, looking intently at Josh. "Yes, maybe you would. Okay, one time, there were some children and their families refuse to pay or maybe they cannot pay for some reason. Who knows why?" He shrugs. "So these children live with one of our families for quite some time. Maybe two years or so. They become part of that family. They learn what it is to live in a hut, to work hard for the landlord every day, to go hungry sometimes. Two years is a good time. Then something happens. For some reason, their families change their minds or they find the money or something. But, they are too late." He smiles. "For by then, these children are no longer ignorant. They had this chance to grow wise. They have experience of what it is really like." He shrugs again. "That is the story. Aside from political change, like Castro's, that is the best way I think how. All those years ago, I believe taking the children to live in the huts is the best thing to do."

"They might call that kidnapping," says Joshua carefully. "Here and now, that's a felony."

"And the hunger, the poverty, that is not crime?"

"Yes, absolutely, that is crime, just not in the legal code." Josh nods, thinking of the talks he has had with his sister. "So education is a good way…to teach through experience. Unless you have a favorable political situation."

"If you have no political hero, what other options? At that time we shoot the landlord, but his son takes his place or his cousin or his nephew. Maybe you feel justice when you pull the trigger, but only for that moment. Nothing more changes. You can kidnap, as you say, the children, hold them for a return of money. But still they see you as the *campesino*, to be put back where you belong. You have no respect in their eyes. You have to invite them, strongly encourage them, to live with you, to see things through your eyes. In this way they learn to respect. A word of caution, some will see, but many, maybe most will remain forever blind."

Josh nods, swallowing the last gulp of coffee.

"You can look to the government, but look closely there. Who is in power, *los ricos* or *los pobres*. Castro was for *los pobres*, but that situation is not so common. At times you have a man or woman who is truly for the people. A champion. That is another way. From Cuba now, we work to include Salvador in *ULA*, but my home government is too tight with your country and that does not help."

"Anything else?" says Joshua. "You try anything else?"

"Back then, we tried everything we knew. Maybe not everything. Now, there are other ideas. Still, education is the way. You have to show *los ricos* their benefit, what is good for them in the change. Do they want a huge house, 10,000 hectares and five cars and to live each night behind the razor wire in fear of their children being borrowed tomorrow by *los desperados*." Salvo shrugs. "Or do they want only a nice house, maybe 200 hectares, one car and to sleep in peace with no wire. If they are wise, they know *los desperados* look at the big land, not the small. But they are people and wisdom does not come to all. Some must be shown, how you say, explicitly. In very plain language. Then, like I say, even if you show them clearly, many are not capable to see."

"Right. Well that is a lot of helpful information. Thank you Salvo." Josh comes to his feet, bracing for another extended handshake. "Hey there's a shela event soon. Maybe we'll see you there?"

"Yes, perhaps."

"I talk with another fellow now." Josh moves towards the door. "A man named Zijad."

"Ah, yes, Zijad." Salvo's face softens. "We have talked a time or two."

"Oh, you know him?"

"He talks too much," Salvo says smiling. "And his English is poor."

"Just a few blocks from here." Josh looks to his tc.

"*Lo siento*, I am sorry. I would show you the way. But I must stay…my grand-daughter and her baby."

"No problem. Shela gave me his address."

"Shela, yes, shela. She is a good woman."

"Right." Josh looks at him quizzically. "Well, anyway, I have to get moving. Thank you so much for your time."

Joshua closes the door behind him, his mind racing.

Chapter 5

Late Friday Morning, June 29

He makes his way down eight flights of stairs, tracking the shadowy alley's approach through the steel grate. Education. Salvo's wisdom confirming the shela outlook. Shela must be communicating with ones like Salvo in some way or other. The real question remains—what type of lesson in life teaches best? For those who would want to skip out on that class altogether or those who have no interest in learning anything new at all.

He pauses at the bottom step to get his bearings, and then turns down the alley towards the next street. He slows, squinting ahead towards the alley's end, carefully going over in his mind the frustration building in his heart over what he thinks he sees. As he walks closer, the scene beside the dumpster becomes ever clearer. A young mother huddled with her two children looks out from under their blanket in a cardboard packing crate. Joshua's heart slows, to a near stop, and in the long pause before the next beat, he hears their lifetimes' unfilled ring of hopeless echoes. His lip quivers violently, his fingers clamoring to form fists. How can this be? Right before everyone's eyes, so opposite of the way things should be. *Sisters, brothers*…the next beat finally comes. Blinking hard, biting his lip, he strains every nerve against his fingers' desires.

He approaches the family home as calmly as he can, squatting carefully down to their level, searching to see their view of the street and from their perspective their small world beyond.

"You know…" He coughs, voice cracking. "We are trying…" Her eyes flicker slightly as he speaks. "…to do something I mean. To make things different…" She looks up with a momentary glimmer, almost meeting his eyes, one corner of her mouth lifting up ever so slightly. With shaking hand, he passes her a full package of food vouchers and stands again to look away, lip spastic beneath his teeth.

Down the block, he has to talk to someone. Pulling his tc, he selects Krino.

"Wat'sup."

"Harsh down here, bud, just harsh." He sighs, wiping his sleeve across his eyes. "Women. It's just not fair."

"Yeah, you got that right."

"Single mothers especially…"

"Bonobos, Josh."

"This has *nothing* to do with sex, Krino, for Christ's sakes."

"Absolutely, Josh. All sexual activity aside, in a troop of bonobos, the females have at least equal voice with the males. That's the trick of it, man. That's what people need is to listen to women at least as much as men. That single mother needs to have a voice equal at least to the talk of the big man."

After a pause, Joshua sighs deeply. "Right."

"Everyone listened to Asha's voice; she was our first female President. And now we're following what shela says, so we on the right track, dawg."

"Just pisses me off. Hey, my first guy Salvo says Knomley needs to move down here; give him a couple years living the real life. With us."

"Yo, right. You just call him up and give him the invite. The man will jump at the chance no doubt about it."

"Yeah, well, how's the alternative source search?"

"You won't believe this, man. These species are catalogued in some very specialized places, a few in bioresearch, some for plastics technology, some even for tactical weaponry. Wild."

"Flowers? In plastics? As weapons? Like how?"

"Not sure, Josh. Listen, I read you this: 'Chemical compounds in biological species of many types can be used for the unexpected'…well, shela sure has us doing something and we still don't know what it is. That's a touch unexpected."

"True, hey, I have to find this next guy. I'm at his building now. I gotta see what else shela has going at my end."

"One more thing, dude. I come upon something else. We can make comparison with more than just apes now Josh; I was telling you about this bio-psych study on the hominid within. That would be within each and every one of us. Remember, we are ninety seven percent DNA-identical with chimps. But these guys are looking at that three percent, a tiny difference but one that makes all the difference. They got numbers like eighty five percent of what we think can be explained by how a Hominid would think."

"Hominid. Now just what is a hominid?"

"I am so glad you ask. We are of the genus homo, species sapiens and subspecies sapiens. But as modern humans developed, there were quite a few other species, hominids, larger brains than apes, apposing thumb, tool making, bipedal—that would be walking fully upright—not living in the trees so much anymore. Hominids. Our DNA developmental background."

"Krino, I'm at my next location."

"We will talk more, my man. Later."

Joshua walks up the sidewalk to the four story apartment. The building door is jammed open, so he doesn't need to buzz in. With no inside door either, he takes the stairs directly up, to the top floor where he finds his way to the apartment. As he knocks, he hears shuffling inside and he revels at his good luck with connecting with the free walking today. The door opens as far as a solid chain allows and an eye appears, peering down at him through the gap between door and frame.

"Good morning sir. My name is Joshua and I have been sent by shela to talk with you today. You know of shela?"

The eye traces him up and down, then disappears and he hears a series of other door locks snapping open along with the chain. The door swings back and the older fellow within steps back, waving Josh in, both eyes now sharpening to a focus on him. "Shela." The man nods carefully. "Please, yes, come."

Fully revealed, this man presents a tall and thin profile with a long nose pointing down and forward offset by those eyes, now surrounded by deep wrinkles and layers of horizontal lines leading up to a shock of greyish black hair flowing straight back. All underwritten by a sad quiet smile.

"Hello, so I am Joshua." He watches the wrinkled face closely. "I was just talking with another man named Salvo."

"Salvo, yes, Salvo." His head nods slightly, hands clasped. "Remarkable man," he says. "I am called Zijad"

The place holds a musty aroma, of age and sour cabbage.

"Salvo says you two talk at times."

"We are immigrants, both of us. He from Latin America, I from Eastern Europe."

"Well he just told me about his life's experiences in Latin America. All the social and political changes that went on. Now shela is suggesting we insist on some social change here. I've come to find out what you know, to hear your story, maybe some bit of wisdom, some truth you might have discovered."

The old fellow's sombre smile deepens. "Prophet may know truth; I know very little. I know most don't listen to Prophet. Politics can make change, but politics can easily be false. What you want to change? Politics here?" His smile picks up ever so slightly. "Or maybe peoples' nature?"

"At this stage, shela wants us to come up with some strategic alternatives. My task is to gather firsthand information, and shela sent me to talk to you. Actually, more to listen to you than talk. We are looking for options you may have been involved with. Like from your background, your experience with social change."

"Excellent research method. I talk; you guide me on topic. You want I tell my personal story?" His eyebrows rise.

"That would work." Joshua nods. Zijad motions towards chairs where they take seats across from each other. Josh places his tc on the small table between them.

"Yes, fine. As I say, I come from Europe in the east. My country is Yugoslavia. It was once country, but not for long time now." He signs, the smile fading. "My country is stable for long time after big war. With Tito we have socialism, good for everyone. Each person has job, each goes to seaside every year. But that is when I am child. Tito dies in 1980. As he is not inspired by God, he leaves no book, no Koran. Socialist ship begins to sink…too heavy with no strong captain. Now I am youth. Next years, I move from Brcko to Novi Sad, from one province to another. I attend university. I study people, most fascinating phenomena. Creature that studies itself, there is only one.

Anthropology is culture, the nature of people. And politics, how they organize. Koran is Allah's guidance.

"Then comes Slobodan. Now we have new captain. He is strong forceful person. The type who pushes his way through. He wants power and he knows how to make fear in others. How you say in English, to intimidate."

"Slobodan?" Joshua stretches his mind, attempting to recall European history.

"Milosovic…our new president. He wants I should be foreigner in my own country. I am Bosnian, living in Serbia. No more Yugoslavia. He wants my friends now be my enemies. Another way he finds to gain power. He makes people against each other, so then they need strong leader. Such as him. Provinces want to be nations. Nationalism. Slovenia goes peacefully, then Croatia not so peaceful. He makes war. For war, people need commander. Such as him.

"I attend University of Belgrade. I am still young. I meet others who do not like Slobodan. Why war, why killing? We talk late in the night, we search books for all we can find. Professor Gene Keenedge from your country—he outlines method. We can oppose Slobodan. He cancels local elections—ones he loses. So we take ballot boxes and walk from Novi Sad to Belgrade to bring truth."

Zijad mechanically, almost automatically, raises one hand as it forms into a clenched fist, like a long sleeping secret sign. "Otpor." He looks firmly at Joshua. "Resistance."

Josh leans forward, feeling his own fists wanting to form.

"Many years. War in Bosnia, war in Kosovo. We resist. Students, youth, any who will join. We must persist. Slobodan talks to people on television, his, how you say, propaganda machine. We bang pots in streets when he broadcasts. We refuse to listen, to be under gypsy spell. We are in streets of Belgrade day after day. In resistance we become like family."

"Family, really," Josh says.

"Yes. As family, we form line. But police form parallel line, many police, yes, we are police state. One in six is with police. Uniform police. Secret service police. Undercover police. Police everywhere. Many stories happen at this time. Some undercover police come, pretending to be with us. As spies. To make trouble for us. There is one with loud mouth on our side, more aggressive, and spies push him through police line so they can beat him. Another time we see one police take off uniform, cross to our side of line. People do these things."

"Right." Josh shuffles in the hard chair.

"Then one day, workers at Kolubara walk out. They strike. They ignore orders go back to work, they ignore police. Notice this one. Peoples' nature. Sometimes they not listen to instructions. People can be stubborn. Then year is 2000. October 5."

"An important day?"

"My friend call me on telephone that morning. Building in Belgrade is burning. I cannot talk I am so excited, so happy. Finally, today will be change. We know it. I and friends run to find someone with car. We go into city. Half million in streets of Beograd."

"Traffic must have been horrendous."

"No traffic problems. Streets are bare." Zijad pauses to reflect. "Many people stay home. Peoples' nature. Here we have two types of people. One stay home to be safe in his garden. Is he afraid or is he wise? Other is angry out in streets. Is he brave or is he wise? Perhaps third type would only laugh now." He falls silent, eyes glimmering.

"Go on…"

"People." Zijad starts to grin.

"Yes?"

"One man acts…you might call this one industrial psychology." Zijad smiles slyly now. "He bring bulldozer to break intimidation chain."

"What?" Joshua squints.

"Ljubisav drives bulldozer into Radio Television building. He does what all are afraid to do. He makes symbol of revolution. When intimidation chain is broken, others follow lead. Others break through police lines on foot. Fear is always problem. People of my country have two fears. They fear nothing change and maybe they die in one of Slobodan's wars. This fear builds into bubble. They also fear police in front of them. Right here right now fear. This fear makes into bubble too. When right here right now fear bubble is burst before eyes, all fear collapses. No more fear.

Fear of police, fear of Slobodan now vanishes. When one fear bubble bursts, all fear is gone. No guns fire. All police join us now, even they know they are part of bubble and they know bubble is burst."

"Wow," Josh says, stretching his legs out.

"Slobodan is finished," Zijad says. "Millennium gift. October 5, 2000. This is change, yes? But not enough." Zijad's eyes sadden again.

"But you got what you wanted, right?" Josh says. "I mean, Mr. Milosovic was out. You said you were happy, even excited."

"Yes." Zijad nods. "Maybe for one day. But tomorrow, we find we only change one man. Slobodan is gone but all others stay. Next day one neighbor wants to find Slobodan's house. He is very angry. He wants we beat Slobodan and his men. But political opposition calls for no violence. They make agreement—for their own benefit. People make agreements. Almost always for their own benefit. So change is small. You want real change; you need change more than one man. You need change many people."

"I am quite curious. How is it the police couldn't stay in control?"

"Ahh, yes. Like I say, the people lose all fear. Slobodan uses fear to control. Bulldozer breaks bubble. The next man, now inspired, runs up steps of Parliament, past police. He lead us through our own fear. Others see, they see flag in window. Power is broken. No fear, no power."

"No guns? No one dies?"

"Lots of guns. No one shoots. They call it Bulldozer Revolution. Next years, others follow. Color flower revolutions. Rose Revolution in Georgia, Orange Revolution in Ukraine, Tulip Revolution in Kyrgyzstan, more after."

"Flowers?" Joshua's mind quivers.

"They make change on politics. No Bullets. You want make some kind of change?"

"Shela is pointing us towards the hill. You know, where the huge houses are."

"Ahh." Zijad smiles sadly. "Muhammad, peace be upon him, warns the wealthy. *Announce a painful chastisement to those who hoard up gold and silver and do not spend it in God's way.*" He looks up at Josh. "Koran. But Koran says one thing; peoples' nature helps them do other thing."

"What are they supposed to do? The wealthy with their wealth? I mean what does Muhammad say?"

"He tells them do right thing. Say: In name of Allah, most Beneficent, most Merciful…righteousness is that one should give away wealth out of love for Him to needy, widows, orphans, beggars. Koran."

"There was this woman on my way here…living right out in the alley with her two little children."

"Yes. Peoples' nature is not listen to Allah."

"My friend tells me women need an equal voice. How can that woman have any voice? If human nature opposes what people are told to do?"

Josh leans forward to listen.

"Professor Gene Keenedge, he say break peoples' nature into pieces to get what you want. Many people not do what they are told. People are stubborn. This also is peoples' nature. If people don't listen to Slobodan, Slobodan lose power. Some are leaders; they break through police lines first. Professor Keenedge writes what is possible is proven by past. He writes of your situation too, he say you can make otpor for that one. For that woman you see. So use one piece of peoples' nature to oppose other piece."

"Otpor? Resistance against the big houses on the hill?"

Zijad smiles. "Why not?"

"Yes, why not. But your story doesn't sound like it was all easy. Any word of caution? Any warning for us?"

Zijad rises from the table, walking away, stretching. He turns back to Joshua. "Some people in power are good for people, no? Salvo talks of Fidel Castro who was poor but became president of Cuba, the native president of Bolivia, the bishop in Uruguay, the women presidents across Latin America. You had woman for president. Asha, yes?"

Joshua nods.

"Asha...name is Arabic, but not Koranic," Zijad says. "Means 'life'."

"Cool, never knew that," Josh says.

"Did she have people behind her? I know you have democracy, but Slobodan was elected president too. People vote for her, but maybe they have gypsy spell from television? Like Slobodan."

"She was pretty popular, there were polls, sort of independent. Maybe not among the big house people, but with most others. The *toorich* definitely are the minority, so they don't matter if you have one person one vote; she did have majority support. Of course the *toorich* use their money—lobbyists and advertising. But majority vote makes the ideal democracy tick."

Zijad shrugs, and then gives him a shrewd look.

"Now she is gone. Like Tito. Maybe that is risk, how you say in English, to put all eggs in one pail. All power with one person, can be weakness."

Joshua thinks of shela. *Oh shit.*

"If you have will of people, you have many leaders. One falls, but many step up to replace. That is strength. More difficulty to organize, but with common goal, is better. If your strength is in only one person or only a few, that is weakness."

Josh frowns. Shela's not one person, but certainly centralized.

"Those people with big houses are few, and all in one place." Zijad goes on. "Use their weakness to your advantage."

The *toorich* have a disadvantage too. Josh's expression softens.

"If people actually want something, that can be strength. Your people, but also theirs. Use your strength wisely. Use otpor against their weakness, but also, don't have same weakness."

Josh nods.

"So bring woman president back to life in some way, but keep her spread among many people. Will of people is power. Some say wisdom of women is good power, one we lost so long ago. Don't let me talk too much, but there were matriarchal civilizations in the past. Prehistoric Crete in Mediterranean, not far from Yugoslavia…Minoan women likely had equal voice."

"Really." Joshua's eyebrow rises. "But I mean if it's prehistoric, how would we know? I mean what the status of women was?"

"Archaeological records show many things even if there is no written testimony."

"What kind of record?"

"Anything made of stone or ceramic or metal. Anything that survives the forces of the elements helps tell the story."

"Yeah, okay, so how would we know from stone and pottery what women were saying? How can we tell if their voice was heard?"

"One might look at religion. Statues are commonly made of the venerated for most religions. Minoans made many statues of goddesses, but no gods."

"Yeah, I see, but does that give them an equal voice?"

"They have palace queens but no kings. They have all priestesses, but no priests. Mosaics show men and women both active in sports. Bull jumping. They grab horns of charging bull and flip over the head to land on their feet behind. Men and women both. All these things suggest equality."

"Right."

"There is evidence of no warfare. When you are at war, you have many weapons—this was Bronze Age so there would be metal weapons. And you build fortresses on hilltops where defence is good. All this shows in archaeological record. Minoan record shows no evidence of war. Suggests strong influence of women. Women do not do war."

"Like bonobos," Josh says softly.

"Pardon."

"My friend is a biologist…oh, I could never explain. Look, I've taken a lot of your time. I better go catch the Bullet."

Zijad smiles brightly. "You go. Build your strength. Use their weakness." He raises a clenched fist again. "Otpor."

Josh walks out the door into the old carpet air of the hallway.

"Otpor." He repeats, playfully descending alternating stair sets, twisting his foot on each step as a child with new thoughts. If shela were destroyed, that would be damaging. Maybe she is too localized. But she represents the minds of many women, the anima of many men too so maybe it's not really a problem. They can't let shela, their leader and organizer, be a risk. But if she's made of many minds, that would be low risk. He'll have to double check on shela's security; bring it up with someone technical.

He twists off the final bottom step, walks across the foyer to the unlocked glass and metal door, and he stops. That woman and her kids; what else he could tell her? Words can be worthless, stick with action he decides. Still, he whispers, 'we're coming'.

Joshua leaves the building, and turns left down the cracked sidewalk.

"Hey Josh," a voice calls from behind.

He spins around, wary. A man dressed in shirt, tie and loose suit jacket walks his way, hand held up in a friendly wave. Josh looks a little closer, and relaxes.

"Josh, right?" The man walks right up to him. "I'm John. You were across the room at the last shela meeting. I don't know if you noticed me there."

"Right, me and my friend did see you. How are you?"

"Not bad, not bad. Hey do you have a minute to talk? I can walk with you a few minutes whichever way you're going."

Josh looks at him.

"Yeah sure. I'm heading back to the Bullet station, then across the river. I'm just finishing up some of my shela tasks."

"Well hey, that's exactly what I wanted to talk with you about. I've been assigned a sort of task through shela as well and I tell you what, it's all about talking with you. You know she gave me a time and place to come looking for you and surprise, here you are. I am actually just on a late lunch break from work."

Josh nods. "Are you looking for info? 'Cause I'll be feeding my new research into the shela databases. If you have access."

"The opposite, actually Josh. My task is to feed even more info your way. More work for you, sorry about that. There are some helpful things I can tell you, it's just that I couldn't have shela sending you over to look me up. Sorry again, but it had to happen this way. It's this job I have, you know. Like on the one hand I'm officially a civic employee, but on the other hand I'm a citizen. So right now, I'm talking to you as a citizen. If we can keep everything low profile, shela promised it would work that way."

"Yeah, okay."

"Will you be at the next shela meeting Josh? Tomorrow afternoon. We could talk after the meeting if that works for you."

"Sure John, we can do that."

"Okay then." John appears relieved. "We know the meeting time and we should have the location by tomorrow. Four hour lead time, right?"

"Right."

John gives Josh a warm handshake and a beaming smile, before walking off.

Josh feels a coffee need set in, and he focuses on getting to the Bullet Train station.

Chapter 6

Saturday Afternoon, June 30

Josh looks over across the wide street. Some young boys are kicking a soccer ball around across in an empty lot where not another soul seems to be around. This would be the place. He reads the coordinates when they show as a blinking 'You are here' on the map screen—that blinker shows a location right across from the spot marked meeting. Except for the shouts of the boys as they play and the far off murmur of city noise, the place has an almost eerie quiet about it. He checks the hairs on the back of his furry companion's neck and finds nothing. Deserted is for sure good for a clandestine meeting, especially with this one in the pure daylight of the mid-afternoon.

"Cum'on, Zaca," he says. "Find Krino, where is Krino? You show the way, girl."

A side entrance leads into what may once have been the office space in this tall metallic industrial building and Zaca whines as he opens the heavy steel door for her. "After you girl." A string of popping neon tubes shine fragmented light along the dim interior hallway and the sound of voices drifts out of the shadows—suddenly escalating into heated tones for a brief moment and then ending abruptly. They walk towards the outburst, and just around the corner pass a man walking briskly their direction. He brushes past them, on his way back towards the door. Josh glances at his face under a shard of light—looks like one of those who stood up to leave the first meeting.

Further down the hall, the one standing at the entrance door, as if guarding the inner sanctuary, turns out to be one known.

"Eli my man." Josh attempts Krino talk. "Wat'sup?"

"Josh. How's it?" Eli's cool with it. "I saw you the other time. We gotta EyeD you. Gimme a look." He holds out the scan pod.

Josh hadn't known of Eli's solid build. "Yeah, you good. Go on in."

Josh steps into the room with the now familiar background music. He finds concentric circles of chairs in one corner of a large open space that drifts off into the distant echoes of a series of huge metal beams and girders running vertical and across. The outer rings of chairs are tiered above the inner, looking down to a large square concrete stepped pit that may once have been part of some industrial process. He spots Krino already sitting in one of the chairs, and makes his way over.

"Hey Krino. Not so easy to get into the room this time. She's tightening up…shela I mean."

"Hey dude, good to see you. Zaca! Come here, you little fur ball." Krino grabs the dog around the head and scratches her hard behind the ears. "Did you take good care of Josh? Did he behave?"

"I was checking her neck fur," Josh says. "Coming here."

"Dogs are the best companion people every found. First domesticated animal to just join right in with us. Pack oriented, just like our tribes, and a very high level of cooperative social skills. Much better than our skills of that type in fact, in more than one way. They easily adjust from Alpha to Beta and back again, depending on the social circumstances. We struggle with that who's in control issue a lot more, especially when it comes to giving it up."

"Yeah, really? Now I know why I love this dog so much. Hey Krino, did you notice? Looks like shela's going to change location every time we meet. This one is random B9, last one was H7. We're about half a mile from Grio's Grab as the crow flies." Josh looks down again to point at the map on the screen lying across his lap. "So did they eye scan our first domesticated critter?"

"Yeah, she gave Eli the look. She good." Krino puts his arm over his friends shoulder as he takes a seat next to him. "How you doin' with that single downtown mother now?"

"Yeah, okay I guess." Josh looks up at Krino. "One's like her keep me going, you know. I've been thinking about one of those Asha truth shows I remember. Nothing about those monkeys you're always talking about but she did tell us we have to think for ourselves and decide for ourselves. And then act on what we think and decide—what makes sense. In that one show she was pointing out all the good reasons for everyone why women should just plain have a voice. No question about it; that would be one truth."

"Not monkeys," Krino gives Josh's shoulder a push. "Man, how many times I gotta tell you, apes. We really gotta start talkin' about hominids 'cause they're an even closer brother, so maybe you won't be using that fallacious classification of monkey. Like I said, chimpanzees are in the same family as us, they just have a different genus and species. They're our brothers, and the bonobos for sure do listen to their females."

"Okay, I hear you man, not monkeys. Anyway, that's what Asha said that time. So I just look around me and I just know for sure we gotta get that mother and her children a voice. She is our sister and she deserves a voice that doesn't just speak, but one that's heard."

"Yeah, brother. So you interview your other dude downtown?"

"Yeah, the second one. And now I got one more guy to talk to right after this meeting." Josh scans the crowd and spots John sitting deep in a conversation. "I voice scanned my first two reports into the databases last night. So they should be available now. You know it may be my own interpretation of some of the info I got, but I had to give shela an upfront warning input as a special report. On her own security. How about you?"

"Same, man, my report is filed. Kind of complex, but I told her we can get what she was asking about. There's a freight supply depot in that one industrial area down by the old dry riverbed. Someone down there stocks some of that kind of merchandise. Whatever shela wants it for."

"Interesting. We should find out more right away," says Joshua. "Not quite so many people here this time. I've been looking at that contraption down there on the floor. You see?" He points. "Wonder what that is."

Krino looks down to see a long segmented piece of flexible pipe all coiled up. Xia is setting up the Virtual. "That's Lana." Krino brightens. "I gotta go talk to her."

"She maybe got a couple years on you bud."

"Yeah, yeah," Krino says, making his way down.

Joshua shakes he head as he watches his friend walk down to the lecturer. He wonders if maybe Lana would be one knowing more on shela security. He checks on John again—they should connect easily after the meeting. Xia appears to have the Virtual set up and in place, and Josh watches as the now familiar Mother7 gradually takes on a faint glowing shape. He feels a shiver, remembering the last time her many faces looked his way. His further back memory wonders if Lana is among those faces—she must have become one of the more influential of those making up shela. He remembers the sparkle in her eye when he would ask his many questions after class. Funny Lana shows few signs of her age, maybe she was a child prodigy. She certainly had good answers.

"She say we gonna meet for one Philli Tea," Krino returns beaming.

"Yeah, yeah, hey why don't you do me a favor and ask her what kind of security they have for shela. Systems access, passwords, crypt code, who does her IT security, you know?"

"Yeah, yeah."

Lana turns to face the group as the background music becomes quieter.

"We have confirmed that you were all in attendance at the first action proposal meeting, so welcome again," Lana says. "We are now gathered at our second location on this street with no name. As each of you has supplied us with a reading of your inner response to the situation presented in the initial meeting, and as some of you have now participated in researching our options list, we will now listen to shela's proposed next step."

The lights have been dimming as Lana speaks her final words, and Mother7 forms into her more solid self, brightens up and moves to center stage. Her multiple countenances scan the crowd, connecting quickly yet calmly with each. Joshua feels his worries dissipate; his fingers relax completely, as her look once again gently touches him.

"My children, it is with a grateful heart we meet each of you here today. Welcome." She pauses, letting her audience take it in. "To begin, we will take care of a bit of housekeeping; we have had to shuffle around our security slightly. We will supply you with a new com channel from this get together, and through it, we will be asking for some random, and some specific reverse feeds. All in good order."

Mother 7 turns her face to speak to everyone, both hands opened towards each of them.

"Now, as we approach our chosen moment of proposed action, we certainly do wish to use our best judgment. In the end, it will be all of us together choosing what arrangement of deeds we carry through with." She raises one hand to touch her heart, as she walks towards them. "At this point in time I can tell you that we have now chosen a day. And, we have come to general agreement on our first specific effort. Still, it does seem wise for us to also maintain more than one other option. Let us recall the organized crowds walking up the hill the anniversary of President Asha's assassination. We all remember the protests on November 30 every year since 2022. The last year was the largest and still we were repelled by their crowd dispersal tactics. Our message was again lost in the confusion, again made distorted and unclear."

She pauses, then goes on.

"So, it will be Parade Day on Citadel Hill that will become our Bouquet Day. That will be this Wednesday coming, in four days precisely. The weather forecasters predict a hot summer day so the crowds should be large, and on that day, we would like to call direct attention to our general dissatisfaction, and to attract a clear focus on our proposal for altered behavior on the part of the *toorich*."

"'Cause we can't pay to sue them." Krino says.

"And we don't have a political system that will tax them." Joshua shrugs. "So…"

"With so much attention concentrated on this one event," shela says, "the parade, we anticipate maximizing our exposure. This being our primary objective…there will be risks, of course."

"Hominids take risk?" Josh says.

"Life in nature's full of risk," Krino says.

"We are therefore proposing to first call attention to our message upon the Hill itself," shela says. "In their own backyard, so to speak, that of many of our target audience. And we see two or three primary ways of catching their awareness at this time;

through our first and hopefully only approach, we will drop in on them by air; our second option, which is a backup, will comprise a physical underground visit; and our third possibility, also a backup, will be an advance through the social underground. So now, we have for you short demonstrations of the delivery methods for the first two possibilities. We do not wish to describe all the details of what is being delivered yet. Please pay attention now…"

A young man who has been fidgeting in the back walks out beside Mother7 carrying what looks like some kind of a toy. He sets it carefully down on the floor, activates it with a remote, and directs its rise up into the air. A miniature helihover. The small craft flips a circle around before the front row of faces, slipping side to side as it goes. Under the direction of the young man's remote controls, it then propels itself the other direction behind the back row this time weaving in and out of the shadows of far off girders, before flying twenty feet above the center of the audience floor and opening a hatch to release a shower of what look like small pieces of colored paper. The craft follows the fluttering paper pieces down to settle with some of them on the floor at center. The grinning young man takes a slight bow before picking up his aircraft along with the remote control box and stepping back.

"We plan to join in with them in their Parade celebration with our own contribution of beautifications for all to experience, both visually and in another way that will be something of a surprise."

"But what will we really be doing? I mean what's with these pieces of paper? Is there a message written on them or something?" a voice calls out from the crowd.

"What you see here as paper represents the flower petals we will deliver on our Bouquet Day, on their Parade Day. Under guise of pretty flower petals we will bring them discomfort." Shela leaves the answer vague. "We can only let you know at this time that our real message will be included in with the flowers petals."

Josh looks to Krino, who shrugs.

"This will be our primary method of approach. As I mentioned, by air. We have a club of young people who are excellent pilots. We hope the residents of the Hill will pay very close attention to the message in the flower petals and we hope we will need go no further. However, we find it wise to also have at least one second plan. Your attention again please…"

A burly man lumbers down the steps between the tiered chairs and on his way to middle stage, bends down to grab the coiled pipe Josh had noticed. He turns to face the crowd and lifts the flexible pipe up over his head.

"I'm Jojo and this is a pipeworm." He speaks as he pivots around to show everyone. "Most recent technology in urban pipeline servicing. This here is a PLR57. It can cut, bore, punch out an intake port, release a cleanse; it has a whole list of capacities."

He sets the pipe coil down on the floor, and pulling a mini remote from his pocket, sets to fingering the small buttons and levers. The pipeworm comes to life, rolling around to straighten itself out, and then forming back into a loop to trace out a figure eight pattern moving at an amazing speed.

"This will be our underground physical possibility, our current Plan B, in case our target audience does not respond positively to our air approach," shela says. She goes on. "So you have now seen the basis of our primary and our secondary methods of message delivery, from above and if necessary, from below. For what is actually our preferred method, but the one that would involve the complexity of the inner workings of people, that of the social underground approach, well for that one we need an inside person or two, and we're still investigating that option, our current Plan C."

"You know that dude?" Krino nods as the pipeworm guy.

"Naw." Krino shakes his head.

"So some of you will be contacted over the next twenty four hours. We have some major and a few peripheral tasks yet to carry out. You'll be assigned to teams…we have your profiles to help us match you together well. And we expect to see all of you out there for Bouquet Day. All pertinent details will be communicated to you."

Mother 7 pauses, scanning her audience.

"Any questions or comments? Unfortunately we can't talk any more to the message to be delivered at this time as that depends in a large part on one of the major tasks yet to be carried out. But on other topics, we have a chance here to touch each other with our voices. Any questions or concerns?"

Josh stands and speaks out. "Hello shela, you know I hear you saying we have improved operational security a lot; I hear all the issues you have mentioned. But what about our security specifically around yourself, your own security. I mean what if they focus on you as a target? What if they try to shut you down in some way?"

Mother 7 nods. "Yes, good question. Believe me, they have tried and they do keep trying; we love them for their perseverance. But the truth is we are your combined voice, the deep down spirit of all people. The feminine of the human super conscience that you see at this moment through me is but an expression of your inner selves via Virtual technology. They have shut down our appearance, suppressed us in many ways in the past, but never can they destroy the inner workings of what we truthfully are. That much we can assure you. So any infiltration at this time will only be a delay."

Joshua sits, squinting his eyes. Yeah, but what if they get into your source code and modify you just a bit, a slight alteration hardly noticeable but just enough to throw things off. Ah, better leave it, he decides.

The silence of the audience is broken again.

"Why don't we just blow them away?" an angry voice calls out. Josh feels his fingers bunching up, his jaw tightening. *Yeah, why not?* One voice inside him asks. *Just shoot them all and get rid of them for good. Real simple.*

"Who's that?" Josh whispers to Krino.

"That one is Cauz. He was in the Marines for a while."

"That is one option of course." Mother7 says unhurriedly. "Many of you should be up on peoples' past choices on that alternative. General wisdom tells us that our adversary would by and large shoot back, and in the end, little would get resolved. We'll send you a historical review on that option with links to database comparables."

"I assume we are going to attempt to get that pipeworm into their pipes?" Another voice asks. "If that is true, however would we do that?"

"Yes, good question, we do have ways. Jojo here with his engineering education will be our expert in that field. He is familiar with several tunneling methods. Our first attempt, however, as mentioned will be the air option…" She smiles warmly at the room. "So hopefully we won't have to dig. But if you want to know more about the potential tunneling option, talk with Jojo or we can give you access to information sets he has posted.

"Anything else?"

The room remains quiet. The audience begins to shuffle around, standing to gather belongings and move towards the exit.

"Hey Krino, can you stick with Zaca and get her home? I gotta talk with one more guy this afternoon."

"Sure thing dude. Me and that dog can be our own pack any time."

Josh looks across to the other side of the stage at John who is looking back and waving at him. He wanders around and across between chairs and the people leaving. John is standing waiting, dressed in jeans yet still sporting a dress shirt today. He greets Josh with a broad smile.

"We can just hang around here if you want Josh. Most everyone is on their way out now."

"Right, no problem."

Josh takes a seat beside as John sits again and they both pull their legs in to make way for a couple as they file past to the end of the row.

"So you work for the City," Josh says.

"Sure do." John's smile diminishes. "I've been there for almost twenty years now. In fact my retirement is coming up, well it should be, but I will have to stay another five years at least."

He looks directly at Josh, then down.

"If I can. You know, I have a lot of family obligations, we have two teenage children of our own, well one is twenty now, and my sister and her kids and I am still the only one with work. Pretty lucky to have it too, you know we haven't had a union contract for six years now. There have been a lot of layoffs, but I am still there. I don't know why I'm one of the few they kept, but that's how it turned out…just a few things I can do with public relations I think and administration is still pretty interested in figuring out what to really do about sustainability. That's my area of focus. No contract, no pay increases, not the way it used to be. Oh well, that's how things go."

"Right, John, I'm not totally sure how this fits in with what shela is looking for. Do you know?" Josh asks. He watches John's demeanor, deducing that someone like John doesn't have the need to clench fists even in the worst of it.

"Well, yeah, okay, it's not just me we actually need to talk about. There are quite a few people I work with and maybe more important, that I have worked with in the past. This one guy comes to mind a lot, Bruce was not far from retirement back when I met him. He was an analyst and I started doing a lot of presentation work on his material. He had this interesting motto that he stuck by, well maybe you would call it a motto and maybe not, but it was pretty simple."

This guy's a talker for sure, so Josh decides to just listen.

"Bruce just stuck with the truth, I mean depends who you are and what you believe, right? But his truth was pretty basic and he would show it with the numbers he used. He would say things like the truth stands alone, non-truths need a lot of support."

"Cool."

"I mean that does sound pretty good, but you know it was difficult to try to make it fly politically so we would always have to soften up the language. Anyway he developed this method of sustainability measurement. Have you ever heard of the idea of human footprint on the planet? Ecological footprint? Carbon footprint? Especially carbon 'cause that is what has given us the climate change we have so far. Well, he pretty accurately was showing the easiest and quite precise method is just converting wealth and income into acres of planet used. No question, the higher the individual or household income, the bigger the footprint."

"Right, so sounds like you and Bruce came up with a different way of describing the *toorich*. And what their way of living does to all of us."

John sits with his hands on one knee, fingers laced together in front. He shifts to face Josh more directly.

“You might say that…but you know, it’s a measure of every household. For me, that really got me going, well, not right away I have to admit, but eventually. Mostly after Bruce was gone. ‘Cause my gig is to talk about and present on sustainability. To administration, to committee, to Council, to the public. I mean we would use words like lifestyle, not ever mentioning income or wealth. It presents better to any audience. But what gets to me is what Bruce would always say, you know, the truth stands alone."

"Nothing wrong with that."

"He was so frustrated, you know, totally peeved off, that I wouldn’t stick with the right up front truth. I told him how you had to be sensitive to what the people were willing to hear. He would tell me things like the laws of physics don’t negotiate politically. And the climate numbers are still going up no matter what you call it. Behind lifestyle, what it truly comes down to is how Robin Hood rich you are. The more gold you have, the more planet you use up. I never used to get too deep into it before, but like I say, I have children, and once in a while I would get it, you know, the idea of what their future looks like. Well, here it is now, you could say, we have it right in front of our eyes. And so I wonder at times about the real truth about what is causing it, their future I mean. And then I always think about Bruce and what he would say.”

Josh leans back in his chair now, looking over to watch as the last of the people file out the door.

“Did he say anything else?”

“You know, it wasn’t my idea. I got this from Bruce ‘cause he said he did this all the time. But the last time we had a vacation, you know we would always get those package vacations to the beach to get away from the winter, my, that last one must be maybe eight years ago now, I did just what Bruce suggested. Just for a day. I walked outside the fence, you know around the hotel compound, and I found my way over to a local taxi stand and took a ride into town. My gosh, things did not look so good. Such a shabby little city, so many of the cars were old and broken, people using horses and bicycles and children running around playing with no real toys at all. I got out on a busy street and just walked around and actually tried to talk with the people and see how they live. You know I didn’t have my digital translator with me and I didn't know the language very well, but I could fumble around with a few words. And then when I got back to the compound, I could see it right in front of me, I mean there we were staying in our comfortable hotel with all our beach toys and buffet meals any old time we were hungry. Us on our side of that compound fence and them on the other side."

John looks down at his hands, silent for a second.

"Right," Josh says. "A fence, kind of like a wall to separate the rich from the poor?"

"Yeah, kind of just like that." John coughs, pauses and goes on. "And now, as Bruce was predicting at the time, kind of the way it is around our own city. Right here, right now. Now I live in a house with an extended family living with me, just like they lived in that shabby little city. Lucky to have one job, lots of mouths to feed."

"Right."

"You know, Josh." John leans over close. "Bruce would always point out to me what I would talk about when I would come back from a vacation. The food we ate, same food we would eat here, the special shopping malls we would go to so they would sell just what we are used to here, the amusement parks we would travel to…you know? Why would we have to fly all the way over there? We have ethnic restaurants all over our city. But we dumped all kinds of carbon pollution in our atmosphere, just by stepping on those airplanes. Our big immature party, we partied my children's future away."

John wipes at the corner of one eye and looks up and away.

"And now I am still supposed to be a speaking expert on climate change. Well, just look at our river. I can tell you or show you on a graph how the water level has changed over the last couple decades. As predicted, where it is dry, it will get dryer and where it is wet, it will get wetter. Well guess what, we and upstream of us is a dryer area. We are dreaming if we think the sunny beach is coming to our doorstep. No way, just bigger weather events. Which is a tough subject to present as well, let me tell you."

"The river used to be larger?" Josh nods. "I kind of heard something about that."

"I mean Bruce seemed to be quite an observant guy. He would always talk about who is responsible. He would talk about the baby boomers, you know, they started to retire en mass about twenty years back. The good life you might say. Or you might say they pissed everything away. He was one of them, but he had such a different outlook. He would talk about who is responsible. The self-centred ones who just partied all our planetary resources away and the more responsible ones who truly thought about their children and their children's future. Anyway, with my children at the age they are now, I am worried. Very worried. I guess I should have been more worried back then when Bruce was still around. I know I am responsible."

Josh looks at him and can't hold back his building string of questions. "So those with more money use up more planet? We only have one planet, right? How much planet do we have left?"

"None, in fact, we have now used up far more than one planet. We were approaching two when peak energy demand actually set in. Some called it peak everything. Bruce was clearly predicting that, from the research he was doing. A lot of scientists were saying so, he said. Bruce kept telling me we crossed over the one planet line back in the 1970's. Can you believe it? I was born around that time and nobody even noticed. Not a word. Another piece of information that didn't sit very well, especially politically, when I was giving presentations. So again, I could only give it general reference and vague emphasis. Especially when I was speaking to Council. They are the ones who ultimately make the decisions."

"Can we talk to Bruce?" Josh says. "Do you have a contact?"

"Sorry, he moved to one of those countries he used to visit. Right after he retired. He's not the type who would stay in touch."

"Okay," Josh says. "Well I can get this input into the shela databases."

"I'll get you copies of all of Bruce's publications. A lot of it was suppressed except at high security access levels for a long time. But I can get them to you."

"That would be great."

Josh and John stand, John stretches and they look around. All of the audience has dispersed, except Lana and Xia standing by the exit talking. A group of young men walk in through the door and start gathering up the chairs. John picks up two of the folding chairs and Josh follows suit. They walk towards the exit.

"You know, my grandfather used to talk about the peace he would find, just going down and sitting by the creek with a fishing pole." John's face looks grim, stretching against his natural smile wrinkles. "My kids aren't going to have that peace. They are going to have a struggle, well they already have it. All because of the big party the rich had…that we had."

"Maybe see you at Bouquet Day?" Josh says.

"I will try my best to be there Josh."

Chapter 7

Early Sunday Afternoon, July 1

"So sounds like we are on the same task force." Joshua communicates with his friend through voice only. "Just different action units."

"Yo," Krino confirms. "Me and a man name of Steve, you and Jojo. Jojo is the man I just talked to; he demo'ed that what-che-me-call-it, pipeworm. Shela assigned him as task force coordinator. So he be our boss man."

"Must fit his profile. What else did Jojo say?"

"Two other things, one is, we got Eli coming on bike; he knows the turf and he knows how to deal with Blades, just in case. So both e-trucks pick up at the same place and then take their load to the same drop off. First thing is, we need to time it out so both our trucks meet at the supply depot for pick up at the same time. Second thing is Eli bringing Xia to you right now. She got some last minute camouflage device or something. She just did an install on our unit."

"So we'll just go as a little convoy."

"Nah, separate routes, dawg. We don't want UPAS looking down on anything looks like we're together; too suspicious, too organized. If they can see us that is, depends on Xia's camouflage."

"So we track each other on plasma map."

"Yes, my man. You will be Jojo's co-pilot so you can take care of that for your unit. And we know the Blades lay pretty low in the daytime, so we go early afternoon. Thirteen hundred hours, what the hell is that man in every day talk, one o'clock? One-barrel water buggies, that's our primary cover on the street."

"Alright. Let's do it."

Joshua finds his riding partner waiting at the designated corner in a little two-seater electrotruck; KoolKleenWater splashed in neon aqua across the side. He slips into the passenger seat, holding out his hand.

"You're the underground expert," says Joshua.

"Whatever." His shake is firm. "I'm Jojo."

Uncrumpling full screen, Josh finds their location softly flashing on the urban map; Krino and the Steve guy show three blocks south. Eli's ICE bike is moving rapidly in on them, and looking up, Josh spots him riding up with Xia on the seat behind.

Eli and Jojo give each other an acknowledging nod as Xia hops off. She walks quickly around to the front of the e-truck, carrying a small white box with lenses projecting from the top and one side. She stands up on the front bumper and reaches over to place the box on the roof of the truck. She spends a second adjusting the position of the box, with the side lens projecting forward over the windshield centre and the top lens pointing up. She then steps back down to the street and comes around to Jojo's window.

"Hi boss." She looks directly at Jojo, nodding over at Josh. "So like we were saying, we just got these camouflage devices so we mostly know how they are supposed to work—we did a few tests and we hope they work. They're real easy to install with only a magnet holding them in place so worth a chance. The idea is they have a camera that takes a running image of the street right in front of the vehicle and retransmits it vertically upward. The devices do not eliminate all shadow effects but are supposed to cloak you fairly well from satellite maybe ninety percent and from UPAS at least eighty percent. I told Eli we do not have one for his bike. They are not perfect, but they will help."

Jojo looks at her and gives a nod. "All right."

"So don't pull up any closer than twenty feet behind the vehicle in front of you if you can help it." Xia says. "Keep the image as clean as possible. Good luck." She turns abruptly and walks off down the street.

"Five more minutes my time," Joshua says.

Jojo leans forward, fingers drumming on the dash. Eli grunts.

"Look guys, I've also been contemplating the bigger picture, you know, we always need to keep our options open, so we should only be making this trip once," Jojo turns to look directly at both of them. “We’re being told to pick up both barrels in the dry flake form, but I believe we need one barrel of nectar. Of liquid.”

“Uhh?” Eli frowns.

“Dry form may be good for our air drop, but liquid would work so much better in the pipeworm. I can tell you that for a fact.”

“But aren’t we going air first,” says Joshua. “Air only, ideally.”

“We got a transfer valve right here.” Jojo pats his pocket. “And we can fly liquid if we need to. There is a pay load limitation issue, but we can do it with smaller loads. Anyway look at me man, this air thing’s not gonna do shit. Just gonna piss them off. Besides, no one listens the first time you tell them something they don’t want to hear. They need a good solid kick in the butt side,” Jojo looks back and forth at the two of them. “And a good solid kick in the arse comes from below.”

“Calm, calm.” Eli says in his boom box voice. “Look, u’m gonna start off with the other buggy and I come find you men maybe halfway.” Eli flips up his lockdown plate and zooms off. Jojo retains a resolute look on his face.

“Okay, Jojo. I got 13:00.” Joshua glances down at the plasma screen spread out across his lap, watching as Eli’s icon moves towards Krino’s. “Estimated time to depot is 52 minutes.”

Jojo pulls them out to join the light Sunday urban traffic. They fall into a stop and go pattern as they pass through the tall apartment blocks of the Lower East. Josh notes they've travelled for maybe ten minutes when a UPAS helihover passes over. *I’ve got to call my sister, maybe that’s her up there now. She could have been a help with this. But would she?* He knows what’s important to Jeira, but ever since she joined the police force, it’s been tricky being completely up front with her. Not that he doesn’t trust his own sister, but he thinks about her peace of mind. He doesn’t want her to have to compromise her position or endanger her employment—a real job isn’t the easiest thing to come by.

“Not to worry,” Jojo says. “Even if that cloaker box doesn’t work, we look like any old regular delivery truck down here.”

“So what exactly is it we're going to pick up?” Joshua asks. “No one seems to be completely informed.”

“She never told me everything, that’s certain. Some non-explosive irritant that comes in dry flake or liquid form, I don’t know nothing else." Jojo shakes his head shrugging. "You can pressure up liquid, like in the PLR57 or in any other pressure unit. The dry flakes, or I guess we're calling them petals, you can just do a dump. Petals are lighter up in the air so you can carry a bigger load, but the trade-off isn't worth it. You just don't have the same options you have with liquid."

"So you want to do something she isn't exactly asking for?"

"I want to make a minor adjustment—to improve shela's plan. And we *are* doin' what she is asking for—keep a Plan B option on the go."

"Hmmm…"

They travel on through the neighborhoods in and out of the intense sunshine. Between each set of building shadows, sweltering heat settles in around them, and when the wind in their hair subsides at each stoplight intersection the sweat beads back up on their brows.

"Wonder if we're passing through much Blades turf."

"I dunno." Jojo shrugs. "Eli would be on top of that one."

Eli comes up behind as they cross under Sky Hill South line. He gives a thumbs-up signal as he pulls around in front of them. Everything must be on track as they approach the warehouse.

They pass along for several blocks beside the dry riverbed.

"Used to go fishing in this river when I was a kid." Jojo stares out past the railing. "Then it was just in the pools in summer time. Not no more, been no water at all for a few years now. Except those flash floods but fish can't live in that."

They turn right and then right again into an alleyway entrance and drive part way down to an old wooden loading dock. Perfect timing as the other KoolKleen truck pulls to a halt around the corner at the other end. Eli zooms down to turn around and wait beside it. Jojo hops out to knock on the corrugated roll-up door above the dock. It opens immediately and he gets into a conversation with someone inside. An e-forklift brings out a polymer barrel. As it bounces into their cargo space, Joshua can hear it sloshing slightly. Jojo smiles as he hops back in the truck. Eli now cruises past, waving for them to follow. Another UPAS helihover passes over a couple blocks south. As Joshua looks back down the alley, he watches a second drum of a different color being lowered into the other electrotruck.

Josh lifts a hand to wave at Krino, staring intently at the other fellow. What did his friend says the guy's name was? Steve or something like that.

"So that other one is a barrel of petals?"

"Yup."

They pull into the street and then left to follow along the dry river, tailing along behind Eli. Joshua sighs, feeling the cooling breeze in his hair as they pass along several blocks without stopping. All three-way intersections beside the river channel.

"All the money they spent on flood control. Very poor design for current conditions, 'cause now the flash floods still come over the banks into the streets. I mean the river used to be high in the spring when it ran regular. That's when the fish would run."

"Right. We used to hang out by the river as kids...never noticed."

Josh settles back in his seat and uncrumples to have a look. All three blinking dots are now moving in the same direction towards the drop off. Back home.

Krino's face appears on screen.

"How's your end?"

"Looks good here bud. I was freaking a bit when that last helihover passed by, but it didn't seem to notice us. Those cloaker devices must be working. Hey, no convoy, no organization, no association. We just cruise on home."

Just like back in the Air Force where there was always an operational plan. Not always a plan that sat quite right with Joshua, but the military sure was organized. He was more interested in finding out what kind of people would join the military. They certainly were an interesting group and he played along with the drills and intense training, just to have the experience for his own interest. Kept him in good shape too. Then those last few weeks, they started cutting some air force budgets. It fit his schedule fine, he had other plans, other situations to investigate, but a lot of the officers in training were not happy to be losing their jobs. Asha had been earlier explaining the truth about military conflict, how little good it did anyone, how there actually never was a winner in any war. But these cuts were for other reasons. He thinks back to some of the flight training classes, and wonders how the young pilots shela was talking about are going to organize their mini helihovers flights. Auto-piloting would be useful for…

"Oh shit, shit, shit, man." Krino's face flashes back wide eyed onto the screen. "We got us some big shit trouble now."

Joshua's focus rivets back on the map. The flashing icon of the other KoolKleen is slowing to a gradual stop in the middle of a block. "Krino, what?"

"Shit man, we done made one screw-up comin' this way. Shit, shit, shit, looks like Blades."

"Calm, strength." Eli's voice comes through. "U'm on my way there. Jojo, you get on over too."

"Yuh just never know what might come up," Jojo mutters. "Okay, let's think and improvise."

"Strength in numbers," Eli says. "Follow my lead when you get there."

Joshua sits up straight now, stretching a piece of the screen out flat between his knees. He watches Eli's symbol turn a corner on the map and speed up behind Krino's icon that now sits stationary. They have two blocks to go. He glances over at Jojo, one hand clenched tightly on the control wheel, the other fumbling back behind the seat.

They enter the narrow street to see Eli off his bike, walking cautiously across in front of three young men, each wearing a long loose red shirt. The three stand with arms crossed in front of an old SUV barricade. Krino and the Steve guy have spread out on either side of Eli. Krino shuffles from side to side, and the Steve guy seems to be clutching something tightly in one hand. Jojo pulls to a stop beside Eli's bike. The three red shirt's stare intently at the new arrivals, their arms dropping in unison. Jojo scrambles quickly around to the back of the barrel truck.

"Yo. You men have good cause. Good strength," Eli is saying loudly. "We have good cause. We need to pass, no more."

He waits.

"I ask you one mo' time, what you carry, nigger?" The red shirt in the middle circles around Eli, keeping his eyes on the others. "You wanna pass, you wanna pay."

The other two red shirts spread out further on his flanks.

"You men shakin' down, protectin' your turf. We passin' through, we got our own shake down happenin'. The man on the Hill be our hit. You want true action you come join us. The man on the Hill got one down on you too. Come, join us. Good cause, put you on the side of truth. Real truth, man."

"You pay, nigger," the red shirt spokesman scoffs. "This Blades turf. We top-man here. What you got?"

"Calm, calm," Eli holds up one hand. "One thing." He raises a finger. "You think you top-man. Thing is, we all pay the man on the Hill. Here, you want to wire your brother, you want to blow out your brother. Even if he your blo-man, what happen when you wire him? He dead. Then you have his brother on your ass."

Jojo walks cautiously forward now, both hands held high. Joshua sees a bright green polymer pistol dangling between two fingers. "Eli," Jojo says. "We can give them a hydro blaster…and we got liquid, so we can give a fill vial."

Jojo and Eli look directly at each other.

"You hold, cracker." The lead red shirt lets his shirt fall open, exposing his whip-wire and a loaded shotgun holster.

"Calm, strength," says Eli, opening his arms towards the red shirts. "You want power?" He looks at Jojo who nods. "We give you this, you give this a try out.

"We have power right here, nigger, this Blades turf where you standin'." The red shirt sneers at the plastic gun. "What that? Look like some children's toy."

"Pneumatic special issue." Jojo eases the pistol up to point over at a brick wall, pulling the trigger to release. A dart of liquid zings into the wall, creating a dull smacking noise like a fist hitting a jaw, and splattering out all directions. "One high quality toy. That's just water to demo; you load it with this." He holds up a small plastic capsule between two fingers. He sets the green gun down on the pavement, beside the capsule.

"You want to leave blo-man drippin' sticky," Eli says. "You put that on him. Put him on his knees. You humble the man, you got respect from the living, not some stiff you gotta dump in the alley." Eli backs up towards the trucks, and the others follow. "We pay. We go now."

They get into the KoolKleen trucks, and Eli swings his leg over the bike. The red shirt has picked up the green pistol and the capsule, and he stares hard at the group with their e-trucks and ICE bike. He points the green gun at the brick wall and pulls the trigger, feeling the abrupt jerk to his arm as the water leaves the gun and again hits the wall. He walks back over to the space between the SUV's, pistol in hand, eyes squinted. He turns abruptly to look at his two companions, sneering, then back at those waiting. He slides the pistol slowly inside his shirt, but quickly reverses to draw it out and point it directly at Eli, then Jojo, snickering. But he lowers the pistol again and flippantly waves his two companions to the side.

The two water trucks pass through the barricade. Eli follows. "You be at Seymour Park Saturday. You want to humble the real top man, you join us." He looks directly at the leader and holds a thumbs-up to all the red shirts as he rides through. "Seymour Park."

Joshua glances over at Jojo. They are both dripping in sweat, though the barricade was in the full shadow of the high buildings along that narrow street.

"Liquid is a good option." Joshua forces a shaky smile.

"Shit, yeah." Jojo calms his breathing. "You gotta have a backup plan. You always gotta keep something up your sleeve."

They drive along for several more blocks.

"We used to come along this way going fishing," Jojo talks nervously. "There were no big gangs back then, no turf and terror and shit like this."

"Yeah, Asha had organized crime rates way down by her second term," Josh says. "Me and my sister used to go hang around along the big river across from downtown. Didn't used to be any fences around the golf course then either. That was before they built the wall around the Hill."

The shadows and hot spots pass by. Josh looks at Jojo.

"You were anticipating trouble," Joshua says. "You knew something was gonna happen."

"Hey, Eli was the man," Jojo says. "He handled that situation excellent. I mean you notice how young those guys are. Why else would they be out on the afternoon shift? They're just trying to prove themselves so they can fit in as one of the Blades."

"Yeah, maybe teenagers."

"Eli says young men like that are looking anywhere to be part of some family or other, so they're the best ones to give another option. Basic human psychology—we all want to belong to a social group of some type or other. So invite them to join us and point them at the man on the Hill. Then they have a cause, just the same as with the Blades, they feel they fit in. And they may just feel more righteous. I figure we'll see them at Seymour."

"Right...but they never met shela," Joshua says. "They have no com channel, no profiles. Looked like they were all walking free."

"Build up the crowd on the street, especially for your air option," Jojo says. "You're gonna need everything you can get. They don't all have to be through shela, they just need to show up on the Day. They can meet shela after if she invites them."

"Yeah, maybe," Joshua says. "Hey, you know that Steve guy?"

"Nah, never seen him before," Jojo says. "Looks like some cult pussy. He holds that black and white cross out in front of him the whole time. What the f' is that supposed to do?"

"Black and white?" Josh says. "It was a cross…you saw it for sure?"

"Yeah, I saw it."

Joshua slips into silence, letting his mind wander in a search for any connection. Gradually dancing puzzle pieces snap into place, at least some.

"Black and white…now I know where I've seen him." Joshua says. "That transition car at the Hill station."

"No shit." Jojo looks at him. "I knew he was some pussy. He probably lives up on the Hill. He better be cool, man, better not have slipped by shela."

Still the puzzle isn't finished—pieces dancing on yet to find a place. *'Cause I know him from somewhere else too. Shit, Jeira, I gotta talk to my sister, why her?*

They pull in to another alley. Not much different than the pick-up place but back on the familiar side of town. Krino anxiously waves them in through an open door. "There he goes now," Jojo says pointing. They watch Steve walking down the alley away from the drop off. Eli cruises past, pointing them to a parking spot. They pull in to the back of the warehouse, parking parallel with the other KoolKleen.

“So we’re all gonna meet on the no name street tomorrow night." Jojo looks at them. "Some flight practice and some organizing. But we gotta split up now, bring no more attention to this place than we need to. You’re staying to unload and repackage, Krino, so Joshua, you can get out of here.”

“Right.”

Joshua steps quickly back out the door, but when he looks up the alley Steve is gone.

Chapter 8

Late Sunday Afternoon, July 1

Staphan walks softly down the alley, a touch of lightness in his step. His lips squeeze tight as he shakes his head slowly, almost in disbelief. The disjointed chunks of embankment clay feel washed clean, revealed to expose a coherent pattern of light rays shining on the now washed threads of the cloth, completely organized and working together. All on track. He rubs his black and white cross gently in one hand, swinging his arms slightly with the rhythm as he steps along, over and past the potholes. That was not so bad, not so bad at all. Thank you Jesus, and you too Buddha, for the strength you give…*feeling just a little smoother in Your Hands,* he hums. He reaches the end of the alley, turning down the street back towards his place.

He can think of nothing but his tc he left lying on the table beside the bread and water when he left that morning. Good work, she'll say. He just knows it; he can figure it out now all on his own. This test may have been difficult and may have been the most critical in her series so far, but shela is giving him a real chance. She seems truly interested in helping him with what he actually needs oh so badly.

He may have a real sleep, perhaps all the way through the night soon, well, that would be asking a lot, but at least he'll be a tiny bit calmer when he wakes up in the late night darkness. The darkness. A darkness without the screaming inside, what could be better? That first middle of the night awakening. Nothing had happened. Nothing out of the ordinary. He had just woken up. And just could not fall back. The falling sensation would not come again like it always had no matter what he tried. Being at the Academy at the time he added insomnia to his research list. He found a book on the subject and read it. He made an appointment with Dr. Holdenstein who referred him to a behavioral specialist. So he had learned to lie quietly for hours on end. Rest is the next best thing to sleep. He practiced focussing on his breathing. Count five breathing in, seven breathing out. Breath out through one leg, then the other, through the left arm, then the right, release your mind to the universe from your heart chakra up through your crown. Maybe that was a mistake—his mind to the universe. For then the voices began to speak.

He ignored them at first, denying their existence. They left him alone for a while, as they were actually quite polite. They started coming back again, maybe he asked them to, he doesn't know. They did seem friendly enough, but who can you trust in such an extensive space as the universe? He tried next to negotiate with them, as it seemed they had a power of some sort, and access to certain information that was somehow appealing. He would trade, maybe, if they could help him sleep again. Yet to this day the negotiating continues. For their agenda, their list of suggestions always enticing, hooked on a promise of peace in the end has turned out to be quite extensive.

Sometimes he wonders if he were randomly selected. Good luck or bad, a crap shoot at the tables. By the Others as he now refers to them, the voices that now give direction to his life. Often unwanted direction. Though he does at times understand after a while. Not always. But right now at least he feels pretty good, almost like he has a slice of that being at peace with the universe on the plate in front of him.

'Cause I did what I true to heart needed to do he chants to himself under his breath. My road to Damascus friend will be a little happier and smiling Buddha will spread his grin out a little further. *I still can't believe shela let my profile have a chance.* Why would she after what I've done, where I come from? He starts to the notice a sinking feeling and struggles to keep the uplifting ones alive.

He notices his real physical hunger now, and he looks forward to his meal tonight. Bread and water it will be, no need to pick up another bottle. He just smashes them anyway. Which is good of course.

Still, the biggest challenge lies ahead. How will he ever tell her, how will he make retribution? He has to believe he is being guided, if he just keeps meditating, if the Buddha is right, the answers are within. More discussion and negotiating with the Others. That fellow in the other electrotruck, that was Joshua. What else can Joshua be but a sign along his path to her…she would be woman now, the one he must find. God is nirvana, God is within, God is guiding him in whatever way to his next encounter. He will go to the park on Parade Day, the parade he has seen so many times from the booth up above the streets.

At first when they were boys he and Paul would chase each other around the seats in the VIP booth hanging high above the plaza with a full view of the crystal cross from the back. Paul always rubbed him out when he caught him. Then when they came to understand competition from an adult's point of view, they vied for a short time for the seat at the right hand of father. Staphan more dreaming of releasing that other person he noticed inside his father from time to time rather than for any love of competition. Their father watched them and never interfered. The first time Staphan did manage to get the right hand seat he wondered what the fuss was actually about. Their father so strong in his business suit. Staphan felt queasy, short of breath and quite nervous while he was sitting there. And of course Paul, with his sly thinking and conniving methods tricked him, making a trade on the right hand seat for what turned out to be another one of his brother's empty promises. That position of power, by all counts, better fit his brother. Staphan only half tried for the seat after that, once in a while remembering the nervous swallow in his father's throat. But he somehow knew it wasn't worth waiting on, he would never meet the other father behind the business mask and anyway the business role was not for him at all.

He sighs. He must find a tree to sit beneath, as the Buddha did for four years. He will seek out his own version of the middle path. Well, it will be a nice place to listen to the next propositions the Others will bring to the table and toughen up for the next task.

Chapter 9

Monday Evening, July 2- early shift

The evening stretches out to the edge of the urban sky. A falling star traces a path diagonally across the skyroof, as Jeira makes that last step up onto the launch platform. She takes a deep breath, feeling her eyes dragged down on task as her hand moves to find hatch-release on her warm-touch control belt. Another quick glance up at the sky as the bubble opens, before she steps down into the cockpit and lock-clicks herself into the flight seat. She unconsciously gives EyeD the required direct look, and clips the standard UPAS com-phone to her flight helmet.

"Ground check," she hears her voice lightly speak the routine words, as her eyes focus in on the control panel. She gesture-selects the index soft touch option, and then moves the main cursor over hatch-secure. As she adjusts to the reality of this part of her life, she clears her throat and consciously hardens her voice a little, taking on the learned pattern of deeper tones to conform to this patriarchal realm. "You copy?"

The plexon cover lowers down to seal her in with an almost inaudible metallic whir, as electromag locks align with their slots and soft blue glow-lights begin flashing their slow way around the bubble-shield perimeter.

"Number seven, this is ground. That's a copy. You are set to release at 21:00." The familiar voice sounds reassuring. "Hey, this is Martine and I'll be your ground partner tonight." Her heartbeat slows to a slightly more peaceful pace and she sighs as a tiny smile rises on her face, soothing her mental focus.

She loads the pre-flight, then turns all her attention to the activity register. Glancing down the incidents lists, she assumes another routine surveillance night—events have been fairly calm the last couple weeks. On top of regular evening visual assists, there were only those two ground chase supports last week, nothing more. Just being the eye-in-the-sky makes her feel good about helping to keep peace in the city. *Show a presence*, the UPAS captain would say; their primary mode of influence. Of course, on which part of the city you shine inspiration decides the real influence the police service can have. But at least she is helping others, she reminds herself. Maybe not quite the way she had at one time planned.

The master screen beeps for her attention and the code notes update begin to appear along the flight line at each pre-selected checkpoint. First, a basic surveillance run over the rough and tough Forest Flats blocks. She shakes her head gently at the name—what forest?—she knows each neighborhood tree by heart. Then, barring any calls, continued surveillance over High Banks—gang conflict activity has been rising there. Across the river after that with a switch to a patrol pattern of the South Downtown. Back across the flowing water again to fly the special priority grid pattern over the Hill, Citadel Hill, and finally a run along the Bullet Train route west to the edge of the urban build-out. Then over the old neighborhood again. Her lips tighten, as her eyes drop and she sighs. Incident stats now flashing help keep her focus as the helihover icon follows the route. Lots of low-key activity along the tracks, some typical downtown events, and that distinct pattern along the river, except where the Hill imposes its security shadow down to the flowing water's edge.

The Hill, a place where she knows her influence from the air is tripled by private security on the ground. Crime on the Hill is non-existent as a rule, an impenetrable fortress of good—at least according to UPAS databases. Of course, they only cover deviant behavior defined by legal code—what else can they do?

The outer cage cover opens above and her helihover tracts out on its release arm, the heliblade now warmed up and running at take-off speed. As the screen counts down the last few seconds, she flicks the one remaining mechanical switch left in the unit. *Release.* Still, not until the traction beam lets her craft go is she actually free of command control's ability to override her decision.

The night blue Boeing Firefly helihover rises gently, adjusting itself into the gentle westerly breeze as the lights twinkle away in waves through the dusk, out across the expanse of the city. She gives her helmet a left-handed nudge as her right hand feels its way around the three-point touch stick while she clears her mind of all but the list. The first route segment will be on autopilot, the switchback cruise over the grid pattern streets of the Flats set to a standard surveillance pattern. Between the tightly packed apartment blocks, medium to high incidents rates translate into the kind of tough neighborhood she has come to know.

The helihover begins its back and forth with a smooth loop-over at the end of each street, it's spotlight beaming down on the pavement on and off to avoid being an easy target. Who knows what surface-to-air devices might be down on the streets? She checks the infrared camera settings, manually fine-tuning out the remnants of evening heat. Gangbangers have been quiet across the city in recent weeks, but history shows this may be peace, or, just as likely, a build-up of something coming. The Firefly follows its path, pre-programmed earlier by ground.

"Number seven, we need an immediate assist at Lytton and Twenty second." Martine's voice breaks the heliblade hum. "Can you take it, over?"

"Yeah, copy," she says, unconsciously still in deeper tones. She shakes her head…absurd boy-soldier language. "Hey, Marti, it's me Jeira. Sorry, I was busy with prep earlier." She moves the cursor to manual override, picking with third-point touch on the control stick.

"Hey girl, can you get this one? I'll connect you with the ground unit. They are, let's see…number 467. That's Randy and Mick."

"For sure. I am on my way."

"Hey, I met those guys at that party Saturday. Cute, both of them. You shoulda come."

"Oh, Marti, thanks, but nightshift, and anyways, you know..."

"Yeah, we'll talk. Now you go for it, girl."

Shifting from autopilot to manual, Jeira lifts the helihover higher and switches off all ground lights. Touching in the intersection with her left hand for location confirmation and quick reference, she moves the flashing patch icon Marti posted to active voice. Exact coordinates with an entrance illumination code show.

"Number seven, this is 467." A commanding male voice booms into her ears through the com-phone. "We've got a situation with a weapons warning and we're making entry in five. I repeat, that's in five minutes. We need a light switch available and a recording. You copy?"

"Roger that." She sighs, deciding to smile past the voice.

She's there with the Firefly in two, picking an oblique angle and backtracking a trace line higher up and away to train the cameras on the tenement door. She picks hover and hold. With one infrared and one visible light camera trained on the door, she leaves the light switch open for the ground unit to flick. "Eyes on, 467. Within your timeframe," she reports. *Randy—Mick, how you guys doing?* She whispers to herself, then aloud, "You got that, Marti?"

"Yes, I'm watching."

Ahead of ground unit schedules as a rule, she relaxes for a minute. Her eyes follow the South Bullet Train as it slows for the Hill ramp, preparing to pass through the security scan in the transition gate. Yet another way of keeping the incidents counts outside of the wall and off the Hill. People want security, she knows, and those who can pay get extra. Those up on high ground; those behind the walls. She watches the Bullet as it slips through its gate hole. Emerging completely into the double bright lights on the other side, it must be clean.

The spotlight switch beeps, now flicked, flooding the doorway in triple bright, with a low beam light up spread over the whole building. The megaphone on the ground is booming and the door opens in a slow response. A man and a woman carrying a small child step out trembling and confused, the man with both hands held high and the woman with one hand up, the other grasping the child's hand. The ground squad officers quickly move in on them to make a secure entry and begin questioning. This scene may not be what the ground crew were looking for, she guesses. The people look very domestic. Maybe another bad lead—it's so hard to know what's actually going on down on the streets.

"Okay, Number seven," the male voice says. "We got it from here. We might give you a call a little later to check on recordings." They will probably want the videos deleted. If they had bad info, why keep a record? They'll let her know.

"Roger that," she replies in form, sorting out the emotional mixtures making their way through her. Who knows what the evening might hold? She swings away, heading off across the Bullet tracks to catch up with the schedule for the High Banks run.

She glances down along the river, watching the tenement towers as they pass under. The parking lots are scattered with abandoned SUVs; most functional vehicles are tiny electrocars, electrobikes, and some old ICE bikes on lock down plates. The visible light cameras see what she sees, but glancing at the infrared screen, she sees where each vehicle shows a heat signature. Electros in light blue, small for an electrobike, bigger for a car. And any Internal Combustion Engine is red, tiny reds for the bikes,—a large red only ever up on the Hill. Then there's the odd red/blue flasher for a hybrid, many of those also from the Hill. Nothing from the Hill would come outside the wall in the night and hardly at all in the day anymore. The Bullet is much safer. And all the people wherever they are, as long as they're warm and alive, sign as soft yellow blips. They are the ones who so need the peace down there.

High Banks is quiet and South Downtown is calm too. She heads back across the river and then over the west end of the Hill itself, looking at the brightly lit golf course sloping down to the running water, the fence cutting through the trees known to be topped by razor wire, and the huddle of yellow blips defining its outside edge. *Keep your back against the wall for better cover and control*, they taught at the academy, and these huddled ones intuitively know how to serve that very same purpose, using the fence meant to keep them out.

She's been down there, of course. It's right beside the old neighborhood. She flies past the trees and out over the trailer park, picking out 253 from the roof pattern on the trailer tops, right there on the second last gravel driveway. They used to follow the footpath behind the trailer over to her childhood playground, where the triangular frame of the swings still casts a shadow from the streetlight. She hovers for a moment, her heart flowing along a memory trail of her earlier life. She and Josh had raced down that less worn path, through the huge trees, down to the river to kick through the gravel of the low water beaches. Those two summers they would meet their friend there, as they gathered to ride forth unto the world as the Knights of Justice. Her heart beats an extra and she smiles; then frowns. Before the razor wire, before the lines were etched in the sand, back when people could at least still choose to be friends as opposed to foes.

Where would Josh be tonight? Down there somewhere; she hasn't talked to her brother in a while. He's been so distant lately, even more than usual, who knows what he might be brooding about now. She worries about him—so indiscriminate about who he hangs with, so angry at the world in so many ways.

She can almost see the school bus they rode together, that first year it showed up, the one President Asha sent. Along with refurbished schools with top grade digital labs of the time, the president gave them a ride to school and a new teacher from somewhere in the suburbs. Mr. Worback was a good teacher; wise in the ways of students, instructing them how they each learned best. And with the ex-military school patrol assistants coming through regularly, the new system sure brought discipline—no switch-knives flicking, no wires whipping, not even pencils flying. Mom said Mr. Worback came for the new proportional pay scale, the more upgrading a school needed, the higher the pay. Jeira had Mr. Worback for that last year of junior high. By then they had the brand new high school built, and most of the teachers there were kind of like him.

Jeira got used to all the aptitude tests; President Asha said if you were smart and motivated, you could do something extra important for your country. Jeira was halfway through her undergrad degree when the first female president was assassinated—and the news channels covered a lot then about the last presidential assassination. They ran profiles on past presidents…how President Asha ran up beside that first president who said *What you can do for your county.* The school buses ran for another year after the Vice President was inaugurated, then they stopped. For Jeira, easy access to scholarships ended when the buses were parked. But, by then, she had it figured; grad school was for her no matter what.

Josh didn't think much of the aptitude tests. What did he always say? *They decide how much I know about what they decide I should know.* He just didn't think much of the curriculum, no matter what learning method Mr. Worback said was his. *My method isn't classroom style,* he would say. He spent time with the rough boys in the trailer park, those Jeira had learned to tiptoe around. Josh found them fascinating; being outside the system, they were a source of real in-your-face human lessons, he would say. And Jeira knew his anger fit in with theirs, though his was of a different sort. Scholarly books Jeira read later said the environment they lived in made them *antisocial.*

President Asha put so many educational programs in place, it took the next government some time to dismantle them, so Jeira did finish her Social Work master's. But it was her minor in Criminal Psych and Deviant Behavior that got her a job—that and the flight simulator.

Joshua did attend college that year he was enlisted in the Air Force. Before President Asha's military cutbacks, Josh took his sister for a ride in a flight simulator, and from that day on she was hooked. Now she flew the dream her brother had, and he worked right up front, directly interacting with people face to face—more her original plan. "He's a freelance organizer." That's what she tells anyone who asks about Josh, unless they know him better, and then she uses the word activist.

She'll have to give him shit for not calling. Again…

She turns the craft back towards the Hill, following up the rising rocky slope to the wall. The digital industrialists, the ones who saw the economic benefits of President Asha's educational programs, they live up here in the heights. *Well-educated youth bring prosperity to all citizens of our nation,* Asha spoke out from the podium.

We can use that training in our corporate strategies, they discussed in boardroom meetings—we need to build Bullet Trains, to compete in the new energy markets, now with those damn carbon taxes and cap and trade initiatives and the like maturing. Not just national taxes now, but ones that had to conform to all the international accords. By the time Jeira had her master's, they had shut down most of Asha's social programs. Fewer social programs increased deviancy, so now they needed special security forces, with knowledge of criminology. UPAS was hiring.

She checks her details screen, watching all violence incidents disappear as she crosses inside the wall. Crime on signed paper would never show up as a V code. With no legally defined violence component, it remains hidden in legitimate corners. Although her brother would list many social side effects clearly associated with nastiness. Socially damaging activity on paper isn't actually crime at all, in fact, depending who you talk to. Legal justice vs. social justice—many broad areas remain open to interpretation. If you talked to Josh, you would certainly hear an opinion.

She flies over the large house roofs, some with helihover cage covers, most with gel-massage tubs around swimming pools, and all with convenient access to the Citadel Hill terminal. Here the downtown Bullet line comes up from the bridge, and another connection arrives from Sky Hill—the safest way between the two on Bullet or by private helihover. Beside the station, the crystal glass edifice with the cross of Jesus pokes skyward. People here go no further down slope from their church than to the golf course. The trickiest for law enforcement remains her own neighborhood, the low security little middle class districts on the East slope. Not far from the graveyard.

She passes over the Knomley mansion set back in the trees—majority shareowners in the Bullet system and FriendlyFission. There at the start, they laid out the grand design, knowing of developing need. Aircraft had barely begun to run on electricity, overcoming battery weight restrictions. With biofuel for competition, KnomCor put a major market squeeze on jet fuel prices—to keep them up! As helihovers can't develop any speed over distance, Bullet trains are the best way to get you there, just as fast as national jet traffic used to. Some of her classmates had gone to work for KnomCor when she decided to stick with more school. Then that one Knomley was elected senator, and led the campaign to improve urban security with the helihover surveillance program.

Her thoughts are interrupted when her subconscious rats out to her peripheral vision and she catches view of *that* house down there. Shit…not tonight. She looks away, humming a little tune she has rehearsed, and she quickly banks left back over the wall to escape, following a leaving Bullet. The trestle ramp this side of the Hill, past the wall, stretches from the almost cliff top edge dwindling down to a distant point, where the tracks reconnect with the ground.

The extra height and distance thrill her, and she dives to follow the train.

Here, even trains almost fly. Anything that flies, anything she can swoosh around with up in the air, always makes her feel better. But, as she whooshes along after the train, the anomaly warning beeps at her from the infrared screen.

Chapter 10

Tuesday Evening, July 3

She watches out the window over her twenty-seventh floor balcony, up the slope to where the lights glow ever brighter, her purring feline on one arm. Her gaze gradually drifts down and across the slope towards Duchess Park just a block away. Certainly one of the best-kept open spaces in the city off the Hill with so many people bringing flowers and mementos to their departed loved ones. The City even has a small maintenance budget for it to upkeep the grass and the flower beds. The walk that afternoon had been nice enough to and from and around the park—one of the places other than up on the Hill where a person can actually have a pleasant stroll. Well, as peaceful as one might hope as all afternoon since she had woken up, she couldn't help thinking about how the night shift before had ended. What would the lab report say about the substance on her Firefly Bubble? Her mind wandered around the various possibilities, everything from irregular deviant behavior to the extreme of all authority being challenged. Sometimes there was good reason for defiance of those with extra clout her mother had always said and she had needed to go listen to her mother again.

So she wandered over to mom's final resting place, to confide her inner worries, and to listen to her mother's voice, so well-remembered within her. She felt a little bit closer and a little more supported, when she placed a big bunch of her mother's favorite flowers near and sat cross-legged as she had as a child in the grass by the gravestone. Living here on the slope, she gets away from what she sees on the job daily and nightly, but even more it is being close to mother's memory and voice that helps get her through so many days. She will never forget how she held mother's withered hand that last time, how she spoke so bravely in such a soft voice of her hopes for her daughter, her hopes for peace and love. For all people, not just certain ones and especially not just those with the power to take it and make it when it suits their fancy.

Her reverie is stirred by the tones of a Central American tree frog. Who could be calling so late at night?

"Identify please," she says.

"Your brother is calling, Jeira." The home butler voice informs in its calm voice. "The image is transmitting, would you like a view?"

"Yes please, view on." She turns away from the window, walking across the soft carpet to stand in front of the wall televiewer where the image of her brother blinks on and adjusts to high resolution. Josh looks like he is sitting on a public bench beside a large tree.

"Josh." She smiles brightly at first. "How are you? Why haven't you called? Did you get the messages I've been leaving?"

"Hey Jeir, yeah not bad. How about you? I'm sorry sister; I've been so busy the last while. I hope you're okay. Look Jeira, there's something I want to ask you."

"Well Joshua, there's something I want to ask you first." She frowns. "A couple things in fact. To start with, when's the last time you were over at Duchess Park to visit mom?"

"Ahh, Jeira, just a few weeks ago. I mean her spirit is always with me, the gravestone is just a symbolic marker; going to visit the graveyard is only our cultural tradition…"

"Joshua! Our mother's resting place means the last time we were with her, our lives together and everything she did for us. It has everything to do with how she cared for us. It's a special place and it needs fresh flowers on a regular basis…in case her true spirit is still close. I brought her a bouquet of violets just today, oohh Josh, I miss her so much."

"Yeah, I know, me too Jeir." Joshua sighs. "Hey, I've been listening to some of her music recently, you remember, that old U2 stuff."

"Of course, how could I forget?" Jeira's feels her hand moving up to touch the spot where her heart beats. "Have you been digging through her disc collection?"

"Well, actually, it's coming from another source. So maybe this is where her spirit is actually hanging around, 'cause it's not just the music; it's the idea behind what the songs say. There's this movement coming together, Jeira, and listen—before you say anything, let me tell you I have a really good feeling about this one."

"Yeah sure, Josh," Jeira shakes her head slowly. "Are they planning ahead for November 30 already?" Those times she was on patrol and the protesters walked up the East slope in long streaming crowds, squeezed into the narrow winding streets. Always on November 30—the day of President Asha's assassination. With the streets weaving back and forth across the slope and the crowds coming uphill, the view of their protest from a helihover was always at least partially obscured to the pilot and cameras. So with security buffers on the ground and air surveillance to watch for any hot spots, the police had generally been able to contain the demonstrations until they lost their energy. Not always easily, though. Growing over seven years now, and she had been on patrol that day as a first year UPAS cadet and the two years after. It was just as big a security risk as Parade Day.

"No, it isn't that at all. Nothing to do with regular marches, this is different. Listen Jeir, you could say this group is trying to put Asha back together through Mother 7 and *shela*, you know, the causes that really brought mom to life? I mean this really could be mom's voice speaking through *shela*, 'cause she's using the nostalgia of the old U2 songs to connect everyone with the same tune. Mom's songs. You know how when we were kids the president would talk about the era of civil rights movements, like Martin Luther King. Mom kinda wanted to be a born again flower child or something like that? And then along comes U2 and I mean U2 is still pretty timeless, so it appeals to a lot of people, you know, ones like us who've heard it when we were kids and older people too."

Josh is standing now, looking at his tc back on the bench. He spreads both hands opened as he looks at his sister's image.

"Anyway, Jeira my sister, this fantastic organization will be attending a party-type contest happening tomorrow, that's Parade

Day…and that is what I wanted to kindly ask you about. What are the chances you would be flying patrol tomorrow?"

"Party-type. What kind of party? What are you getting into this time, Josh?"

"Cum'on, Jeir. Like I said, I do see it as mom's spirit and she's speaking through shela. The voice of all women. Her voice combined with Asha's voice. You know, like a combined voice that actually cares. Okay, I mean, I'll tell you, the basic idea is to show the people up on Citadel how we feel about the way things are structured, like who is responsible for everyone and who we truly want to be responsible. And I promise you, we plan to do everything in a completely peaceful way, no V-codes for Urban Police. But shela is being quite clear, that the message has to be firm. A message that has to resonate. Really be heard."

"Like November 30 two years ago. We had long lists of V-codes that time. How's your anger, Josh, have you done any more of those Virtual emotional adjustment sessions?"

"Not the same, Jeira, no violence. That doesn't work. I know that personally. And now shela is repeating that over and over. Just an outdoors afternoon street party…they even have a name for it, the Seymour Park remote control contest."

"Go Sheba." She puts the cat on one arm of the couch. She raises her arms to her hips like she's always done with Josh, and turns to face him directly. "Did you say remote control?" Jeira feels her eyebrows furrow. "Josh, were you guys out at a street party last night? I got smashed by a little remote control, a helihover Firefly, right into my Bubble-Shield. And it was filled with a putrid purple liquid. It was the most disgusting smell; I almost vomited. Was that you and this new group?"

"Where were you patrolling?"

"It's an unnamed street, a dead-end along the west bullet trestle. There were a whole bunch of people, mostly young men, down there. Two of them climbed up that trestle, that's what brought me over."

"Oh God, Jeira, that was your patrol?"

"Yes, Josh, that was my patrol. So tell me again about the no V-code. You know, that was a misdemeanor. Basic obstruction of the UPAS service." Jeira shakes her head. "And that pilot looked like he was just a kid!"

"Timothy. Yes, Timmy is a teenager, but teenagers have voices to be heard too, you know. And he is one excellent pilot, didn't you notice? It's like he can visualize from all directions at once, a skill that should be developing in flight school setting, Jeira, not out on the street corners. That's real natural spatial intelligence, a real ability waiting to be put to good use."

"So what about that purple liquid? It's at the lab right now, unless you can tell me what it is. Is it toxic? Preliminary analysis says they might use it in some overseas locations as a backup for extreme crowd control."

"No, Jeira, not toxic at all. I mean I don't actually know everything about that, it's not my task, and I'd have to run it by Krino or Jojo. But pure organic I am quite sure. Look Jeira, that's what this party is about tomorrow. I mean, I don't want to get you in trouble with your captain, you know that, so I shouldn't tell you everything. But when we were driving across town to pick up that liquid, I kept thinking, we could use a live view from above like the ones you have. I mean you're the eye in the sky, keeping peace on the ground, right Jeira? We were in a real tight spot with some Blades, and you could have helped us, guided us around them. To help keep the peace, sister."

"So who exactly are *we* this time? Come on, Josh, tell me everything," She sighs. "I know you won't. Tell me what you can at least." Jeira paces back and forth in front of her televiewer now, looking sideways at her brother who is doing his own pacing in front of the bench.

"Okay, like you know Krino."

"Krino the endless flirt."

"And a few other people, sister, there are some older fellows I was interviewing, a woman who was one of my instructors for a few weeks, Jojo and the Steve guy..."

"What exactly are you guys doing? Why are you going out into gangbangers' turf? Josh, that's just plain dangerous."

"Hey, Jeira, that reminds me, I have to ask you, you might know the Steve guy. You know from back around the trailer or something. He seems kind of familiar to me, but I haven't talked to him yet. Yeah, so his name is Steve or Staphan, he's a tall light haired guy. Ring any bells?"

"How would I know someone by a description like that?"

"Okay, there's this other guy too, Jeira. I have to tell you about this guy for sure 'cause you would really like what he does. His name's Eli and he works with the Street Angels, so he knows how to interact with the Blades. We didn't have you guiding us, so anyway, not only does he talk our way through, he's trying to enlist some of the younger Blades onto our side. To give them something to do, but in a much more positive way—isn't that a crime prevention strategy? I mean it makes a lot of sense to me, there can be potential natural talent in any group, so it could easily be there in some of those street gang guys."

"Yes, that does sound kinda cool," she says slowly, feeling her heart soften with her voice. "Remember that time Josh when President Asha was talking heart to heart—you know, in one of her truth talks. How she told us we all have a lot of cultural beliefs that aren't the best for our own good. That there's pretty clear social science and statistics showing us what damage they do to us. I mean to glamorize criminal activity in films so it looks appealing, almost culturally promotes a career option, especially to young men. I think that time she was talking directly to young men, telling them they have options, and what you always say, that we all have a talent or two we can use to help our country, to help our family and our own people."

"Of course, Jeir, that stuff goes through my head every day."

"Oh Josh."

She knows you can cut back on crime by cutting back on the reasons young people, especially young men, would turn to criminal activity. Lots of young men aren't naturally drawn to deviant behavior, but the cultural and socio economic factors can have a large influence on choices young people make. If your career options are few, you may choose the excitement of a short term in the underworld. What Asha had said that time...reinforced in the classroom for her, and for Joshua in the streets.

"Jeira, are you having a thought?"

"Yes Josh. Your Eli friend does sound like he's involved in a pretty cool effort."

"So are you on patrol tomorrow? Look Jeir, if you are, maybe you can try to get an assignment so you're patrolling the Hill. Our event has to do with the Parade, I can tell you that much. You could be our view from the sky. I tell you, Jeira, I really got a good feeling about this one. It's quite well organized and it would truly help the people…you know who I mean."

"Yes, Josh, I know who you mean." She sighs. "Yes, the Parade is tomorrow and yes, I am on an extra early shift to help cover. That's a high security event, so they always assign extra shifts. Look, no promises, but I'll let you know."

"Okay, Jeira, if you bring your personal tc with you, I can give you our frequency code. We can talk on a secure connection when it's happening. It would be just like helping mom's spirit Jeira, really. We don't want to lose your job for you; you with one of the last of those middle class incomes."

"I'll see what I can do."

"Love you sis."

"Bye Josh."

Chapter 11

<u>*Wednesday Afternoon, July 4, 2029*</u>

Joshua and Krino saunter along the concrete path through the roped back shrubbery, stepping quickly out of the way as two mini race cars chase each other past their feet. As they approach, the beat of music becomes louder and louder and they sense the festive mood of the crowd up ahead.

"Stand down, girl," Krino says, crouching to grab Zaca by the collar as she strains to take chase.

"Stand down." Joshua repeats, cocking his lower jaw sideways. "Is that a basic dog command?"

"Yes, in fact, it is. This canine is familiar with a broad repertoire of basic dog commands. She is one knowledgeable animal." Krino pats Zaca's side, clipping in her leash. "Good girl."

"The amazing thing is you have a dog mastering prepositional phrases." Joshua looks sideways at his friend. "Remarkable."

"You make all the jokes you want about the dog's intelligence. Fact is, when it comes to social intelligence, Canis lupus domesticus has a far superior sense of pack bonding than Homo sapiens sapiens. That would be us, dawg, you remember? People."

"Dawg me? Or dog me? Or me people?"

"Why do you think so many people have dogs? They get the affection they need that just isn't available from other people. People are so focused on themselves, they have nothing to give. They fight with each other over most everything. Then when they look to each other for love, there's nothing there. So they find the love they actually need in their best friend—and that be dog, my man."

"Hey, Krino, listen, I got a monkey story for you."

"Our general topic of conversation was centred on apes, like when you spell it, it starts with an A, not an M." Krino sighs, shaking his head. "Apes, my furless large-brained friend, not monkeys. Fact is, we actually need to be picking up on what I can tell you so far about the hominid that is a part of each of us. Within us."

"I did hear you last time, Krino," Josh says calmly. "But this actually is a story about monkeys with an M, not apes with an A. Listen, there're these hundred monkeys living on an island somewhere in the South Pacific."

"What island? Most South Pacific islands only have birds and lizards; the pigs, dogs and chickens all come along with the people when they arrived. That means no monkeys."

"Listen for a minute! This is an analogy. There're these hundred monkeys living on an island any old where. Just for you, what that means is they're totally isolated. One day for whatever reason one of the monkeys on that island starts to wash her food. Maybe in the creek or wherever. Before she eats it. The rest of the monkeys living on that same island watch her, and one by one they start to wash their food before they eat it too."

Krino looks at his friend, shaking his head.

"Okay, here's the thing. When the hundredth monkey starts washing her food on that first island, the monkeys on a whole bunch of other islands around there start washing their food too. Spontaneously." He looks hard back at Krino. "That hundredth monkey was critical mass. I got a feeling this time with shela we are gonna hit critical mass."

"You are quite the story teller, my man." Krino kicks a shoe into the sidewalk, making a scratching sound. Zaca looks back at him. He raises an eyebrow at the dog, giving her a wink.

"Now your turn. Tell me about hominids. With an H, right?"

"I'm gonna try and keep this one simple just for you." Krino puts a hand on Joshua's shoulder, giving him a look of deep compassion. "Now even someone like you just might probably have heard of the one name of Lucy 'cause she is still the most famous. She is named after a classic song, and that might help your memory. Lucy in the Sky. With diamonds. Australopithecus afarensis. Okay never mind that part, that is her genus and species but too much for your brain to handle no matter what size you got. So focus on this word, family, she is still in our family, she was a sister. Most importantly for her, and for you and me at this very moment of explanation, she was alive 3.2 million years ago. That was a long time ago, brother, and even then she was quite a ways along her way of getting' to be us. That is the evolutionary process—some folks don't like the idea, but whatever. The important thing being, that our three percent unique DNA started to develop millions of years back. You with me?"

Josh nods dutifully, mimicking a military salute.

"On the other hand, now listen to this, when did us people start building cities? 'Cause cities got neighborhoods for the upper class and neighborhoods for the lower class. Only after we developed agriculture, no more than nine or ten thousand years back. Before that all those millions of DNA development years, we were hunting and gathering no matter what our species. And our social structure was more like a pack of dogs. There was no big man, no king or emperor, no *toorich* or anything like it. So let me be clear, most of our unique DNA developed before cities, importantly, before social class structure came along. Most of our uniqueness developed when we were all together hunting and gathering, all of us. Even the *toorich*. What I'm saying is, having any *toorich* is not in our genes, man."

"You spin a pretty good tale yourself, Krino." Josh wraps his arm around Krino's shoulder and looks into his face. "So how did it happen, then, after we learned about life on the farm and then life in the city, that we now have this social class structure? And the *toorich*."

Krino pats Josh's hand, then picks it up and throws it off his shoulder. "Don't know, never got that far yet. But I tell you, my man; it is not in our genes."

They pass through a row of tall hedges where the ropes are wrapped around to form an entrance gap, coming in to view of a large grassy open area with scattered trees and clumps of bushes. They pause as they step through to the beat of the music no longer dulled by distance.

"Looks like they have a centre set up. Over there."

Krino looks up from Zaca to where Joshua points, distinctly the music source. A large booth pokes up beside a brick plaza where groups of people sit and stand and mill around. A booth-wide Liquid Crystal screen with a popped flex-frame has been erected above, rippling slightly in the breeze. As they approach, they can read *Seymour Park Fifth Annual Remote Contest 2029* flashing around the outside edge. One group of teenage boys finger their control devices and all around them little Fireflies skim above the brittle grass while another group controls the movements of StalkWalkers picking their way through the deeper thickets.

Other folks stand scattered around the booth and along the concrete paths while some sit cross legged in circles on patches of dry brown lawn, avidly chatting together in their little clusters. Joshua scans the faces for anyone he might recognize.

"Shit, shit, shit man, get us a gun." Krino shakes his friend's shoulder. "Look who Eli and Jojo are talking to."

"Jesus, I see Krino, that's one of those Blades, isn't it?" Josh squats to scratch Zaca's chest. "I mean, Eli did invite them, and they are talking to each other. So calm, like Eli says. It must be cool." He stands again. "Come on, let's check it out."

"Shiit. Yeah right…alright. Zaca, you lead out girl."

They walk at a calculated pace up to the side of Jojo and Eli standing both with folded arms in active conversation with a man who's hands talk with him—dressed today in a distinctly out of uniform green dress shirt. Hard to judge his age.

"Joshua. Krino, my man." Eli greets them as they approach. "This here is Ed."

"He was just filling us in on the liquid option," Jojo says, looking at Josh and then Krino. "How well it works."

"Good afternoon, gentlemen," Ed smiles, spreading his hands wide with finesse.

Joshua looks him over closely…definitely not the spokesman from the SUV barricade. His voice sounds so out of place, a political diplomat speaking from an off-the-streets face. Josh's eyes brighten. He can't help thinking about all the people in the larger flock; the one from the other end of the herd may not at all be what you thought when you get up close.

"As I was mentioning," Ed goes on, "I do admit it was I who came to have the green 'toy' gun you gentlemen so graciously left with us. Sting, our apparent leader on the scene, cannot truthfully be classified as an open-minded man. Now that turned out to be quite fortuitous in my case."

"So you loaded up the vial?" Jojo says. "You put the liquid in?"

"Yes, I did take the opportunity to transfer that bit of the mixture you provided into the weapon. Then, as Sting and I have not been on the most amiable of terms, I chose him. He has been rattling my cage bars, so to speak, ever since I affiliated myself with the Blades. An aggressive man, quite without couth. Consequently, my desire to initiate a fracas between us. You may express it as a squaring off or a setting of terms. When I challenged his command, informing him that I would take over for the next shift, he didn't quite see the situation as agreeable. So I discharged a couple squirts into his lower midsection." Ed grins. "All appearance portrayed him as if he had wet his pants…all in good humor of course."

"This is excellent. A real practical field test," Jojo says, grinning. "How did he react? How did it affect him?"

"The man simply has no funny side to him." Ed raises one eyebrow, pursing his lips. "He pulled his whip wire, intent I believe on piercing my very being with a bleed hole. However, he had not taken two steps in my direction when his face distorted in a most peculiar manner. He simply wilted on the spot. Lee and I, Lee's was the other man there, were wisely stepping aside to avoid the wire, but then as far away as possible became our ultimate priority. Gentlemen, what an offensive odour. What could you men possibly intend to do with such a pungent perfume?"

"Come," Eli motions over towards the back of the booth. "Come see."

Josh and Krino look at each other, and then fall in as they all follow Eli around the booth, looking to where his finger points. From just behind the booth stretching out to a large tree, a string of remote mini-but-extra-wide helihovers floats in a line, one behind the other. There must be ten or twelve of them. Eli motions them out onto the grass along that line walking up to the first of the hovering crafts.

"This our gift for the man on the Hill," Eli says, smiling slightly. He indicates the colorful flower petals visible through the transparent cargo hold covers on the tops of the helihovers. "These flowers. For his Parade."

"These are helihover carriers." Jojo takes over, directing attention out along the line. "Each one has capacity to hold a two quart volume..." His voice falters, shifts to a mutter and takes on an irritated tone. "And there should be liquid in some of them. Man, are they all loaded with the dry stuff?" He walks abruptly down the string of crafts all the way to the large tree, looking intently into each cargo hold.

"He really doesn't like flower petals," Josh says.

"He likes Ed," Krino says. "And the squirt gun."

Jojo returns to the group, scowling.

"Yeah, anyways, we have some of these little flying units already up there with cameras," Jojo says. "We need our own views of the parade, so have a look at the screen." He waves a flustered hand to point.

Xia, scurrying about amidst her arrangement of digital devices, has the LC main screen divided into a matrix of sub-screens. City News comes through on one with a live presentation of their Parade Day broadcast. The commentator is speaking with the parade marshal at the moment. FFT reveals their coverage on the screen beside. But it is on the sub-screens below where Jojo jabs towards views of pristine street intersections with gathering crowds. Leaves flutter in the foreground of one image looking down from a high angle, as if the camera is positioned high up in or close to a tree."

"Timothy has some observational HH's already in position," Jojo tells them. "These are strategic points along the parade route, viewpoints selected to both observe our flower delivery and to use in our own calibrated triangulation for positioning. Looks like we are almost set up to make our drop. Four observationals, ain't that right Tim?"

The boy nods, keeping his focus on the assorted collection of remote controls. Joshua recognizes Tim's incessant grin from the evening of the dead end street practice session. The excellent piloting skills he had seen. The smash into UPAS, his sister's unit as it turned out. Reminding him, he can't forget to call Jeir.

"You becha. First run will be all on AP, autopilot." Timothy giggles as he glances up from the scatter of devices. "When they blast off their confetti, we blow our flower petals right then and there." Two other young men begin to fasten colorful streamer paper to the tops of the helihovers, disguising the units under a jovial look of celebration.

"Liquid, we should be using liquid," Jojo mutters, shaking his head. "These dry petals might catch everyone's eye, but ahhh, whatever on this air thing." His voice trails off behind the excitement of others as more people crowd in around the string of carrier helihovers.

Joshua feels extra tingles of eagerness for this flock, those who are now seeking out those ever-elusive greener pastures. He glances around the booth area, breathing in the atmosphere, the energy. Definitely like a move towards more fertile pastures. To his surprise, in the shade of another tree, he picks out the familiar faces of his first two interviewees. Talking to each other. As he looks a little closer, he notices they seem in a heated discussion. He smiles. "Hey Krino, see those two old guys over there? Those are the two I talked to. Downtown. They kinda said they knew each other."

"Looks to me like they know each other," Krino says. "Good enough to maybe take a beatin' on each other."

"Yeah, I gotta go listen to this." He wanders over towards the shade tree, carefully approaching the two.

"Ah, Joshua, come, come. I need help, *ayudame*," says Salvo as he walks up. "I am try to show my friend how to improve his English."

"Not language spoken matters so much, Salvo, action matters much more. What do people do. Peoples' nature give them no choice. Always same story."

"Human nature, you old goat. I tell you and tell you, not peoples' nature." Salvo turns to Josh. "Is this not correct? In English it is human nature."

"What difference?" Zijad raises his hands imploring the above. "Look on what a people do. Rich and powerful man stand high on top of hill. Poor man stand on bottom of hill. But poor man look up. Same story from centuries. Man on top, fear there not be enough. He want keep all. Man on bottom fear there not be enough. He want to take for himself from top. Both have same fear. Big fear. You give either of them answer, neither one listen."

“Not the same story. Look at the technology, you old fool.” Salvo stares at his comrade. “Look what the poor man has now. Am I not right Joshua? Look around you Zijad, my friend. When I was a young man at the bottom of the hill, we stood there with our battered old guns. Maybe bullets, maybe not. That was our technology. Now look what they have here.”

“Technology make no difference on peoples’ nature. You want change, people have to make change on themselves. On inside, many peoples are good nature. But others, you must trick. You must use one part of man’s nature to be stronger than other part. Give the ambitious man something he can conquer and control. Give the self-important man what makes him important. You have to trick these ones.”

Salvo stares at his friend for a moment, looking over at Joshua.

“Yes, that one is true, you must capture his mind and his soul,” says Salvo. “Then you must bring his soul down from the hill. I tell Joshua what is best. You must bring the man down from the hill to visit the bottom. Not as the man he is now, but as the child he was at one time. Only then he will change on the inside.”

“Ahh, Salvo, you talk and you talk.” Zijad jabs his finger at Salvo. “So you will not only bring man from hill, you will bring him as child?” He raises his hands on high again. “As your prophet Jesus said, bring them to me as children. How you will do that one, my friend? How you will bring him down from hill and make him child again? You are not Jesus I am sorry to say,” He pokes repeatedly towards Salvo’s chest. “And if you are, most people not listen to prophets. How will you do this one?”

Joshua shakes his head, like listening to the interview analyses after he voice scanned them into database. He can’t get a word in edgewise here, but the jumble of ideas from this conversation mix in a swirl with the memory of those analyses and then gradually settle to form a first draft shela rhythm. Her VirtuALL feedbacks. The virtual world, designed to entertain, where people know the preferred version is an All Links Live connection, a true feelings integrated familiarity, designed to give a person a vicarious experience of each character’s life at that very moment. The way they experienced the Knomley and the citymen news clip, and gave shela her emotional feedback, recording each person’s response to each moment of the drama. Could that somehow be applied? To the people of the hill? As children?

"Now the poor man has lots of education." Salvo is saying. "These ones are not illiterate campesinos. Asha gave the people knowledge. Now they can think and plan for themselves. Now they know what they are doing. And they have technology to help with their plan."

Joshua steps back smiling, leaving them to banter on. His face straightens and his mind churns as he wanders back towards the LC screen, half noticing what's around him. If there were just some way of convincing Mr. Knomley to come down the hill in virtual; one that would keep him prim and proper but still give him the experience. Connected only to feedback lines, now that might make things more possible. It wouldn't be kidnapping if he were doing it of his own free will. Big if, that. The free will part lingers in the way. How would one get him to actually want to stick his wrists into the pickups? Some form of mild deception. He shakes his head clear, and looks up in surprise.

"Hello Joshua. How are you?" The grin beams at him. "I had a chance to drop by the park here for a minute and I saw you."

"Oh, John, hello."

"I just wanted ask, did you get those reports I sent?" John says. "From Bruce?"

"That's all in the shela database now, yes."

"Excellent." The smile spreads wider. "You know Josh, I finally feel as if I've really done something. I sure know Bruce would be happy, even ecstatic about what we are doing. I mean, compared to all those official presentations I've given, this might actually have an impact."

Josh tries to focus on this new conversation. "Have an impact, yeah, that's what we want." He looks over at Krino and the group, then back at John. "For sure, but tough to change people, isn't it?"

"Yes, it is, I know that. I feel terrible about how much it took to change me. As much as I have changed. I mean, I would listen to Bruce talking all those years, but I didn't actually hear. All those things he would bring up, he was so angry a lot of the time. Pushback, I would tell him, that's what we are dealing with here.

Patience, we need to be persistent and patient. But now I see how the audiences were all so much like me, listening but not hearing."

"Right." Josh has a distraction ringing in his mind.

"Denial is what Bruce would call it. People in audiences would be tuned out, even when they were officially there."

"Denial John, I hear you." Josh's mind alarm is ringing louder. "John, sorry, I want to ask you more about that but I have to call my sister. When can we talk again?"

"Oh, hey that's fine 'cause this is a pretty public place for me to be." John holds his hands up, backing away. "No problem Josh. Maybe at the next shela meeting."

"Right, talk to you then..." Josh pulls out his tc as he hurries over to the booth.

The crowds gather around to watch the screens where the parade has begun to move. As they follow the decorated floats, some point over at the fleet of cargo carriers hovering off across Seymour Park in a wavy string; their streamers blowing gently in the breeze. They each follow the one ahead in an identical pattern over towards the far-off west trestle. In the distance, they ascend becoming insects with long trailing legs up the side of the iron grid, and then turn to follow the tracks up the steep slope to disappear from sight. All focus now switches back to the sub-screens, and as the crowd squashes up close for a better view, Josh keeps to the edge.

The parade has reached main street on one of the observational camera screens while City News and FFT compete to comment above the blare of the lead brass band on the news screens. Sister, sister, sister Josh drags his eyes away from the distractions, pick's Jeira's private number on his tc and waits for her to recognize.

"Where are you Jeir?"

"Josh!" She sighs. "I thought you would call earlier. Never mind, I'm on a patrol right now that is over the Hill. I'm assigned to a viewer posting, mostly hover and hold positions. I'll patch you my main camera so you can have a look. Everything's going smooth so far."

"Sorry Jeir. Yes, I can see the parade now. Can you just keep that feed coming through…I know that's gonna help us."

"I can do that."

"Hey sister, I'd introduce you to the young pilot from the street party. But you might still be a little pissed." Josh glances over at Timothy. "He's right here but he's intensely busy. Real talent right here, Jeira, just like Asha said. And it's what he can do for his people."

The formation of cargo carriers now appear on the screens, no longer insect size, but bright and colorful like the parade floats and they pull into line as if a late addition, hovering along above the floats and bands, mingling in with floating helium balloons.

"When they pass the Crystal Church," Jojo says. "That's when they'll start the confetti poppers and firecrackers."

"We need more spread," Timothy tells his friends, fiddling with a master control. "We wanna maximize our coverage."

The group of folks around the LC grows, as mini Fireflies, StalkWalkers and racecars pull over to park in their respective pits. The high point of the Seymour Park Contest seems just ahead. The first floats approach the Crystal Church on the screen.

"Alright, here goes." Timothy's eyes widen and his tongue pokes halfway out curled up over his top teeth. He pushes a button as the first carrier passes below the observational helihover hugging up beside the spire. All along the length of the parade the rose pink petals drift down in a series of swirling clouds as each carrier makes its release. Folks along the parade route, the people of the Hill, raise their arms and cheer as the lead band salutes their town square.

As the petals settle down amongst the crowd watching the parade on the Hill, those gathered at the LC screen watch intently. No one says a word as the minutes pass. Josh squats to scratch Zaca's ears. Krino drums his fingers on Josh's back.

"Well? What's happening?"

"They should be noticing, shouldn't they?"

"Shit," says Jojo, shaking his head. "I knew it…I mean, the sense of smell depends on humidity…this is a dry day and we're dumping dry petals."

"So now what?"

"We bring the carriers back," says Timothy in his more mature voice. "We could squeeze in a second dump." They continue to stare at the LC screen. City News happily comments on the bright sunny day. Then it happens. Bang! The sharp explosion comes through the sound system as one of the sub-screens goes blank.

"What the f…?"

"Look, look. It's the Hill cops." Another sub-screen shows a cyan motorbike below its tree with a Hill security guard standing beside, shotgun pointed directly at the camera. Another woof of gunfire through the sound system accompanies the immediate static signal on another sub-screen.

"Shit. We're losing our triangulation network. We have to try to decode their scrambled GPS signal up there. We got no time for that. Or go by eye." Timothy and his friends scramble to adjust their remotes.

"Okay, forget all that—I recorded my path on the way up," Timothy says with a new authority. "I'm gonna transmit the route to you guys so you can follow it back down. I'm gonna reverse my unit and back track. You guys follow."

The crowd squints hard now, jabbering, whispering and looking off towards the west trestle where the carriers went out of sight on their way up. "There they are," a voice cries out. "Good eyes." The line of fluttering dots looms larger and larger. "Now I see them too." Until the line of streamer hangers hovers back to its place in Seymour Park.

"At least those cops didn't spot our carry birds."

"Thank God for the streamers."

"We need to load them up again, right?"

"Yo, but what's the best option for position now?" Timothy and this helpers banter back and forth. "We only got one observer left." "We gonna fly same formation?"

"Look, just load them up. All of them. With liquid this time." Jojo takes control now. "Joshua, how's your connection with your sister? Give Xia your tc. She can get your transmission into our network; patch it through to the LC. We need her positional network too if you can get it."

Jojo instructs those around to load liquid capsules into each carrier hold. "Timothy, you figure it out? What's our best approach now?"

"Like I thought, I can't break their GPS scramble signal on the hill. I can fly by previous flight path memory to get back where we were." The boy has another grown-up moment, turning to his two friends. "You guys each fly a lead unit, so we have three separate formations. Lock the rest on as auto-followers just like last time. Both of you lock on to my lead, but pick up a random offset to define your routes and follow me to get back up the Hill. Then we separate."

"How do we do a liquid release," Jojo mutters, shaking his head. "We should have had this all pre-planned. You should always have a back up. We'll have to figure something out. Get those little birds up there first. Wait, wait, wait, I got an idea. Rip those streamers off; we want them to stand out this time. Any flashers or sirens they got, turn them on."

Timothy and his buddies grab their controls, gathering around the image coming through from Jeira and the remaining observational still up beside the spire. They each pause to have their bellies sprayed with an evil orange face, then zip off along the trestle back up the Hill with Timothy's unit in the lead.

"Joshua, what's going on down there," Jeira asks. "There was such a beautiful shower of rosy pink. Almost like little flowers."

"They are flower petals, sister," Josh says. "Please hold where you are Jeir...you're our best observational point now. Can you patch us your positional network?" He looks blankly at Jojo, shrugging.

"Sorry, Josh. I couldn't give you exact position even if I wanted to." Jeira says. "That is completely classified."

"Never mind then. Get her to spot out the Hill security police," Jojo says. "The shotgun boys."

"Hey Jeir, you see any cyan bike cops on the ground? Can you point your camera their way?"

"Yeah…okay Josh. There's always tight security with a regular patrol around the Bullet station. The middle of the parade is just looping past it now. I'll hover higher and give you a pan shot."

"Timothy. Fly straight up to the Bullet station," Jojo says. "Past where you were last time. Join the parade there. Keep right out in the middle of the street, out in the open. Position the carriers just above Citadel Station. Maybe a hundred 'n fifty feet elevation. Wind's comin' from the south, so get them flying in a circle around the south side."

The string of helihovers follows the litter of the parade route gone past, looming bigger and bigger on Jeira's camera. Timothy leads them into a hover circle above the crowd awaiting the grand parade finale when the last float reaches the platform. "Okay, now turn on the flashers and sirens. Loud. We want some negative attention this time. Now you, Timothy, I want you to think like a dive bomber, you know, like in those old war plane movies. Pretend you got machine guns and can do a strafe attack." Two cyan motorbikes, patrolling along beside the parade, spot the helihovers. The officer who shot out the camera they all saw is pointing his finger up at them.

"Josh, something strange is happening," Jeira's voice comes through on her brother's tc.

"What is it Jeir?"

"Hill Security is putting out a Bulletin now. There's a high alert warning coming through. There're disturbances close to some water sprinklers. People are tripping over each other to get away from those areas. They're getting concerned about possible crowd panic."

"There they are…they got us sighted." Jojo points to the screen. "Now crank those sirens up to max, Timothy. Form a tight circle above them, nice and slow. Buzz around like a swarm of lazy bees. Now you see that cop? Dive right into his face, Timothy, just you. Really piss him off."

"But they'll blow our drop birds out of the air," Timothy cries out. "Like the observationals."

The two Hill Security Force men have dismounted, shotguns drawn. As Timothy's helihover dives down within feet of the Hill officer, and then veers off to the side, he quickly pulls his shotgun and fires. Then, like a day at a skeet practice shoot him and his partner pump shell after shell into the air and blow the buzzing flock of carriers out of the sky, one after another. Timothy's last, as he makes one more valiant dive bomb run. And a dark pinkish mist starts to descend on the Bullet station, carried by the breeze as the parade begins its grand salute beside the Crystal Church.

"Exactly," says Jojo quietly. He grabs Timothy in a bear hug, lifting him off his feet. He then clasps his hands over his head, dancing in a tight little circle.

“Josh, the folks up here do not look happy,” says Jeira. “At all…I don’t think there’s going to be any crowd panic; they don’t seem to be able to even form a crowd.” She zooms her camera in on different groups of people caught up in their efforts to get somewhere else. With hands over faces, eyes wide in looks of sheer disgust, they stand in fits of coughing. Some crawl on hands and knees through mist covered grass, having lost any concern of grass stains on their exotic clothes.

The two Hill Force security men, having holstered their shotguns, stand with hands on hips after a mission completed. As a swirl of the mist drifts their way, one raises his sleeve to cover his mouth, and starts running for his bike. The other races coughing close behind.

Chapter 12

Wednesday Evening, July 4

They sit huddled together in small groups, talking in hushed tones, waiting for the latest inside information to be revealed. The downstairs improvised theatre hums with the beat of the U2 music and the anticipation of the crowd. Mother7 waits with them, the all women avatar visible, yet patiently immobile as if she had been there for all time.

The brick walls of the old industrial office tower above tremor slightly, even into the solid concrete floor beneath their feet and Krino and Josh look at each other.

"That's gotta be the eleven o'clock Bullet," says Joshua, pointing. "We must be right beside the trestle, one of those buildings on the street where we had that remote control practice party. I'm sure we just came another way this time."

"Yo, man. On the street that gots no name. I look for street sign posts on my way in and there is none. And that is the song been playing here this fine evening...listen. *Where the streets have no name.* It's like I get it, man. Shela's rhythm." Krino scratches Zaca behind the ears. "So double check our coordinates. On that map you always looking at."

"You are right, bud. This place is D4, right on that same no name street."

"Ts'what I said," Krino says.

"Hey, you been keeping up on FFT? What they've been talking about since forever, they're finally going to do it. They're going to be FFM now. They'll have to change the name of the Mag too."

"What?"

"Yeah," Josh says. "Fortune Five Million instead of Fortune Five Thousand."

"So what's that supposed to mean?" Krino scratches his cheek.

"The *toorich* class is getting a lot bigger, not actually, but just by definition," Josh explains. "Median income will be a lot lower, actually, but many more people will be in this social class. Since we learned to farm, and then forgot that and moved to the city."

"No shit."

"Hey, looks like she's gonna talk." Josh nods towards the theatre stage.

"We have made a statement." Mother7 has brightened and risen. "We have shared how we feel with the *toorich;* we can consider them now informed." Her subterranean eyes follow the edge of the crowd. "We know passive submission will bring us nothing, so we are actively expressing our needs, our desires, our requirements. Through special messages. Our bouquet delivered over their Parade tells them directly how the current arrangement smells to us. Our bouquet calls out, quite clearly, offensive."

A cheer slowly rises among the less tired in the crowd, energizing the others and escalating as it circles around the room and then around again. Many come to their feet in applause. Zaca barks.

Xia's LC screen, set up on the back wall, runs and reruns clips of people rushing from the Parade, from Citadel Station, tears pouring from their eyes, choking on pink tinged air. Both City News and FFT have picked up detailed coverage, simply having swung their cameras from parade float shots to the spectators. One clip of a woman in her Parade Day best has been trending, and they zoom in on and show in slow motion her dishevelled face portraying directly into one camera a day gone bad. Though she isn't able to voice words, other voices background to her speak. "This can't be happening," a woman's voice shrieks. "This cannot be allowed," a determined male says. "Our community must remain safe and peaceful." Then another man. "These terrorists must be apprehended and punished."

Mother7 opens her hand towards the clip. "This final voice is clearly dating himself to the times of terrorist labels; pinning the views of the community on the no longer relevant past. Our message must continue, so an addendum will come out in tomorrow morning's publications, after we let the bouquet influence sink in. Hill folks may wish to change their clothes, to sleep on it perhaps. This further public notice will be quite explicit, defined and written in clear legal terms. We have taken out a full-page ad in the soon to be FFM Mag, detailing what we expect from all non-participants on the Hill. Full financial support for education and health programs for all, no less than Asha had in place. This message includes required amounts and a deadline for the *toorich.* We have financial accounts waiting for their donations…which will of course come from the depths of their newly compassionate hearts."

The cheer soars again, higher this time, all rising up now to join in with many arms reaching up in celebration. Some begin to dance around, to boogie with each other.

"So we do appreciate the improvisations some of you made to adjust our air delivery plan." Mother7 raises her voice. "Thinking on your feet has paid off." Josh looks around to find Jojo; he wants to give him a pat on the back at least but the man is busy swinging a chair around. "Some slight miscalculations had to be dealt with in the field to pull things off as planned. Thank you for your innovations."

"Still everything is not settled, all is not final." Mother7 holds both hands up, waiting for the din to calm. "The struggle continues. As we both wanted and expected, there are some disgruntled people on the Hill. We have caught their attention, as intended. Most excellent. But now many have retreated to other urban hills, to rural estates, where they may presume to be visiting with friends and family. Reports have it most late afternoon Bullet Trains were full today and most private helihovers are posted as on vacation."

Jeira must be noticing that Josh thinks, he'll have to ask her.

"So as historical evidence indicates, people first react in a defensive manner. We recall the Asha anniversary protest walks up the Hill. We have done well here today, not hurting anyone, not maiming anyone, not causing any real damage, but at the same time calling attention where it is due. We are following the policies and protocols of what we have learned from past uprisings, past calls for change. Let's review the November 30 protest marches. Last year the marches were met with taser guns and rubber bullets. Now, we are not being affected by that type of retaliation."

Krino nudges Josh, whacking that spot on his shoulder.

"We stand on distinctly different ground this time." Mother7 pauses, glancing at each of them. "We have essentially slapped their face; we have caused them shame."

A muted murmur runs through the crowd.

"So what are their reactions? Now there are rumors they wish to raise their wall higher. Their plan to enclose the Hill community in a virtual Plexon-Bubble has been revitalized, to keep any recurrence of anyone dropping off another bouquet. Complete control of all air traffic down to midge size in and out; an added annoyance for them but perhaps no more so than their concrete wall. As well, they are proposing to suspend the economy sections of Bullet Trains this week, maybe next, maybe indefinitely."

Josh feels his face drop to a frown.

"So these are general policy proposals, but it is the reaction of the individual people we must also pay attention to as well. Though we do have a period of relaxation for the moment, we must remain vigilant. Be attentive, be observant. We must not become negligent at this time of maximum attention. We must continue to implement our alternatives. So we will form new teams, again based on aptitude and orientation profiles, and we will continue. We must be prepared for any response."

Josh looks to Krino who signs a thumbs up.

"To help us understand what we might expect from them, we now have a presentation from one of our social experts about the best prediction of people's reactions. And after that we will hear updates on our other options."

Lana has made her way down the steps between the chairs to speak. She turns to face the crowd. "The flower revolutions of early this century and late in the last did bring change, but not always in the ways expected."

"We goin' for that Philly Tea tonight," Krino winks at Joshua.

"Really," says Josh, sighing. "Good for you."

"Why would that be?" Lana questions. "Let's take a look at people from an innovation theory perspective. It is innovation or change we are asking of the *toorich*, so the well-documented studies of people in situations of broad proposed change will apply here. We are propositioning an innovative and completely new manner of not just thinking or believing, but much more importantly the resultant behavior. We want people to wilfully, or at least obediently, respond to our social pressure, to submissively modify their conduct. Historically, in many situations where an innovative idea has been brought forward, the response has been analyzed, and keeping human nature in mind, the results are understandable."

She looks at them, stopping for a second. She raises a finger.

"People are not all the same; in fact they vary considerably on an individual basis. But fortunately within a group of people across the variance of human nature we do find consistent patterns. So it isn't hard to see that it is not just us and them, it is rather two opposing cultural beliefs grinding up against each other. It is, as with most human issues, complex."

"Brains dude," Krino says. "She's got 'em."

Josh nods, listening.

"When it comes to innovation, let us divide people up in say a statistical manner," Lana says. "Considering innovation theory, in any representative sample, there are the Innovators. These are a very small group of two and one half percent. Innovators come up with new ways on their own as these are the ones who change for change's sake—it is their nature to constantly try out new ways. This very small faction leads. The next group, thirteen point five percent are the Early Adopters, they will look at what the leaders have done, they'll say 'hey, educating everyone, supplying all with the basics of health, yes, I have the resources, I see the benefits there, good idea', and these will then follow. But now things get dicier. Progressively as we climb the bell curve, we meet more and more resistance. Within the next standard deviation, people start analyzing. They get out their accounts sheets, and they need to see real returns. When they find the benefits, when they see that what others are doing is actually working, when enough data has accumulated showing repeatedly the same results, they do gradually come to make effort to modify in line with the innovation."

"I wanna get innovative with her," Krino says.

"Shh..." Josh quiets him.

"Now let's jump ahead for a second and skip the next group—we'll come back to them. When we start at the apex of the bell curve, that other full half of any part of humanity, well, for them there never was any change. Nothing, in fact in their lives changes—they are unaware of any innovation. This large group is actually not a problem for us, not part of the solution, but not a problem. It's the group we skipped just before the apex, the group that puts up the greatest resistance, the Early Majority that delays the longest in their analysis—they are the ones we will have the most challenging time with. And we do have data on them. These are still quite unpredictable on an individual basis.

"So this is just a quick overview of what we are most likely up against. We have tried an innovative method of bringing social shame to the forefront, and applying it directly in the interests of our desired outcome. We must also consider ourselves; we would have patterns of our own. There are those among us, who deep in their hearts are furious, angry to the nth degree at the social injustice, who simply want to see literal blood on the streets."

Joshua feels the familiar indents where nails have pressed deep into his palms, and he softly tells his fists to chill. "Calm." He uses those Eli words. "Strength."

"We must be careful that we stick to our policy of resistance," Lana concludes. "A slap on the face, a good solid slap, but nothing more."

As Lana steps to the side, she nods to the ever attentive Xia.

"She's one intelligent woman," says Krino. "That was one fine little lecture."

"Yeah," says Joshua. "You better go congratulate her."

"Yeah, see you later, man"

"Thank you Lana," Mother7 says. "Now, we will have an update on our other options."

Jojo bounds down to the presentation area, turning to face the crowd. "You all saw the pipeworm," he says. "You know we have the technology to move through the underground, through the public piping systems. Now, all communities have three piping connections, those are water, storm sewer and sanitary sewer. Yes, that last one is the shitty one. And in the room next to us, we are thirty feet from the main utility right-of-way going up and down the Hill. So in anticipation, we have begun tunnelling straight across. We expect to be punching a tap into one of those lines in a couple days, depending—it sounds like on what their response is to our bouquet and published message. Through that tap, we have access to any household or any group of households. These pipeworms were designed to move through fluid over a wide range of pressures and we have knowledge of each worm's location at any time. And our tracking system cannot easily be blasted out of the air. The worms can carry a load that we leave at any household, a load of one or more off a list of discomforts we can deliver."

"Kick in the butt," Krino says.

"Yeah," Josh nods.

"I cannot emphasize enough that the pipeworm option eliminates our need to go through the air again," Jojo says. "This underground signal won't be a slap in the face, but a good solid kick in the posterior." He looks at Mother7, catching her many eyes. "If need be," he adds. "So we can tap in to any of those three lines. Then our delivery options depend on which line. We can make their whole community stink again, through the storm water catch basins, we can make their drinking water give them a certain gag effect or we can blow their toilets backwards and let them live in scented effluent for a while. That is a choice we have to make while we wait."

"Bubble-Shield or not," Josh says.

"We got 'em enclosed," Krino says.

"I wanna let you know as well, that the air drop we just carried out was an indiscriminate dump on everyone, all those statistical groups of Lana's," Jojo says. "Now up on Citadel, that's a pretty good selection of our target, but with the underground approach, we do have schematics and line diagrams from public records, and we can narrow our target down to the individual household. Or even the individual, if we choose the water or sanitary line for example and if we know or estimate their personal washroom patterns. If we were to take a gentleman like Knomley who may have an ensuite facility, we have direct access to his shower water and his sanitary drain."

"So there we are," Jojo says, moving back down the steps. "We can pick who we want."

"A word on our third option," Mother7 says. "For our social underground initiative, we do have a potential candidate selected, but we want to keep that identity anonymous at this time. Our candidate has great potential. We'll keep you up to date over the next few days as we wait. Patience, my children."

She bows her head and her illumination begins to dim as the volume of the music slowly builds. The crowd stands, stretching, many yawning and begins to dissipate. Josh rises, glancing around for Krino but feels a tap on his shoulder. He turns to find John behind him.

"Hi Josh, how are you?" The guys flashes on of his bright smiles.

"Hey John."

"I am so sorry I couldn't take a chance on staying longer at the Bouquet Day, but, hey, it seemed you were a little harried too. Did that go great or what?"

"Sure did." Josh unwinds Zaca's leash from the chair.

"Hey, I know Bruce would be so happy about this." John went on. "It so fits with his expose-the-truth ideas. Now those things he worked so hard to get out, well, they seem to have a voice now. And surely not the voice I could ever give them officially. Like I was saying, I could never have publicly expressed what your group here is saying with this kind of message."

Josh bends to clip Zaca's leash onto her collar and stands again. "Right." He nods, listening.

"You wouldn't believe the struggle Bruce had trying to officially get the planetary hectares idea through to Council. He used maps a lot for display and acres are pretty versatile when you put them on a map. I mean an acre of residential property looks the same on a map as one of his planetary acres—we knew people truly connected with the idea."

"So could anyone like me, say, put my own or anybody else's planetary acres on my screen map?" Josh asks, politely.

"Sure enough. If you know their income—combined with wealth if possible—or some proxy for it like house size, you could easily do an accurate estimate and then pop an acres sized circle up there on the map." John nodded avidly. "Just that we never got it to public engagement. Even if you cast your talk in terms of lifestyle, they ask for your source and no one ever wanted to talk income and wealth equals consumption equals ecological footprint. Endless pushback. All those people would see was an attack on their own personal lifestyle. They had plans. And if something looked like it was going to interfere with those plans, they would just not want to talk about it. So even if the sustainability clearly pointed to was of their own biosphere, our planet, their own life support system, and say we showed them clearly using real measurement the broad impact of the higher income on sustainability or lack thereof, they would rather pretend it wasn't happening."

"Is that the denial you mentioned?"

"Pushback, but exactly, denial Bruce would say." John nods. "Too big of a problem, so there is no problem."

"Right."

"They planned on having a bigger better lifestyle than their parents, just like their parents had a better one than their grandparents. That's the way it happened all along and that's what they came to expect—that's definitely what they wanted. The way it had always been, they'd say."

"Yeah, I've read about things like that," Josh says. "Attitudes like that."

"You want to hear about attitude, my goodness; you need to know what it was like talking to the City officials. The senior administration. I mean, they were well educated people, quite intelligent, but you could see what they did at work, how they carried those personal lifestyle beliefs right into the city design they would approve. A complete reflection of the attitude they carried in their personal lives. Bruce pointed that all out to me. Pathetic, that was one of Bruce's favorite descriptive words."

Josh guides Zaca around the chair, picking a walking path between the other groups of people gathering to talk. John walks along beside.

"You know, Joshua, I have been looking around at the audiences that show up here," John says. "You guys are also quite well educated, very intelligent by my observation. If you don't mind my saying. This difference is, most of you guys can't be much older than my kids."

"Everyone can have a voice." Josh looks at him. "Don't you think?"

"Oh yes, of course, everyone, you are right Josh. You know I'm just kind of curious, I mean how do you guys live if you don't mind me asking? It seems like a lot of you are students."

"Personally, I find the formal education doesn't fit for me so well," Josh says. "So I read a lot, but mostly, and I did learn about this originally in one anthropology class, I do research by the participant observer method. That is one of the standard methods of anthropologists. I love to learn that way, like for example, the way I talk to you and learn about what Bruce thought."

John nods, eyes widening.

"But you know, a lot of my friends are part time students—some older ones are still finishing off what they started in Asha's day. You can learn a lot online, and some know how to get that recognized officially. There's part time work when you find it, you know, to eat and have a place to live. We cooperate a lot, like as a community. We all walk wired, so we stay in touch about whatever's going on. Yeah, it's pretty cool."

"Wow, you know Josh, I am starting to like this whole outlook. Are you heading off now? You know, I think I am going to hang around here a bit and talk with some of your friends."

"Cool," Josh says. "See you later."

Josh glances around for Krino as he follows Zaca towards the exit.

Chapter 13

Wednesday Evening, July 4

Jeira's afternoon surveillance shift was extended into the evening, almost a double shift, pushing the limits of UPAS safety on allowable piloting time. Her thinking is a complete muddle, and she runs on instinct. The Captain's office seemed to be stretching interpretation of regulations during the confusion, or possibly the confusion was the deciding factor. A chaotic sequence of reassignments came after the parade's untimely ending and the quick loss of parade goers. First there was keeping an eye on the residents of the Hill who had attended the parade and directing emergency medical teams to the locations where need was most insistent. For a while she was almost directing her own assignments, when Martine at ground was busy with the coordinating chaos. Going by what her perspective view allowed her to judge best, she flew back and forth picking up real time traffic imagery to assist medical aid ground units coming from and to the crystal church square. Just as the medical situation came under control, ground sent her for a hover and hold at first one and then a second Bullet Train wall transition station. They wanted video footage of the gate holes, on top of the security scans as the final allowed Bullets entered the Hill for the afternoon. That request held high priority, a directive straight from the Captain's office. In the late afternoon, when the demand for traffic out from the Hill became intense, and new Bullets had to be allowed in to supply trains for the outbound traffic demand.

"You sure Martine?" she says, her mind fighting fatigue.

"That's what they sayin', those incoming are empty in the economy class. They are not letting anyone board the back sections. After these last few trains, no more trains at all."

"But how are most people going to get around, get where they're going?"

"I know girl…hey, I've got another call."

Amidst the afternoon confusion Jeira wondered who she was actually helping. After returning to base, exhausted enough by then, she heard after a required one hour rest, she'd be back in the air.

On the second shift, as the sun settled low in the horizon, Martine also on extended shift directed Jeira to join other UPAS helihovers patrolling an observational circuit along the wall, the perimeter of Citadel Hill. They flew a weaving pattern, recording all movement in the streets on either side of the wall. She was pulled from that circuit for a hover and hold over a construction site as crews arrived with large machinery to erect a temporary pillar station—that's what ground called it, apparently one component of a partially put together plan to have a virtual plexon shield over the whole community. Martine revealed bits and pieces. She had heard some talk of that in the past—an extra security feature of some sort.

Now she wonders.

Hovering, she scrambled to file report data, all the time thinking about the whole of what was going on. Talking to Martine on the Captain's office perspective, she shared a few items on what was really going down.

Now, with the pillar station finally in place, Martine busy, Jeira's concentration sags under the heaviness of the extra flying hours. Officially there's still a piece of the shift left she'll dedicate to Parade Day security reports to be on the captain's desk by morning. But other assignment type unresolved questions won't let her alone, maybe not exactly official UPAS, but she knows she can't return to base just yet.

She selects recall list, and lets autopilot take her back to hover beside the west trestle, looking at the spot where that tiny Firefly wove its way through the girder beams. Resting her eyes, she lets her mind drift. Who knows what conversations might be happening inside the building walls or inside the minds of people. This dead end street where she had the collision with her miniature duplicate. Triggered by the moment, she swoops down to look around at street level, finding no one on the structural grid, not anyone on the street tonight, not one burning barrel with a warming fire. A deserted place for a surface level cruise.

Someone right here had been playing with a remote control helihover then, and now the reports from ground say small suspicious flying aircraft were seen and destroyed this afternoon right up over the Hill. But destroying them had only exacerbated the situation on the ground. She had reported her collision two nights ago, but ground didn't seem to be making a connection there yet. Should she speak up and inform them? Who is Josh involved with and whose side is she on now? How will peace ever come about—on or off the Hill.

She knows her brother and his folks are doing what her heart has always told her was right. He always has good intentions when he gets past his anger; she knows her brother well. But not all people have that kind of outlook. Not everyone spent their early summers down by the river talking about the knights of old—their courage and honor. Josh and Sas had agreed to total boy-girl equality all the way. A lady knight is completely equal to all gentleman knights. Nice then, so idealistic. Criminal deviation studies reveal all people have some tendency towards deviant behavior, even if at a very slight level. She just worries about him, the risks he takes, and the lack of security across most of the city. If they confront the people living on the Hill, the ones with the real power and resources, the ones who give direction to her Captain, could they ever have any influence? And would they survive?

At least they have the courage to face their fears and look at the truth; she has always given the protesters that. Courage they talked of long ago. Courage she should have.

In her weariness, but now with eyes partially rested, the voice that had never left her in total peace demands attention. With resistance weak, deep inside memories call her back to that long ago house party, the one she's spent a lifetime trying to ignore. And the parking lot on the ground she's been avoiding for so long. She knows she has to face that with courage, for her own peace of mind, she has been told. She zooms back up to cruise height, and spontaneously calls up the coordinates of the house in the Knomley neighborhood.

Her craft takes the most direct route back up the Hill, and like a trusted steed given head, reins itself in when they arrive at the steel gate entrance. She stares down at the hated place, forcing herself to relive that past. Two large red dots on infrared chase each other tonight down the long driveway and she guesses what types might act in such a way. *That* driveway. No matter how she's tried, she will never forget her visit to *that* house—*that* party, around *that* island pool.

The summer just after senior prom.

For not only did the digital industrialists want the cream of the crop for their businesses, the more daring boys on the Hill had their eyes on the prettiest girls living down below. Where the rules were much more lax.

The parking lot with the abandoned grey executive SUV after...she shudders but keeps her focus now.

After that party, after the drinks they teased into her and who knows whatever else they slipped into them. She still can only guess from the symptoms; that sense of carefree wonder, that temporary state of euphoric glee. She felt like a child goofing around with those three boy playmates who gave her that ride home.

Almost home.

She traces the road they most likely took back down the Hill, through the wall where there had once been a vehicle gate and through the more familiar streets around the trailer court.

Her struggling-for-control adolescent mind thought she knew one of them; it felt vaguely safe. But they pulled into that parking lot, stopping among the abandoned SUV's at the stretch grey luxury unit. At first the toying continued as they tried to tease her in, but something in her strongly resisted, and the game switched to serious. They became more than just verbally encouraging. One grabbed her quick when she tried to scream, stuffing his driving glove roughly into her mouth—she can still taste the sweaty leather mixed with the blood on her tongue. Another held her arms behind while the third ripped off her blouse, to tie her hands with. She bites her lip now, feeling those hands all over her, and each of them having her, then leaving her crying in the wrecked auto.

As an older mentor now, she consoles her inner teenage self and the pain diffuses somewhat. She looks down and the executive grey has been salvaged to somewhere else, another help to heal the past. Time makes change, yet still she must face her deepest fear and do what she knows to be right. Today. She holds her lips tight, releasing all in a heaving sob.

She finds refuge in her professional outlook most days, but back then, she cut her pretty hair, and followed Josh around for the rest of that summer, learning to dress rough. And act tough. Her mother was so worried, but she made up a story like Josh's. She developed a glare for those boys in the trailer park that summer, keeping her hand clenched tight around her new mini whip wire. She carried it with her the first year at university. And she never did tell anyone she really knew the whole story of that night, not her mother, not her brother. Just the councillor later, when she began learning techniques.

She can only ever process so much at any one time. She returns her thoughts to the academic, her refuge—deviant behavior is more prevalent in younger cohorts. If her trauma showed as a V code incident, its location would be conveniently down below the Hill. And of course that's the way the ones on the Hill would like to keep things. The ones on the Hill…she had made her pledge to the UPAS and honesty was one word in the oath. But talking to mother with a bouquet of flowers right there two days ago had been so real. Almost like mother truly was there. That honesty word works on her conscience…who deserves and receives the truth?

Her fingers fumble over the control panel, touching home. She slumps back in the seat, eyes half closed and lets the helihover fly her back to the cage.

Chapter 14

Wednesday Evening, July 4

Joshua pushes the heavy door opened, stepping up onto the street. He looks up at the sky, and there it is, the expected west trestle. That was Jeira up in the air over this street two nights ago. This is the same dead end street, the one everyone is talking about, the street with no name. Big sister protecting the Citadel, but protecting those down below as well. The door clicks closed behind him and he hears the footsteps of someone to his side.

"Hello Josh." The one speaking walks up towards Joshua.

Joshua swivels his head, half startled by the somehow familiar. "You're Steve, you were in the other electro-truck," he says carefully, turning to look up at the tall thin man standing there, hand in his pocket, clutching tightly. Josh looks even more closely and his eyes narrow slightly, hands twitching. "And...and you were walking across the station at Citadel last Friday morning, you were getting into the transition car—dressed in that black and white shirt."

"Shine out in the dark, surround the dark with light. We are all invited," the guy says with a flourish. "So you noticed me those places…but there was another time, even further back. When life was so much more pure."

"Yeah, I do know you," Joshua squints hard, "but from where…"

"When we fared forth, Sir Knight…"

"Sas! Jesus, Sas, that's you. God you look different. Down around the river, when we used to hang out…you, me and Jeira." Josh's eyebrows rise. "Yeah, we were going to carry out the most honorable of deeds, weren't we? We were gonna save the world. How the hell are you Sas?"

"The Savior's name is not to be taken lightly." The voice sounds familiar, yet somehow rings hollow. "Yes, I was Sas. Staphan now, or Steve if you like."

"Oh, I see. But how did you ever get a transition pass? You pretty well have to have a home address on the Hill for that." He pauses. "You are from the Hill, aren't you? We never talked about it back then did we, we just met down by the river all that time."

"I was afraid you wouldn't like me if you knew. And it didn't matter so much back then, in those more untainted times. Yes, I did live on the Hill, in the *master's* house. One has no choice of where one is born, does one? But no longer, my friend, no longer."

"We never saw you the third summer. Jeira and I only came a couple times that year; I guess we had to get on with growing up. Well, whatever have you been doing with your life since then? Did you finish school and go to college like most everyone?"

"Well, yes, I did attend Sky Hill Academy for four years. I am officially educated in the field of liberal arts. But much more important, I have also had an experience that has started me on an intense training in the school of the spiritual. The challenges of the Academy pale in comparison."

"Oh yeah…" Josh stares for a moment.

"You must be talking to shela…she assigned you to that KoolKleen delivery task," Josh says. "You understand our efforts here. Has she given you more?"

"Shela, oh yes. She is my guide and my light—along a new path." Staphan spreads his hands wide, palms up. "I have *Others* as well, other helpers may be the best way to describe them. They have shown me the way, a path down off the Hill; my home is here now. Shela assigns me tasks, as I must be tested for purity. The *Others* give me direction that I often don't understand."

"You must have been at the first meeting then. I never noticed you."

"With shela? Yes, I was there—the crowd was large."

"Oh man, Sas, you got me so excited. I mean I can see it now, we stopped meeting by the river when Asha's administration was putting everything we were talking about into place. Then things fell apart when she was assassinated, so now we're back to square one. Shela is right there and we have another chance." Josh takes a deep breath, slowing his chatter. "So, where do you live now?" Joshua searches his eyes…they seem distant. "Which way are you heading?"

"Yes, just above Grio's Grab. But Joshua my friend I have only a minute. It is Jeira I must speak with, your sister." He falters. "The truth be told, I am not sure how to go about this. How could I speak with her?"

"Right, sure," Josh says, looking for Sas in that face. "Open me a put point on your tc and I'll give you her contacts."

Staphan's face looks blank.

"Here, hand me your tc." Staphan passes a device to him. Josh looks at the screen for a second, then at his own. "Okay, I will send her contact to you now, there you go, done."

Staphan's voice becomes quieter. "She is well, I hope." He reaches out to retrieve his tc.

"Jeira, oh yeah, she finished two degrees, one master's in the right field to land a real job. She became a UPAS surveillance officer. She flies one of those helihovers that are always buzzing over. Hey, we'll have to all get together again."

"I would like that, yes, very much." Staphan pulls the cross he grasps from his pocket. "But I must go now."

"Wait Sas. What about your family?" Josh tries to connect. "Look, if you live up on the Hill, or you used to…I mean they must come to visit you once in a while."

"Oh no, my path down was a solitary journey."

"So you have gone prodigal. You don't talk to them at all?"

"I can return to the Hill if necessary. My mother and father always have a place for me—if I can ever get myself straightened out they say. We have contact. They just don't understand…as you might imagine."

"If you straighten out they would kill a fat calf for you and have a feast."

"Something like that, however, my brother would not be appreciative of my return—as you seem to be familiar with the original story."

"I never knew you had a brother," Josh says. "How come he never came down by the river?"

Sas doesn't say a word, shaking his hanging head.

"Ohhkay, well let me tell you this," Josh says. "There's this idea floating around; this wise old man shela sent me to talk to. I mean you were guided down here by the others you say, so maybe you could guide your family down. For a tour at least. Maybe just in Virtual. Or even in VirtuALL. This brother you have...how about him."

"Oh, yes, my brother. My dear sweet brother Paul." Staphan's face crystallizes. "Perchance a million eons in the future, but not ever one instance before would he approach this place. I am afraid, Josh, that is completely out of the question."

"Someone else then, one of your parents or someone else you know from the Hill. Just to get a start, others may follow."

"I wish I could help you there, my friend, but I highly doubt it; I can't imagine one soul that would even consider the idea. No one in my family has any inclination towards this venture I am on." He recalls the way his father would swallow at the table some times. "Well, maybe long ago but now I don't think so. Anyway, Josh, I must tarry no longer."

"We'll have to talk more."

"Yes, Joshua, I would like that."

Chapter 15

Thursday Afternoon, July 5

"So you went for Philli Tea?" says Joshua, heaving a bag of dirt up on the pile. "How did it go?"

"Never mind." Krino breathes hard. "Zaca is my only girl."

"Josh's lips tighten, as he wipes his forehead. "Well you must have talked. You found her so compelling, her intelligence and all."

"Talked. Ohh yeah, man, we talked, all of us talked." Krino grunts, dropping his bag to start a new pile. "We had us a group discussion. She brought the whole neighborhood along."

"To the Tea Shop?"

"Those two old men you was talkin' at." Krino glowers. "Both of them."

"Zijad you mean? And Salvo." Joshua looks at Krino with concern. "Well, I was wondering how they would get back across the river. So they were there too? I'm glad someone was taking care of them. Hey, did you get a chance to ask her?"

Krino looks at him with a blank scowl.

"About shela's security. Zijad was warning us shela might be a concentrated target, remember? And what if it's a sly modifier virus or something like that. Effects we would hardly notice. Did you ask?"

"Yeah, that is one thing she did speak to in my direction. On everything else she only talked to everyone but me. Those two old dudes were getting along with her just fine." He winces. "She even took them home with her. That should make you happy."

"Krino!" Josh grabs his friend's shoulder. "They needed a place to stay. How would they get home last night?" He frowns at his friend. "With the Bullet shut down because of us. So what did she say about security?"

"Maybe you should talk to her yourself."

"Maybe I should."

Krino looks back dully. "She said yeah. Your idea may be of concern. Run that possibility by Xia, she said."

"Really. So she does think a security breach is possible." Joshua's eyes fall. "One of us has to talk to Xia then."

"Yeah, right."

"Could be you," Josh says.

Krino's face gradually brightens. "Yes, my man," he says. "That Xia is one fine looking woman. I do feel a need to help her with all those tasks she's assigned. No doubt she would be setting something up for shela's next gig."

"You'll do it then?"

"I had enough of this dirt bag activity; I need a clean shirt. Come on, Zaca. Let's go." Krino makes a slow turn back towards Josh on his way out. "You go talk with that Lana, Josh. You like to ask questions and she got a lot of answers."

As his friend turns away and walks towards the stairs leading up out of the basement Joshua stares off into nothingness for a moment. Then he turns and heads back to grab another bag of dirt, past the neatly stacked pile of excavated bricks into the forming tunnel. They have already reached the storm line; it looms large and blue overhead. They just need to dig a little farther to access the smaller sanitary and water pipes, Jojo says. Several people are working with square shovels to fill the bags; others use picks and sharp shovels to dig in further behind the storm line. Josh can see Ed in there beside Eli, each of them placing decided blows into the clay. He heaves another bag up on one shoulder.

"Strength and honor."

Joshua turns. "Sas. Hey, you come to help?"

"Bread work," Staphan says. "Always good for the soul. Something my father never did once in his life. Nor my brother. Yet it is my soul I must attend to, not theirs. For am I my brother's keeper?" He looks forlornly into Joshua's eyes.

"I couldn't tell you, Sas." Josh squints a smile. "I only have a sister."

Staphan blinks. "You are blessed."

"Have you checked in with Jojo?" Josh sees a negative in Staphan's eyes. "No? See, we're digging in to access those water and sanitary lines; that's what Jojo says. He's an engineer so he understands how all this works. Those guys are digging, the others are bagging the dirt, the ones over there are building supports and I'm on the moving crew. So you have a choice here, or actually multiple choices for your bread work." He smiles brightly.

"I noticed you just lost a worker on your moving crew, so would it be safe to assume you need a replacement?" Staphan says. "We would not want you working too hard, my friend."

Joshua steps carefully back, waiting as Staphan hoists a dirt bag up to his chest. "Your father is a hard worker is he not? Maybe a little selfish, but we are out to educate him. And your brother must have some kind of a good side to him." They follow each other back out of the tunnel.

If you only knew of my brother, Staphan rests his chin on the cold bag. *But I cannot tell you, not you, nor anyone else, not ever.* Staphan cannot himself accept the latest directives coming from the *Others*. He so far has ignored the voices no matter how they persist. *There has to be another way.*

"Yes of course my father does fit well into that highly praised hard work ethic," Staphan says. "So commended as the highest of standards by we, the people. Covetousness brings glorified liberation from the deadly sin of sloth. You know, he may work hard, Joshua, but his culturally ascribed *success* has been so dependent on the phenomenal advantage he has had over the average person. Success being achievement of the oh-so-aspired-to status of the well-to-do."

"Advantage?" Josh says.

They amble side by side towards the dirt bag stack.

"How so?" He can guess, but feels curious about Sas' story.

"My particular family has been well-to-do for six generations. Our distant ancestors owned factories in the seething boom of the last 20's a hundred years ago. When one starts out wealthy, one can't help but continue to be successful with hard work. Lots of people not so well off work just as hard as or much harder than my father. When a person is in a family like mine, family financial accounts allow many mistakes, many fresh chances to start anew. For a rags person, no matter how the myth persists, chances of attaining riches remain so very unlikely."

"So the wealthy beget the wealthy."

"That is essentially the truth. The advantage of the descendent is not just large, it is huge. You may wish to investigate the statistics on that."

"Yes. But Sas is everyone like that? There must be some exception. Take you, for starters. Whatever are you doing living down here now? Where is your advantage?"

Sas heaves his bag onto a short stack in the pile, stretching his full body over the top to push the dirt bag all the way back. Tiny pieces of clay tumble down the sides of the pile. He turns about and hoists his rear up on the bag to sit, breathing heavy as a trickle of sweat runs down his forehead.

"No, all persons are not the same. Not at all." Staphan stops to catch his breath, shaking his head. He then goes on. "To be extra successful, you must be of a certain type."

Joshua throws his bag halfway up a higher pile, turning to hold it in place with his shoulders while he rests in another rain shower of dirt particles. His face drips as he listens.

"You must have the commerce character, the business acumen," Sas says. "You must be able to ignore all the Noble Knights teachings, yet at the same time present yourself as if they are your guiding lights. You must be an actor, one way on the outside, another way on the inside. On the inside, most importantly, you must befriend deception. You must be ruthlessly aggressive. Then you have the necessary advantage over others who may also have family bank account insurance."

"So your father can be aggressive? And the deceptive aggressive ones climb higher up the well-to-do pile."

"Oh yes deceptive and aggressive he is, or has at least learned to be." *But not near as ruthless as Paul who comes by that naturally, no learning necessary.* "So it is. So the world is."

"But still, what of you?" Josh hears noise at the entrance and looks up at the top of the stairs to see Zijad opening the door for Lana. She steps through smiling, and Zijad holds the door further waving Salvo in as well, before stepping in to follow them down. Josh waves at them, gazing at Lana for a moment as she descends, then when she looks towards them and waves, he turns back to Sas.

"Ah, my trip to Damascus," Sas says. "My saving grace, my curse. There are *Ones* who interfere with this world rather than leaving it run as it might. They once in a while give direction to the fortunate or unfortunate passerby. For *They* would at times have the world dance in another fashion."

"Damascus Sas? In Syria?" Josh paces his words, forehead creasing as he focuses on his old friend. "Yeah, okay back then, I think I follow. Look Sas, you have always been more different than most as far as I can remember. You are of the noble honorable type; non aggressive."

"Much depends on the direction *They* give. *They* may wish to use aggression to counteract aggression," Sas says. "*They* never give full reasons for their methods and one has no choice in the matter."

"You are a prime exception to the rules you describe, Sas." Josh turns to push his bag of dirt all the way into square position, blowing out to keep the dirt specks from his face. He lifts his arm to wipe his sleeve across his forehead, turning back to face his re-found friend, smiling.

The three newly entered arrivals walk up to join them. Joshua catches Lana's eye and she winks and smiles brightly. He feels his face flush, glad to be hidden behind the dirt and sweat, but he speaks. "We're chatting about societal reasons for excess wealth."

"There have been exceptions to any rule across the span of human history." Lana stands there beaming. "In each paradigm in which a major pattern has come to exist, or where circumstances present what appears to be an all-encompassing unalterable blueprint, there has consistently been exception."

Josh attends to the lecturer's voice, thinking of the clean shirt Krino went for.

"This is the field of soft science, the realm of human beings, not physics or chemistry," Lana says. "Consider again the statistics of human behavior across the innovation distribution. The Innovators are a constant exception to the majority. And the Early Adopters are a relatively small group as well and act consistently at variance with the mainstream."

Joshua looks at Sas with one eyebrow raised.

"You see my friend," Salvo says, facing Zijad. "I would advise that you listen closely to this intelligent lady."

"Peoples' nature is complex," Zijad says slowly. "Predictable, unpredictable. Miss Lana say many truths."

"Human nature, you old goat," Salvo mutters under his breath.

They shuffle in a group away from the dirt bag pile, making room for other workers carrying full bags out from the tunnel.

"So what we are doing, our bouquet drop, our tunnel, that is innovative exception is it not?" Josh says, looking at all of them, then at Lana with his own smile. "We pursue just cause as innovators or adopters against the backdrop of the status quo. The Early Majority, is that what you called them Lana?" He looks directly into her eyes, feeling his heart beat a little faster.

"Yes, yet even if we are successful in our pursuit, will justice be completely served?" Lana's eyes sparkle. "Across the spectrum of human history, there have been only a series of progressive steps, albeit usually in the right direction, but with many regressive steps as well. I pose we are attempting but another small move forward." She pauses, "Assuming we do succeed in this instance."

"Perhaps we are yet to heave our deep sigh," Joshua looks at her carefully. "Progressive, yes, we are doing it differently. We aren't shooting anyone, no killing like in El Salvador's past, right Salvo?" He glances at his interviewee. "Or a thousand other struggles like that. I predict we might have a progressively deeper sigh."

"Is then we are happy?" Zijad asks. "The deeper sigh?"

"And is happiness what we look for in the end?" Salvo says, squinting at Zijad. "Is this the final nature humans look for?"

"Let's check the historical record of the near recent past to help us define happiness," says Lana. "To start with, how about our antagonist Mr. Patrick Knomley. Does anyone believe he is happy?"

"He's my father," says Staphan.

"Oh. I'm so sorry," Lana says. "Hello. My name is Lana, have we met?" She stretches out her hand to Staphan. "It's just that if you, Sas, right?, that if you are here at this time it may be acceptable to you that I should apologize only to maintain superficial politeness. Everything personal aside, if you allow us to view circumstances in that fashion, is your father happy?"

"Huh! What can I say?" says Staphan keeping his eyes up. "Sometimes he has seemed happy, or content at least with his own values and sometimes not."

"Ahh, all people are this way. That is part of human's nature." Zijad glances sideways at Salvo. "Some people have happy, how you say, disposition and some not so happy. This too is part of human nature! This nature has variation each individual."

"We must bring them down the hill for a long visit, you old goat," Salvo says, turning to Zijad. "Now you speak better English, you listen. Our friends here have technology. Bring them as children; that is the way. You can do that, yes Joshua?"

"I'm not sure yet," says Josh. "I mean Sas here came down with no technology at all. He just came down." He looks Staphan's way. "I know you were explaining your reasons, but were you influenced at all by our youth, our Noble Knights days?"

"I come not on a completely honorable quest," Staphan says, grimacing. "Like you heard me say, there have been other influences."

"In many cultures, in many nations where youth serve commonly two years in community service, their attitudes are affected," says Lana, looking down and then up to meet Joshua's listening eyes. "Elders and statesmen have often recognized the wisdom in this. Especially those youth who serve in a missionary capacity become distinctly more mature than their counterparts."

"What Salvo said," Josh says.

"Yes, Salvo and Zijad have wise insights," Lana says, nodding. "Attempting to retrain older people has no effect. As Zijad says, Milosovic was confined for years in prison, defending his human rights violations until his last breath. Much longer than two years yet with no effect. Focusing on the more easily influenced childhood psyche, or using one part of human nature to influence other parts, those are the innovative ideas we speak of now."

"To combine the effective influence on youth and the tricking of human nature, one part with another," Joshua joins in, searching Lana's eyes.

"If we could somehow merge these gentlemen's ideas into action," Lana says.

"Exactly what I was thinking," Josh says. "But like you say, can we do that somehow?"

"To have one like Mr. P. W. Knomley fulfilling one part of his childhood needs with another," Lana says excited. "I can't fathom the logistics, but the ideal resultant would be a BMG on his part, and voluntarily which is important."

"Yes, yes," Joshua's eyebrows crease. "But a BMG?"

"Oh, sorry." Lana's eyes go wide. "In the #tags and pages just before Asha's time, a BMG was a Bill and Melinda Gaetz. These two had attained the status of the wealthiest in the world at that time, yet they personally chose to become philanthropists."

"Yeah, that's right," Joshua says, nodding knowingly. "They were Time persons of the year in '05 along with Bono. That's the year I was born." He looks sheepish now. "So anyway my mother would always tell me about them, like she thought my arrival had something to do with what they did." He brightens. "They caught the attention of the public eye back then."

"Well, perhaps a case of serendipity did occur that year. You do follow their lead in a way." Lana beams at Josh. "We all do I mean, in this group." Her lecture voice falters slightly. "The Gaetz couple did eventually sell their mansion. Again, by personal choice, they transferred to an authentic middle class lifestyle of the time."

"They do almost what Jesus told the young rich man," Salvo says.

"We cannot permit ourselves to be influenced by Christian teachings too closely," Lana warns looking down at the dirt floor. "Turning the other cheek, as our composite conscience shela pointed out, cannot be an option."

"Jesus did not always turn the other cheek," Salvo volunteers. "He threw the moneychangers from the Temple."

"That may be a preferable paradigm to emulate," says Lana kicking a small stone back and forth with her foot, focusing on its movement. "We cannot crucify our opponents as the Romans did; we must be more civilized than that. Perhaps we must throw the moneychangers out." She raises her hand, almost as if to touch

Joshua's arm. She holds it in midair and from it he can feel the slightest warmth. "The concept of childhood influence, that I believe we must evaluate more thoroughly."

"How about in Virtual," Joshua says with a shallow breath. "Or even VirtuALL? The thing is, would it be voluntary? Or does it have to be?" he goes on, turning to distract himself by talking to Sas. "Zijad says you only have to trick some people. But let's just say you trick one part of a person into doing something a different part of the very same person would never do. It's still the same person, so even if you influence say the child inside, it is still voluntary right? We haven't crossed shela's slap in the face line, have we?"

"I would suggest at this point," says Lana, "that we consult with a systems expert."

"Well some things we do know. To start, we all know how VirtuALL works," Josh says. "You get emotive feed hookups and you truly experience Virtual as if you were actually there and as if you really were the person whose role you experience. An emotional avatar. Lots of people can't tell it from reality—it is truly not just seeing but experiencing life from another's point of view."

"Technology," Salvo says, poking Zijad with his elbow.

"Otpor," Zijad raises his clenched fist. "But how can we make a man as a child again?"

Josh lets his own hand rise, and form a fist, trying hard to see it in a different light.

"You ask the Nicodemus question," Salvo says. "Jesus told him he must become a child again, to be born again."

"You are not Jesus, my friend," Zijad says. "And if you were, who would listen?"

They all look at each other. Joshua breaks the silence, looking at Staphan.

"Good sir, could it be you have a mission upon the Hill in the near term? You could perhaps return to your family castle once more." Joshua looks to his fellow Knight of Justice. "You could maybe get a feed on your father or your brother somehow. Would that be possible?" He shrugs. "If shela approves."

"Well, I don't know but I suppose. My father, perhaps," says Staphan slowly. "He does often use BusinessDream to work through the night." *Paul? Never, he was never any different as a child.* Feeling eyes on him, he hears voices flowing from his meditative visions, the waves of abyss, the darkness flowing up over the edge from the depths below. "Maybe," he says. The *Others'* give imperative suggestions, directives swelling up from those depths. Oh, if only these wonderful ideas were coming from *Them*—but they aren't.

Chapter 16

Friday Evening, July 6

Josh cautiously follows the steps down into the basement, squinting over towards the tunnel entrance where a dim light shines. He can't believe he's back at the place of the bread work as Sas calls it. He had been invited out yesterday for further conversation with Lana and the old dudes—fascinating dialogue in all three cases, after followed Krino's suit in going home for a fresh clean shirt. Maybe Krino is right, maybe there is something special about the feminine. But now he's been told the final pipes are exposed, and this evening has brought him out on inspection though shela's reasons for a visual check seemed vague. Shela must know more than he does, of course she does. As he walks past and around the stacks of brick and then the dirt bag piles, he hears loud voices from the tunnel's end.

"...you can just keep a case of it on the side, goddam it," an angry voice shouts. "You wanna give it to them hard from the bottom, so why not use something they'll really feel?"

"Look, Cauz, I'm with you." Josh recognizes Jojo's voice now. "I'm just as pissed as you are, I mean, someone like Patrick Knomley could have done what we're asking on his own long ago. But we just can't use something that harsh. Our strategy is to listen to shela. She was hoping just a slap across the face, but her next plan, the one I know he truly needs, is a good solid kick in the ass. And us sneaking down the sewer line and up the vertical pipe below his throne puts us in position to do exactly that. But a boot in the butt never draws blood like you're talking. That's too much; we just can't go that far."

A moment of silence hangs heavy.

"Why is shela a she? Women!" The other voice says. "Look, these bastards deserve it to start with. They aren't gonna listen to a slap and they aren't gonna listen to a butt kick. Think about it. The trains are shutting down; the plexon shields are coming up; their defences are becoming impenetrable. This is our last chance to get a real message in while their guard is still soft."

"Joshua." Jojo looks up as Josh walks hesitantly into the light in the tunnel. Jojo stands leaning on the broom for sweeping the dirt floor under the three pipes now exposed overhead. Worm cases lay neatly stacked below. "This is Cauz. He wants us to use K-5 or RDX in the worms. I try to tell him the direction I am pretty sure we're getting from shela."

"Shela is female," Josh says, walking up with hand extended, "just like Mother Earth is a mother." Cauz's hand is smooth steel.

"Fuck that," Cauz says, stepping back. "My mother thought she knew everything and she didn't know shit."

"Really?" Joshua looks him over. "Some people should never be in authority. Especially over a child."

Cauz stares at him with a softening face.

"I dunno Josh," Jojo says. "Cauz says he supplied shela with his VirtuALL feed." He shrugs. "I mean she has his profile, but shit, listen to him."

"Of course I gave her a feed. Check it if you want, they're all group domain public. I can even describe it for you right now." Cauz stares hard at them. "When madam shela showed us those city men, I was devastated. I wanted to scream out loud but I kept my scream inside like my mother told me to." Cauz's eyes swell and his voice cracks. "'Cause they are us, don't you see?" His face contorts into a hard-corner sneer "And then I see that fucking Patrick W. Knomley. I want to slap him blue, kick him 'til he can't breathe, pummel his fine fat body right down through the concrete."

"Krino said you were in the Marines," says Joshua, putting on that calming smile he knew from his own mother. "You know, Cauz, I hear your anger loud and clear. I was pretty pissed too at Knomley's attitude." He looks at Cauz carefully. "So you think we should beat the crap out of him. Or—maybe take him out."

Cauz's face relaxes, mouth curling up. "Depends how we set the blast to go off, might knock him off, might just blow his fat face off—you never know. Get their attention for sure though, so why not? Why waste time trying to change him. Look how old he is, he's had endless chances to do it different. He's a waste of skin wrapped around a bag of shit."

Josh looks at Jojo, keeping his eyes calm.

"Yeah, pretty frustrating, I know. Hey you gotta talk to Salvo—have you met him? He's been in conflict zones, around killing quite a bit." Josh squints over at Cauz. "How about you, you seen any combat duty?"

"I was in special ops strategic planning. No personal action; but I know what we had the front lines men do. And the shit that happened to some of them." Cauz's eyes go hazy. "Anyway I'm a front line soldier in my own raging battle; one that's always been oh-so-real to me. Been waging war deep down inside as far back as I can remember." His eyes clear. "I got a lifetime of battle strategy planning. I can definitely tell you what we can do with the strategic advantage we have now. We can pack a couple of Jojo's worms here with just enough K-5, or RDX, I can get that too. I heard you Jojo; we can use the pipeline schematics to pick and choose who we want to take out. One at a time starting from the top of the list. When they see the next one just above them going down, that's when they start to listen. And believe you me, they will listen real close."

"We're gonna load liquid," says Jojo firmly. "The rankest stench ever." He shakes his head, staring hard at Cauz. "No explosives."

"Listen, this flower strategy comes off all wussie-ass." Cauz squints and frowns. "It limits our options—we need an alternate plan."

"Alright, give us an alternative." Jojo leans the broom up against the worm cases and turns to stand, arms folded across his chest. The three stand facing each other, almost in a circle. Jojo looks at Josh. "We should always have a Plan B; that's what I always say."

"Okay, then." Cauz becomes enthusiastic. "I can supply a box of K-5. Just a backup." He grins broadly. "Leave it in the corner. Just in case."

"Let's say you go somewhere and you have a gun in your pocket just in case," Jojo says, lips pressed hard. "You leave the ammo at home. Or you think a little more and you decide to bring a couple shells but you keep them in your other pocket." Jojo blows the dust off a plank. "Or maybe you have a brainstorm and you put those shells in the chamber but keep the safety on. Or..." He looks wildly at both of them. "How about if you just shut the fuck up and leave the gun at home altogether."

"You know shela's history profiles." Josh keeps his voice at a peaceful tone. "If we use violence, we have to expect it coming back at us. And then we get nowhere, things become counterproductive."

"You, Cauz," Jojo says, shaking his head. "Are playin' with fuckin' insanity, man."

Cauz stares straight at Jojo. "Yeah, well I am familiar with lots of history profiles. I have my own history profile." Cauz's left eye drops a large rolling tear. "You want to talk about violence? All right, let's take a look at one small portion of the *toorich* profile." Jojo looks back, following Josh's calm. "Did you know they live longer than us?" Cauz says. "Now why is that? The fact is, they have the money to pay for better doctors and medical care than us. You see those MediVAC helihovers taking some ninety year old bag of bones into the Private Downtown Revitalize for a gene clean to add another decade on to his life. How much does one of those gene cleans cost now? Man, its five grand just to do your gene read before they even start. Who's got that kind of liquid cash? So while they extend their lives 'cause they can afford it, we who don't have the cash, don't get the health care and therefore we die sooner. We live shorter lives. So they take part of our lives, don't they? You follow me? Of course that's never gonna qualify officially as violence, but in the war in my head, they are killing a part of us. What about that profile?"

Joshua and Jojo look at each other, and then back at Cauz.

"All my life," he goes on, "every time I ever looked up at any line of huge houses on the ridge, all I ever saw was targets. And now's one optimal time to start picking them off. They may be pretty smart at making money, but their defence strategy shows zero intelligence. They're set up like one row of big fat sitting ducks. All lined up, just a'waitin'. So we can blow them to pieces the way I've done it in my head a thousand times, or we can do it even better now, your way using these pipeworms. We pick and hit targets with more enhanced precision. If we start taking out those houses one at a time, they'd have to be real stupid to want to live like that anymore."

"We all want that kind of change...we're on the same team," Josh feels his mother's soothing voice come out of him. "It's just the method that's at issue."

"Exactly, just the method," Cauz says. "So like I've said before, we could use surface-to-surface missiles, hell, good old ground artillery fire, but now that you guys got 'em, why not these underground mobile worms? I do want to cooperate; I do want to be part of shela's team. So I'm with you guys."

"Yeah, good," Jojo says. "So cooperate. Let's do it shela's way."

"Why not just load some K-5 in a couple worms? Just two or three." He shrugs emphatically. "That would be our Plan B sitting, waiting just in case."

"That's where we start to differ," Jojo says, glancing at Josh. "I know it was me who pushed for liquid but that was only a slight change in delivery format. Still no real lasting damage."

"Okay, okay, before you say another word, just listen," Cauz goes on. "Now's our chance. Just in case. You agree we need a backup plan, right? We all agree there. We can load the backup worms with PVCmelt too. That would melt down their pipes. Say the sanitary lines. We do the select houses, lots of them so their civic crews can't keep up with repairs. We put K-5 in the same worms. PVCmelt neutralizes K-5 so if we release the melt the K-5 is gone. That would give us two choices in each worm. Depending on the status of those plexon shields we either blow them sky high if they don't listen, or we swamp them in their own shit and pretend we never had no explosives. How's that for a two-in-one strategy?"

"I suppose I can see us having the PVCmelt in a few worms," Jojo says shrugging. "That is a viable backup strategy we never considered yet. In case we lose control of the worms or they block us in somehow. I mean, no one gets hurt by a melted down sanitary line."

"No serious health issues?" Josh looks at Jojo. "Cholera and the like?"

"They'd have to be pretty careless or pretty stupid," Jojo says. "It's exposing them to their own stench mostly. I'd say it fits shela's policy."

They all look at each other. Cauz starts again. "Well then why not just hook the sanitary line directly into their water line for that matter? Send their shit right back at 'em."

Jojo thinks for a moment. "That's insane. We could really infect them that way. Anyways, the logistics are against us there. The water line is pressure fed from a compressor. The sanitary line is a gravity feed. We'd have to move our own compressor engine right in here to boost the sanitary line pressure. We just don't have the time or resources to do that kind of hook-up. Wouldn't work. We gotta stick with the pipeworms."

"So K-5 then?" Cauz's eyes narrow. "I'll get a box over here right away."

Jojo looks to Joshua for calm, his face screwing up in anger. "For the last time no Cauz, absolutely not." He takes a deep breath. "You can get us some PVCmelt if you want to be involved." Jojo looks at him directly. "No K-5. No RDX. No explosives. No way."

Cauz turns to Joshua, hurt in his eyes, then back at Jojo, with equal determination. His face sets into a contorted decisive mask. "You can get your own fucking melt." His features explode into a sneer, as he glares back and forth at both of them. He turns his back on them and stomps off down the tunnel. "I got no more fucking time to piss away here," he voices back over his shoulder. Kicking boots into each step on his way up the stairs, he slams the door at the top behind him.

"He's one crazy guy," Jojo says. He picks up the broom again, silently sweeping around the worm cases.

"I suppose we're all crazy in some way or other," says Josh. "There's a part of me that wants to go right along with him."

Jojo stops sweeping, looking hard at Joshua.

"Jojo," says Josh quietly. "We're gonna have another meeting with shela tomorrow night. I was just sent to give her an independent personal status update. Looks like we're all ready to go?"

"Ready to rock," Jojo nods.

"All right. I'll get that report in to her."

Joshua walks slowly back out of the tunnel. He feels a shudder growing inside. If this Cauz guy has a profile, like he says he does, approved by shela, well, holy shit. *A controllable virus insert, not to destroy her, but to slightly modify.* A software virus or a piece of bio-digital ware, a person, maybe someone kind of like Cauz. Or maybe that hidden away part of him, maybe the rage inside him's the virus. Forcing his hands to relax, Josh reaches for his tc to call up public group domain.

Chapter 17

<u>*Sunday Afternoon, July 8*</u>

"So you see what I mean?" Krino says. Josh gazes about the brick walls of I2, half listening. Blocks away from the last location, shela must be minimizing attention to the tunnel. "When a child sees you," his friend goes on, "who they never met before, a new person comin' into the room, their first reaction is one of distrust. Do they come running over, big hug, how's it goin' you adult you? No, they hold back. They check you out. Brain thinks survival, that's what comes first."

"So this is the hominid instinct?" Josh shifts his look to Krino. "The distrust?"

Eli and Ed are pulling metal chairs off stacks and setting them out in circles.

"Makes sense, don't it?" Krino walks up to Josh. "We had to survive. You know it's a dangerous world out there with all them other competing tribes around, let alone the carnivores, so first comes distrust. As the brain develops in a growing child through the same stages as it did as our species evolved, a young child in modern times would be physiologically at an earlier phase, depending how close they are to the pivotal age of six. Age three might be somewhere between Lucy and homo erectus say."

"Lucy, oh Lucy, up in the sky." Josh turns away. "Hey Krino, let's go back to talking about monkeys. Wait, I know you don't like monkeys, but cum'on, let's drop Lucy and talk about someone like Asha say." What Josh has been hearing on his friend's latest subject is ringing a little too true.

"Yeah." Krino brushes Josh away with a sweeping motion of his hand. "You will comprehend what I am telling you one day my man."

Josh moves to hold up one end of the LC screen while Krino helps Xia unravel the digital displays gear. Salvo stands facing

Zijad, waving one hand about to emphasize a point in the private lecture of the moment. Josh can get them in on Asha.

"So you guys remember Asha's last Truth address?" Josh asks, extra loud. "I mean I sure remember where I was that day we lost her, but when was that last Truth session?"

The room goes quiet as everyone thinks back in silence. Up on the third storey of an empty loft tower this time, they are readying for another evening with shela. Above the stage assembly area, the room oozes a pattern of mortar, fading as bricks climb up close to the ceiling. Windows, boarded or not, circle the perimeter above. A curious afternoon breeze follows the beaming sunshine, blowing lightly through the odd open window.

"I know that day whoever it was took her out." Krino speaks first. "At one fifty-seven, November 30, 2022. Was just another day at college for me until I heard..." He steps back to unroll a spool of wire and stands, shrugging. "I was over in the study hall cramming for a midweek Biochem exam. Then my roomie give me a call that changed everything. So her last address was three days back from that, on the Sunday before."

Each of them pauses at what they are doing. A breezy gust swirls down through the room from above, reminding of stormier days, maybe when the last *a la derecha* pushed its smashing howling way through the glass.

"My mother was a bucket of tears when I arrived at home that afternoon," Ed speaks out. "The principal at our elementary school had announced the demise of our president over the PA and we all were sent home. I don't believe I fully understood so mother attempted to explain the implications to me. I know she always followed Asha on Sunday nights. My mother made a valiant attempt to instill the ideals of truth into me." He winks and nods at Josh. "When I was but at child."

"I write immigration exam three months before," says Xia. "I study English. That day I learn new English word. Assassination." She hands a wireless insert to Krino, pointing at a socket.

"That Asha had a lotta good shit goin'." Eli booms out louder than usual, his voice ringing off the stack of metal chairs. "'Cept for her, I probably be out bangin' the streets right now. Truth is righteous."

"My mother said she was the first president to ever truthfully express feminine values in public," Ed says. "She could publicly put across compassion for not just some of us but all of us. She never said anyone was bad or evil, she just said some had more potential for change than others. Especially during those addresses."

"Yes, exactly. My mom was so touched when Asha spoke, and terribly sad that Wednesday," Josh says, helping Krino raise the LC screen into place. "For weeks after too. During the conspiracy theories times...I mean the Taylor brothers got life, right? But who knows. Me and my sister were at home that Sunday night watching with our mom. Asha was talking more on her wealth series, the real truth about excessive wealth. I learned a lot from her, better than any college class. Remember, she was implementing her wealth cap legislature that had been going before Congress those last few weeks. Like always she talked about being a responsible citizen, and in that address she was emphasizing how the extra wealthy have a huge potential for change. She said if we have legal statutes in place to keep it all fair for everyone, even the ones who resist do change in spite of themselves. Even if it takes a generation to make the difference. If we don't have legislation, some always take advantage…even if the majority wants things to be fair."

"That wealth cap was her downfall, my mother thought anyway," Ed says. "Her plan was to take all that advantage away from the wealthy. And no matter how clearly she explained why and all the reasons it was good for the majority, those wealthy people just could not get happy about it. Who would want things to be fair when it takes away your personal advantage?" Ed raises his hands in a shrug, and then grabs another chair.

"She gave pretty good reasons, I thought," says Josh. "She planned to use that money to finally eliminate poverty, mostly through education, but health care too and what did she call it, guaranteed income insurance. She was going to use it to pay for all the school upgrades and finally move teachers up into the socio-economic class where she said they belong. Not just by income class like the lawyers and doctors, but so teachers are the folks treated with the most respect. Remember her teacher of the week award, how they profiled one from a different city or county each time. She made it pretty clear how important teachers are, how they are the ones who actually make or break our future. And she gave us options on what kind of a future we really wanted. Our first madam president was picking up on what our first ethnically diverse president mostly just talked about."

"He was way before me," says Ed.

"He talked in a positive hopeful way," says Josh. "Would have been so good if he made some stronger decisions. But his misjudgments then may have helped Asha's campaign later. It always seems like you need a government that looks poor to show potential for something different. Almost like an endless cycle if you leave it up to the political system alone. Therefore, we now make change without depending on any election. We the people show our will through shela." Joshua looks around at the others, his fellow shepherds in his mind. He goes on.

"Everyone knows some things are simply true but a lot of traditional cultural rules keep people from talking about what is actually true. Asha showed us it was okay to reframe cultural beliefs, break traditional rules and talk about self-evident truths like our forefathers. All men are created equal. She even started talking about unacceptable subjects like birth rate. Maybe abortion was a moral political wedge topic then, but the truth is education of girls and easy access birth control turns out to address the biggest part of the problem."

"Who can afford to have kids?"

"We only have one planet, and John was telling me we were using almost two planets worth of resource at one time. That varies by person or household or neighborhood, up on the Hill, some of them use over ten planets worth. *That* info never went public even in Asha's time."

Josh looks at Salvo and Zijad who have been listening. "She was our democratically elected president. And it seems like someone didn't like how our democracy works, so they took her out."

"You have one form of democracy and you also have capitalism," Salvo says. "Maybe some of your businessmen did not like who the people elect. Ones like Asha had social ideas that are not so good for business. Castro had the same problem. He always said he would die for the people of Cuba. One must be careful what he says, as they tried to kill him many times."

"Asha would talk about capitalism and democracy," says Josh. "How they compete. How big business and corporations were winning then and now again shela says. With big business interests in control, the voting majority become just one more item to keep restrained."

"Some have a clear advantage in a capitalist system," Salvo says. "The ones who do well in a competitive business environment. And some others too, certain types of people. The ones who do well as CEO's."

"The more aggressive?" Josh asks. "The ones born wealthy?"

"Yes, *amigo*," Salvo says. "Some are born into traditional wealth. The advantage of the wealthy class in Latin America was always there. Part of the historical hacienda—the patron and his campesinos. The patron wants to remain the patron. Keep same tradition. Human nature, no?" He turns to Zijad.

"Human nature is what do people care on." Zijad says. "First is self. Next is family. Then is community. Last is everyone else. Not all people this way. Prophets teach all people to care for all—to oppose their own nature. But aggressive one interpret prophet to fit his own way. If you let all people free to do what he wants, aggressive one rise to top. Do not depend on prophets. You must have political system. With good leader—this is key factor."

"Wasn't that communism they had in Eastern Europe?" asks Krino.

"Socialism in Yugoslavia," says Zijad. "Marxist Leninism all over Eastern Europe. But never true test of what Marx say—what you speak of, truth. Autocratic system get in way. Strong man such as Stalin with total control. Tito was better, he didn't kill millions but system not guarantee good leader. Milosovic was elected at first but later he became tyrant."

"You say Tito was a man of the people," says Salvo.

"Yes, how you say, somewhat. On one side he live like king himself with many palaces, but he make good life for everyone also. He was simply hero from war in right place at right time," Zijad says. "Problem in Yugoslavia is people get good life and then they get lazy. They don't work so hard. After some time, expression is they can't pay me as little as I can work."

"So capitalism is better. It forces people to work hard. If not, they don't eat."

"Marx says capitalism produces lazy people too. The bourgeoisie. They are classic example. They own everything and produce nothing."

"Knomley?"

"I dunno. I mean he does work."

"We need Asha's ideas back like some type of cap on capitalism. Some other kind of socialism. People have to be forced to care about more than just themselves. Politically. Legally. Culturally. That's where we come in. We are creating a cultural influence."

"You say Castro try new system," Zijad looks at Salvo.

"Castro called it socialism. He promoted cooperatives. People own part of the company they work for—just like you own a business or shares in a business. He educated everyone, just like Asha...he eliminated illiteracy. He gave everyone free health care, and he sent doctors around the world."

"John says Cuba was the only country living a one planet lifestyle," Josh says. "Really cool, if they did that too."

"Fidel Castro was a dictator," Ed says, looking around. "Wasn't he?"

"Never. His government was always elected. By the majority of the people and all elections were open to international scrutiny, not like Milosovic," Salvo looks at Zijad to confirm, then at them all. "The majority are the poor ones to start, but they keep voting for him even when he makes them not so poor. He strongly encourages neighborhood conversations; get together with your tribe, like we do now. He gets people politically involved, involved in their community like in early democracy here in this country. They lined the streets for his funeral."

"We are showing Knomley and his tribe the advantages of equity," Krino says. "One thing is it's so much more efficient to educate the poor. You can educate ten or twenty or more poor people for every rich kid in the fancy private schools. Asha showed us all the numbers on that."

"Until the poor become rich," Ed says.

"No room on the planet for that according to John," Josh says. "Anyway, illiteracy has to go first, full education has to come next. Then let's see what the people want."

"We are waging war," Krino says. "War on *toorich* terrorism."

"The moral equivalence of war. William James called it that," Ed says. He looks around shrugging. "I merely quote Lana. We go to battle or perhaps we simple engage minus the traditional weapons of war; we shoot no one."

"Now I'm thinking of her no growth economic plan," says Krino. "When you talk on population control, the economy and population are so intertwined. Take any animal population. If it grows as they are designed to, it eventually reaches the limits of its ecosystem. What happens? Population drops off radically in a very short time. Easy to state in theory, but not a pretty sight to observe. Lots of death. But an adjustment that's necessary to rebalance the ecosystem. But now you got this supposedly intelligent animal reaching limits, way past the limit of one planet from what Josh said, aware of what's gonna happen. That would be us. You choose to stop growth 'cause you know what's coming. I know she was telling us that."

"That would take a lot of grownup thinking," Josh says. "You remember the presidential idea of putting aside the things of childhood—you know, time to grow up. You tell me Krino, what animal is more mature than people."

Krino looks at his friend. "I gotta think on that one a while," Krino says. "I get back to you."

"The *toorich* cause our society to be as it is. Capitalism creates wealth yet without regulation also causes poverty. And capitalism is the primary cause of the carbon back taxes our entire economy pays now," Josh says. He's been checking out John's data. "Eco-warriors point out Knomley's tribe and the like; the way they live has always been harder on our planet."

"Explanation please," Ed says.

"The analysts have pointed out that one for decades now. Asha was talking about it in one of the other Truth shows. The wealthier you are, the more resources you use, and most people choose to spend their money on having a good time and the fashion of the day including travel. You know early this century, they used to actually fly off to other countries to go to the beach just to have their wedding there, bringing the whole entourage along. Just because they could, no thinking, no good reason. They needed to flout their social status."

"Really. Do they still do that?" Ed says. "I mean those on the Hill."

"Not even them—international flights are so restricted now," Josh says. "All globally regulated. Back then, they didn't think twice about all the jet fuel dumping carbon into our atmosphere. Instead of spending their extra wealth to support the more fragile bio-fuel aircraft industry or just get married in the local church and spending on a net zero house. You have to have legislation to motivate people to take care of their own back yard. We all breathe the same air. Getting rid of excessive wealth gives us a cleaner future too."

"So the more wealth you have," Ed says, "the bigger your footprint."

"Precisely. Unless you choose to spend your wealth on environmentally friendly technology," Josh says. "But who did when they all had the choice? With all the green wash advertising."

"Woulda had a lot to do with women; they got their inherent gather-turned-shopper tendencies," Krino says, voice dropping as he looks at Xia. "Consumerism would've been driving our planet over the brink."

"I'd guess that's who arranged the wedding on the beach," Ed says, looks to Xia too. "I mean, that would have been a woman's idea."

"Where I come from, we cook goat instead of chicken and extra bowl of noodles for wedding," Xia says. "We go shopping for food. Meat is our luxury."

"Still, some of us want more than that James guy's moral equivalent," Josh says. "They want to use good old weapons of war. There are rumors floating about a guy named Cauz."

"Shela's in control," Krino says.

"I don't know…she doesn't exclude everyone," Josh says. "She notes in his profile he has an extra tendency to carry the traits of the little boy in every man. The little boy who plays with toy soldiers and their weapons that blow holes in castles of sand."

"Well I hear that little boy is setting up his adult version of those weapons," Ed says. "As we speak…exact opposite of the shela directive as we've been told."

At that moment, the door bangs open and Staphan walks in.

"Hey, you're just in time…we're just finishing setting up." Josh looks at his old compatriot. "Did you make journey up the hill?"

"My valiant crusade to the master's abode," Sas says. "Yes, I made journey and you may wish to hear the tidings."

"We're listening," says Josh.

"I can speak to everyone here?" Sas questions Josh, looking around.

"We are all with shela," Josh says. "You got a profile now, eh Ed?"

"You bet."

"Shela may not be a complete test of honor," Staphan says. "But I will get to that last. First, my father. My father is a very competitive hard working businessman. One requirement and consequence of that status is that he uses BusinessDream to fill his mind with numbers reviews while he sleeps. So I ported a bottom of the hill VirtuALL tour to his Dream system last night. That part was easy. 'Cause insane as it may seem, I also slipped into his room and put a pickup wire on his wrist. So we have a reading of his reaction to the tour."

"Really? So he's been down here in VirtuALL now," Josh says excited. "He has experienced the feelings down here. So?"

"I am so surprised myself." Staphan chokes a bit. "Deep down, as a young child, he has always had some level of compassion for people. The problem is he has layers and layers of cultural influence squeezing that compassion down, down, down, out, out, out. His mother, from her mother before, her voice is there, turning her nose up as she walks by the lower class. She tells him thousands of times, in a thousand ways 'we're better'. Shela says it would take dozens of trips down here for that little boy's compassion to break through to surface." *Then there's Paul, but that's a different story.*

"We don't have time for that many trips, that kind of psychotherapy," Josh says. "Time is what shela keeps saying it will take. Maybe she has endless time, but not us if we want to make it happen now."

"We're ready with our underground option," Ed pipes in. "Just sayin'"

"The physical one through the pipes he means." Josh looks at Staphan. "What can we do? That's such good news and bad news, Sas, but what can we do?"

"One thing you must tend to immediately is this man named Cauz," Staphan says. "You people know him, yes? It may be wise to find him. Based on my information, he is arranging his own manner of influencing the Hill."

"I heard talk," Ed says. "Like I said, some want to stick with the good old weapons arsenal."

"You know where he is?" Josh says.

"He may have set up a bunker," Ed says. "I could investigate more through a call and find out where."

"Call," Josh says. "Now."

Chapter 18

Sunday Afternoon, July 8

The four walk as a tight group along a broken pathway beside scrubby trees protruding from the base of a steep rocky uninhabitable slope. The Hill looms above on one side while crumbled apartments and ramshackle houses look their way from across the street on the other. The street and parallel walkway weave along the indents and protrusions of the Hill bottom until they come around a tight bend to a new view. Eli leads the group and they have been sharing their eyes looking ahead and behind and across the street as he instructed. They stop for a moment, all looking ahead now.

"So what your man say?" Eli asks.

"We are entering the neighborhood," says Ed. "Not the best place to be, you know, but I kind of appreciate having the Hill on our one flank right now."

"Yeah," Eli says. "We close."

"How does our location show on the map?" Ed glances back at Josh.

"Another two or three blocks to that first address." Josh looks quickly at his small screen. "Those mega-houses up there on that jutting out ridge just might be the ones he's looking at."

The wall at the top of the ridge appears clad in fine stone, punctuated with small pillars, matching in texture and appearance the buildings behind. A solid line of high houses crowds towards the front, vying for best view and the most prominent position. A picture perfect community designed by an architect's fine eye.

Josh and Krino, following along behind the other two have been deep in conversation. Josh talks about his concern of a virus in shela to Krino's developing knowledge of bio-digital technology.

"So you thinking Cauz could be a virus himself?" asks Krino.

"I'm kind of worried," Josh says. "More like he's being influenced by the offspring of a virus in shela. I mean he's got an approved profile with her, but his actions just don't fit shela's agenda. Something is completely out of whack. Look at what he's talking about. He set up exactly the opposite of what shela wants. What we want."

"Yeah, sounds like the dude is way off." Krino nods.

"So one question in my mind is, to who's benefit would this situation be?" Josh says. "I mean, if the police find him set up with weapons right now, that would be exposed to the media and our whole non-violent approach gets destroyed. That would help things stay status quo. We would just be posted as some radical group that needed to be suppressed. And they'd do it real quick."

"Like Urban police comin' in with one of their tactical assault squads."

"Exactly," Josh says. "But whoever the strategy, I'm wondering how they went about penetrating shela? How would they set up Cauz like this?"

"Well my friend, shela to start is a completely digital record no matter what the complexity of the biological source, that being us," Krino says. "People put their deep core thoughts and beliefs together into a massive digital database. We all know the technology for Virtual and VirtuALL. Basic emotional and deeper intuitive signals read in and out of people in digital format. If someone controls Cauz at least partly and somehow implanted a false record into him for shela to read...well, I just do not know, dude. We gotta talk to Xia again."

"Yeah," Josh says. "Interesting and scary, but, okay Xia."

The two ahead of them have stopped again. "That building there." Eli grunts, pointing across the street.

"Up on the third floor," Ed informs them. "Number three oh seven."

"Okay, well we all worked together to scout the place out, and for travel protection, but I don't think we should all go up." Joshua looks at the other three. "Maybe one or two of us. Cause I mean he's pissed, like really pissed."

They walk along a little further, until standing directly across the street from the complex. Elegant Ann's Apartments is written in paint-chipped wooden letters high on the front of the building.

"You talk at him before," Eli rumbles at Joshua.

"He was in the tunnel talking to Jojo," Josh says. "Like I said, he wanted us to pack the worms with some kind of explosives. K-5 or RD something. But he was so pissed off when he left." Joshua looks at all of them.

"You go," Eli says. "Take Ed."

"Just two of us then," Josh says.

"Uhh!" Eli grunts.

"Eli my man," Krino says, "We can find us a spot right here in the shade."

Josh and Ed cross the hot potholed pavement, stepping along the front sidewalk to the steps with mailbox keyholes. Ed lifts the broken door to shift it back over the sill and they step into the building. Stairs lead them up to the third, past broken glass and scatterings of refuse along the edges and in corners. Joshua knocks beside the faint 307 outline, and he has to bang twice before they hear any stir on the other side. The door swings gradually opened, stopped abruptly by a boot to leave its chain dangling and a vertical slice of Cauz appears standing there, a raised burp gun hanging in one hand.

"You again." He looks at Josh through hard-lined eyes. "What?"

"We want to talk. If you have a minute." Josh gives a calm smile. "This is Ed, he's cool."

Cauz stares at them, chewing his lip. He edges the door closed a fraction, looking intently at Ed, and then pushes the latch back allowing the chain to fall. He opens wider, still with his boot kicked in holding the door in place. He hesitates again, staring a Joshua with both eyes now, lower jaw hanging below a slightly open mouth. Deciding, he steps back abruptly, waving them in with the gun hand, giving the two full view of the apartment.

Pizza boxes and empty bottles are neatly stacked, lined up in arranged piles along the walls. Wide beams of sunshine, laced with floating dust particles, blaze through a large window with no blinds. The light gleams off and casts shadows from an array of military gear laid specifically out across a table. A neat display of small rocket like projectiles stand beside a tube of the same diameter with a shoulder brace and a miniature screen folded out from the side. Each rocket bears a brightly painted word, what appears to read as a surname. Josh takes a few slow paces, gradually looking up through the window to catch a hazy view across the beams of sunlight. Up above the rocky cliff, the top halves of the mega-houses stand protected behind their fancy wall.

"So you gonna blast them?" Joshua says.

"You fuckin' rights," Cauz says. "This was an air option no one ever discussed. Don't know what shela was thinking. It's so obvious. Surface-to-surface ticker babies, with whatever we wanna load in the carriage."

"Right," Josh says casually. "So what have you got loaded in these?"

Cauz just smiles, shaking his head. "Last chance to do it right, I tell you. I got my good old mama SMAW you can see right here and her ten little children ready for a visit; one each for the top ten soft targets on the hill. And then I even got an old M224 mortar he points over towards the bedroom door, but that's mostly for effect." His grin broadens in a satisfied way. "You know, a backup plan. Always a good idea to have a plan B."

"What is SMAW?" Ed asks.

"Hey, an inquisitive young man. Good question. That's standard issue; Shoulder-launched Multipurpose Assault Weapon." Cauz laughs, placing one hand on the tube with the shoulder brace laid out on the table. "Note that multipurpose adjective, 'cause we're gonna use it here for our own very special purpose."

"Ed was with the Blades a couple days ago. Now he's met with shela," Joshua says, cautiously measuring his words, looking at Cauz. "Now he's with…us."

Cauz drops this hand off the assault weapon to his side, his other arm swinging lightly with the weight of the burp gun. He walks around the table like it's been his only patrol for an extended period of time.

"So at one time he was following one set of ideas, that of the Blades, and now he's up and changed his mind to follow us and shela." Josh looks straight at Cauz. "We can all do that if we choose to, you know."

Cauz stops cold, stares back at Josh, then looks Ed over. "Hi," he says, shifting the burp gun over to his other hand to shake. "Yuh gotta do what yuh gotta do."

"Yes sir. Like you say, sir, it is most wise to have options," Ed says. "I do have to admit though, it was more by chance than anything other that I am now engaged with shela's group."

Cauz's smile widens and he looks back at Josh, then he squints at Ed "Come over here. I want to show you something." He puts his arm over Ed's shoulder and guides both of them over to the main window, behind the table with the little rockets and the SMAW. He motions out the window.

"See those extra large cribs up there on the ridge?" His lips puff out, squeezed tight. "Disgusting. That is one disgusting display of unnecessary wealth. Those are our options now—which one goes first? Well, we have to start at the top of the list. Prioritize them. You might think the biggest would go first. Well that's kinda right. The bigger they are the more likely they're at the top but there can be exceptions."

"Yeah okay," Ed says.

"That's how we make the ones at the top nervous, get them thinkin' to themselves why would they wanna be at the top," Cauz says. "Fair to assume they know their position on the Golden Glow FFT lists, everybody knows those lists, so if they're smart and they want to stay at the top and be safe at the same time, they know they have to ship some of their assets down here."

Josh tries to follow the thinking, and the mood.

"So the Golden Glow gives us their priority status and blesses each of these children with a name. They should catch on pretty quick after a couple or a few visits by these kids. They've got some choices to make, and we can help them make the best choice—for us and for them. We'll see who listens." Cauz looks at Josh now, his mouth hanging open and his eyebrows both raised. "Like you mention, everyone has a choice to change their mind…some just need a little coaxing. Right?"

"Shela is giving them all forty eight hours to respond to our messages," says Joshua quietly. "That would be starting early tomorrow when the Monday morning FFT Mag comes out."

Cauz looks intently at him. He walks over to the ledge, picking up what looks like a withered piece of fruit. "You know, I put this apple here over a month ago when I first moved in with mama SMAW and the children. Everything was nice and fresh back then. Every day I been watching this little piece of fruit shrivel up just a little bit more. But look, it's still here. Interesting, eh?"

"We could load those children with our liquid," Joshua says softly. "Jojo says it'll go into any sealed unit."

"You see that child blessed with the name of Knomley #1? That's a ticker baby designed to collapse a soft target. Not just giving the target a bad odor day, but eliminating the problem completely. Neutralizing, as we used to say. Now that one has a thermobaric core." Cauz smiles grimly. "Sorry, already filled up. As for the other children, sorry, they're full too. All ready to carry their loads to new nests up on the hill."

Joshua swallows, cocking his head sideways. He walks to the window, looking out into the bright sun. "You saw the film clip, Cauz, the city men. The one shela showed us." Had Cauz been at the first meeting?

"There should be no such a thing as a city man. That's upscale slang we use for the homeless; the down and out. There are city women and city children too, while the fat cats eat caviar in their rooms with a view."

"You are right there, I mean, I agree totally with you on that one." Josh comes back to lean on the table. "There shouldn't be any city children or women or men either, but unfortunately, there are. I sort of picked up from the clip the options we have to try to change things to the way we both want them. The way we all want them. No more city people. Remember there was the guy with the blade, the other guy with the brick and those guys who took a leak all over the Patriot."

"Yeah, I got that message loud and clear." Cauz leans up beside him, gun in hand on the table. "But listen to me, you pissed all over their Parade. What did that get you? They just hop in their executive Bullet Trains and their little personal helihovers and they leave the problem behind. They run away, no different than Knomley hopping in his Hum V and driving away in that clip you're talking about."

Cauz had been there, meaning a shela approved profile. "There's this one old guy I've been talking to." Joshua changes tactics. "He's studied people and human nature all his life. He says people usually have to be told things more than once. Usually a lot of times. They don't get it the first time. Why not reload your children with stinkobaric instead of thermobaric? Sort of a new way of engaging in military type activity. You could add another voice to the many voices telling the same people the same message. 'Cause just think, if you eliminate the people who actually need to hear it the most, how will they hear the message? But if we persist, they will hear I am told."

Cauz looks at him through expressionless eyes.

"I mean, okay, there were the blade and brick options," Josh goes on. "But if you think for a minute, you have a couple challenges yourself. Are you gonna launch when they're at home or just torch their houses when they're away? How you gonna know who's at home. Even a military moron like me has some understanding of collateral damage. Anyone who's seen the news on any military conflict knows that one. Why not keep it blood free, I mean, upscale kind of to the brick, but hold off on the blade."

Cauz looks at Ed, who has been nodding along.

"You say the Mag coming out tomorrow?"

"Yeah, the weekly Monday version," Josh says. Cauz scrunches his face. "Tomorrow morning. Officially at 10AM."

"Forty-eight hours from then?"

"That's what shela's giving them."

"And?"

"Then we go to phase two. Our brick will be the set of pipeworms you saw in the tunnel. Jojo's kick in the butt option."

Cauz wanders over and picks up the apple, rolling it over and over, examining its wrinkled skin. He looks at his watch, then glances over at Ed, and then Josh. "You know, I been waiting on shela so far, even though she is a woman." A wavering smile crosses Cauz's face. "I can give it that forty-eight starting tomorrow morning. What you see here stays as it is. Our blade option stands." He thinks carefully. "Unless, of course, they start raising their virtual plexon. Then we'll have to compress that time frame, no question. You guys will be happy to have this option in place too. Check shela's history files. The blade option has resolved many situations in the past—when people get tired of askin'."

Josh looks Cauz square on as they shake hands at the door. "Good luck, you," Cauz says. Josh almost sees a mirror deep in the mist of those eyes. He follows Ed back down the stairs, then across the street to where Eli and Krino, sit on a low brick wall.

"What happen?" Eli asks.

"He's standing firm as our blade option," Josh says. "He'll wait the forty-eight hours to match shela's schedule. We have just over two days until Wednesday morning." He hesitates, looking at Ed. "Unless they get the big Bubble going up. Then, deals off."

They all look at each other. Joshua sighs, feeling the weight of it all.

"So I presume we will all be attending shela tonight." Ed breaks the silence.

"Uhh!" Eli grunts.

Chapter 19

Sunday Evening, July 8

"Sorry I was late John, we had a couple tasks on the go."

They step quickly together up the stairs, now familiar to Josh after helping to set up earlier that afternoon on the third floor.

"I really admire how together you guys have it, so hey that is no problem at all. You know, like I was saying, Josh, I talked with quite a few of your associates at the last meeting. You are not only well organized, but organized in a very interesting way."

"Like, not the old ways, right?"

"I hope you aren't tired of hearing my mentioning Bruce, but you know, I honestly believe Bruce would have fit in quite well with your group. He did not think much of the people he worked with, not at all. Especially his direct supervisor whose decisions he knew the best. He found that fellow so frustrating, quite intelligence in the traditional sense but with a real lack of interest in facing the reality Bruce would bring his way. Classic case of denial, Bruce would say. Not just his own supervisor though; Bruce was not very approving of the hierarchical administrative structure in general. He saw so many things differently than the way they were, and he actually questioned who was making the decisions."

"Kind of a misfit," Josh says knowingly.

"And what kind of system put those administers in the positions to be making those decisions?" John says. "He'd endlessly joke about the CEO. You know, that is one thing I repeatedly notice about your group. You guys don't exactly have a leader, do you?"

"Well shela is our group conscience, all of us, all our thoughts and feelings, well with a lot of filtering, are what go into the database, and then she comes out of that. Ideally the peaceful, compassionate yet insistent side of our human conscience. We follow that, so that you could say, is our leader. Otherwise, with some help from shela, we all do what we do best."

"Bruce would be so excited about that, that way of organizing."

They open the door to find the circles of metal chairs almost full, the audience attentive to Mother 7 speaking from the improvised stage, sheets of plywood on top of a solid array of wooden crates with a metal step stool for access at either end.

"We better find a seat," Josh says in quieter tones.

"Yes, yes" John whispers.

"All of you have been informed that our final warning message to the *toorich* will be published tomorrow morning," Mother7 says. "So they will have forty-eight hours to make change; that is our schedule. As we await their response, wisdom of the ages suggests we bind ourselves more closely by sharing our deepest thoughts and feelings, our developing insights. Clearly we share a sense of deep-seated anger, a frustration that is helping fuse us together in our common cause. We are very aware of our humanness, the inner knowings we have of what is right and what is not. Of fairness, of justice. Of what resonates with our spirits. We share a belief that change must come about, but we also appear to agree that we must address our need for change in a mature fashion. Who then would come forward and speak?"

Salvo stands close to the stage, ambling up the aisle between rows of chairs to the square center and steps with care up one step stool onto the stage. The plywood cover creaks and he fumbles with the mic Xia hands up to him.

"I talked with this gentleman," John whispers.

"Right," Josh speaks softly back.

"In the politics of social change come name Jesus the greatest socialist of all times. Though my Muslim friend Zijad warns us that people do not listen to the prophets, those who inspire me say religious teachings do show the path. Maybe some choose to listen. I have seen many die in the name of justice and I now believe in a better way. We must come to the Creator as children, ask Him through our childish hearts what to do. This is the way that has best served true revolution. Children change most easily; we are the children of change and we can invite all others to join hands with us as children."

"To be born again," someone shouts out.

"Si, yes, like that." Salvo looks around the room. "So that is my experience I want to share with you." He bows his head, passes the mic back to Xia and makes his way down the step stool. Moving back up the aisle, he passes Lana on her way towards the stage. She quickly steps up on the stage and turns to face them, waiting for her moment of hush.

"Yes, records do bear instruction from that moral Lecturer two thousand years past," Lana says. "He advises also that those who live by the sword die by the sword. We consider His tuitions, reflecting on them with practical consideration. We choose not to live by that proverbial sword; however, neither do we turn our face to be slapped on the other cheek. What is our compromise then? We must engage our adversaries with an attitude of compassion, yet we *must* insist on having our voice heard. Clearly heard. So we must be insistent to that point, ensuring our voice falls upon awakened ears. Many of these ears will require time and repetition before they actually hear, but the message must be voiced until measurable indicators confirm modified behavior."

Josh glances sideways at John, wondering what beliefs the old guy would hold.

"I will add in further to the child idea," Lana says. "Psychologically, it is within the first five or six years of people's lives when their brains and personalities are initially forming that many decisions are made. Young minds are highly influenced by the adults around, the parents, the family setting and the cultural context. The time comes when the brain is hard wired, so to speak, and decisions have been made and adulthood has been reached. There was that childhood time when other options may have still been under consideration, however, and we may be able to appeal to those childhood alternate options still deep within the adults. The inherent better nature of people remains buried beneath the belief baggage of surrounding adults."

Josh hears a murmur run through the crowd.

"Compassionate insistence. That, I would suggest to be our maxim." Lana looks around at the crowd. She repeats,

"Compassionate insistence." She walks across the stage, handing the mic to Staphan as he comes up the steps at one end. Josh's look traces her figure as she makes her way to a corner at the back of stage.

"You might have something to say," John nudges Josh.

"Right," Josh says, nudging back. "But I think they need to hear a Bruce story too."

John looks at Josh, and then rests his chin in his hands, thinking.

"Really John," Josh whispers. "Cum'on, let's get over there." He stands, edging towards the aisle and John hesitantly rises too.

Staphan is now speaking.

"Through a movement called SonofMaNirvana, my kind seeks out the best in both West and East. Buddha teaches us that all awaits us within, that through meditation we find the middle path, the Way. The Messiah teaches love thy enemy as well as thy neighbor, yet with tough love he threw the moneychangers from the Temple. Many of His parables revolve around wine, while the Buddha teaches avoidance of all alcohol. To look upon the teachings of the Savior with discretion fits the middle path. As Lana has said, we must be compassionate with their ignorance, yet insistent with their enlightenment.

"But I bring to your attention the inherent dark side of humans, the Satan who challenged Christ in the desert. There are those in the world born free of the inner discrimination between right and wrong, with no idea of what justice is. The questions stands, what is to be done with these ones? I would suggest special treatment must be given certain people, those closest to this Evil if we call it that. Some of these may require confrontation in a more insistent manner than others. Perhaps a much more insistent manner. My *Inner Guides* inform me that this is true, so I pass it on to all of you to keep in mind."

John and Josh edge around to stand at the end of the stage.

"And I also wish to reveal the truth about myself. I was born on the Hill and lived most of my life there. My father is high on your list, and I will let you know I have approached him in VirtuALL, in his dreams state, where the six-year-old child still is. And I can tell you, as Lana suggested, at that age he had another disposition. A kinder, better side that could be appealed to—that side, however, is buried deep. Accessing it is not easy. So those are my thoughts."

Staphan walks, head bowed, to step down from the stage. Xia meets him to take the mic and she smiles brightly as John takes it from her. John makes his way up, peering down in thought and clearing his throat.

Josh makes his way over to Lana, giving her a little smile, a look she returns.

Walking up to the edge of the stage, John looks up with a practiced smile. "Hello, I truly do thank you in the audience and shela for this opportunity. My name is John, and as you can probably tell by the color of my hair, that I am quite a bit older than most of you. You might be able to guess a few not so obvious things about me by the color of my skin not just my age."

Josh glances over at Lana—she might be thirty.

"I come from a demographic that was the cause of a big part of the concentration of wealth problem," John says. "Which, without going into detail, I can tell you is strongly tied to our biosphere problems as well."

He pauses, letting his words settle.

"Being somewhat of a professional speaker, I have a broad familiarity with not making politicians and senior decision makers feel uncomfortable with the inconvenient, but still getting a message through to them. Diplomacy, yes, I am sure you are familiar with the word. Anyone familiar with a film quite a few years back, about an inconvenient truth? The truth you guys are speaking of here truly is inconvenient, but must really be heard, so I congratulate you on your efforts."

John takes a pronounced breath.

"Anyway, I am up here to apologize for what I didn't do, for not making the decision makers feel not just a little but a *lot* more uncomfortable. You guys are doing what I didn't do. I am so sorry about that, and in their absence, I want to make that apology for my whole age, gender and ethnic group. Again, real sorry. Thank you for hearing me." John steps off the end of the stage, handing the mic to Xia.

Silence ensues, as no new person steps up next. Mother 7 begins to stir and then a voice calls out from the crowd.

"I wish to pose a question to you, my most respected elders," Ed stands up on his chair. "I am fairly new to this whole endeavor and quite young as you may have noticed, perhaps by the various colors in my hair, but you people are fantastic mentors. This effort makes so much sense to me, but there is one thing that does not make any sense at all. I just wonder why we even have this struggle; I mean what is it that drives a person to want to be one of the *toorich*? Why would anyone want to be so extra wealthy? Would that not be simply an endless hassle? I mean I just don't get it. But hey, you people are my elders, so I await your answer."

Ed stays standing, looking around the room.

Mother7 has moved back to the center of the stage, patiently waiting. Joshua follows Lana as she makes her way back to the stage side step stool. She looks at Josh, eyes questioning, and he waves her to go first. Her smile brightens as she takes the mic and faces the crowd.

"A perspicacious or insightful view of human inception would be in order to address that question. We have an accurate record of our biological story, but our cultural beginnings, the nature of humanity, that would be more subjective. Let's use biblical reference in this case, why not, though all original cultures have a creation story. When we were evicted from the Garden, then, we found ourselves in the harsh world of nature with all its natural laws. Out of the Garden, people have inherent needs for survival, the basics, nutrition, attire and habitation. Once survival becomes more assured, many patterns of humanity then show an economic preponderance to enhance, to progress further, to develop, and then on an individual basis to improve one's socioeconomic status, and depending on the situation, often in competition with one another. The privileged emerge out of the varying patterns of circumstance, out of the ruckus, and they become symbols of success to that inner drive to improve. Big men in tribal times, then the passionately feudal lords and dukes and then those cloaked in the garbs of royal purple—kings and queens of nations."

Josh finds himself totally absorbed, listening, hearing her. Krino had no problem with older women.

"Historically landowners were the well to do—essentially the cultural ancestors of the digital lords who we now call *toorich.* They are lauded as having acquired a desirable status, a now enviable position engrained over generations. In our times, the millionaire, or now, due to inflationary effects, more realistically the billionaire has emerged as the cultural idol. What initiated itself as a set of basic human needs has in many instances far exceeded its original intent. So to succinctly answer, it is actually instinct gone astray."

*Not in our genes…*Josh recalls Krino's biology.

"Most have now long forgotten why they pursue extreme wealth, but their fear of hunger lives on deep within them, and the cultural designation of successful keeps clamoring in their ears. They have strong messages, both internal and external, to strive to maintain status quo. The All Mart kids are notoriously known for self-perpetuation of status, a status they simple inherited, through no effort on their part. These results of an earlier instinctive drive, are what we strive to re-educate."

Lana nods to the crowd and glances at Joshua now standing at the edge of the stage. She walks directly towards him and with a flourish and bright smile, passes him the mic and gives him the center. His heart beats twice.

"I have a comment, no more." Josh starts, looking over his people. "I have spoken with many of you and we are on track towards showing the benefits to the *toorich* of striving to modify their instinctive drive as Lana has defined it. We are their college and their clinic, as well as a hungry, angry mob surrounding their fortress. As Ed rightly asks, why would they want to live under these extra stressful conditions, under siege? If I were one of them, I'd be losing a lot of sleep right now," He holds his free hand open and up. "So I would believe they have to at least be doing some reflecting. What I mean to emphasize, is that if we show them an option and keep making the status quo increasingly uncomfortable for them, they will cede eventually."

He looks at John.

"Kind of like the carbon taxes John says when they first came out. You have to make what *you* want a part of the economy so people make choices to their own benefit that are also to the benefit of everyone," Josh says. "If we all don't cooperate on carbon pollution, John tells me, everyone dies in the end with the *toorich* just dying a little later in whatever sealed emergency structures they have. So we have to make *them* be smart enough to want to change now, and see it as their own idea to their own advantage. Diplomats, we must be a new type of diplomat."

Josh walks off the squeaky stage and down the rattling step stool to join Lana at the side.

Mother7 moves back to centre, patiently looking over the crowd for a long moment. Silence reins across the floor until the gently evening breeze can be heard rustling through the unboarded windows above. She speaks. "As we mentioned earlier, we have yet to hear a response from the Hill. Our final ad will be posted in the FFM Mag tomorrow morning, and we are closely watching the accounts. The response to this hour is nil; they appear to be frozen. We must wait up to our deadline and be ready for our next step if no change shows." She pauses. "So unless there's anyone else to share, we will reconvene tomorrow."

Joshua sees Staphan talking to Salvo as the crowd mingles around. He points them out to Lana and they walk up on the pair as Staphan is speaking.

"…yes, my father. You were the one who informed Joshua then. To have influence at the childhood stage. I took my father on a VirtuALL tour down here in his night time dreams and in his dreams he came along in a childlike state."

"But will it change him—that is the defining question," Josh says as they walk up. "It's not a two year influential visit like you talked about Salvo, and it's virtual, not real. I mean what actually awakens the ears of men?" Lana waves Zijad in to join them too.

"A religious experience is one thing," says Staphan," that can have a profound effect on a person. Just that God seems to decide on the where and when of it, and we have no influence over God's decisions."

"Personal tragedy," Lana speaks unnaturally slow," or…"

"A gun pointed to the head," Salvo breaks in. "It has good effect but only in the short term."

"That's Cauz's idea now," Josh says. "And he says it has had real effect in the past."

They all look at each other.

"Is near death, how you say, experience has effect—proven," says Zijad. "Not blow out brains, but if bullet pass through but not kill. Die for minutes—then bring them back. In ancient times Egyptian pharaohs require to put them in sarcophagus and time how much air they have. They want pharaoh with wisdom, and near death bring that. They practice with slaves—the ones who survive are wise slaves. But pharaoh must be wise one. Now days people in hospitals modern medicine bring back alive. This changes people outlook—the human...nature."

"We have to work with other technology—we can't use a sarcophagus but we want that effect," Josh says. As silence settles in again, Joshua looks towards Lana. "What else were you going to say Lana?"

"Ohh, I was just thinking about when people get involved romantically, you know, when they fall in love," she says softly, looking up into Josh's eyes. "That has historically had profound influence over personal behavior...and outlook." Her eyes flicker as she giggles a little.

"Yes..." Josh stutters, "I know what you mean."

"Women mature faster, as girls, yet live longer as women," Lana say. "A long term relationship between a man and woman matches better when a woman is a little older."

Josh nods, smiling silently.

Jihad and Salvo have fallen into a heated discussion.

Staphan watches Josh and Lana as they mutually absorb each other. He thinks wistfully of the contact he has now made. He will meet her early in the morning; he must try to sleep before that. He lifts a hand in goodbye salute.

Chapter 20

Early Monday Morning, July 9

He wakes with a start to a thundering subliminal roar. The clamor surges louder, driving sheets of an inner storm in blasts of fear, then anguish against the walls of his inner being. Sitting up straight in the midst of the turmoil, chest pounding, he reaches for the water. Fumbling the glass to his lips, he pours the liquid in absorbing swallows to seep into the cracks of his parched throat.

Oh for pure simple emptiness, oh for nothing at all. But the undertaking awaits with no choice, the alternatives looming ever more dire.

Sas rises, stumbling into his clothes and heads out the door, essence dragging in torn pieces as he forces himself to walk the sidewalk. He barely notices the early morning's promise of a fine day, the contrast with his mind too great. He shuffles past the now dead Grab, ambling down the deserted streets to where he must go. One all night teahouse she talked of where the officers gather after shift, but it's the other one, further down on Sequa.

A quieter place. He finds a seat in a wooden booth and sits to await.

The ups and downs of life, one struggles for an up and drifts back to the next down. Why? Nirvana, Creator, maybe these are but human created concepts. The Savior had his ups and downs but so many people seem to have a nice steady hum on the up side. He looks around the Tea House, noticing the few other patrons. All going about their regular lives, free of his turmoil or anything like it he is sure. What it must have been for Jesus out in that desert for forty days and nights or hanging up on a wooden stick for how many hours. Why would a Creator allow such things to happen? To prove faith in tasks assigned? Is that the only reason?

From the corner of his eye he notices a dark uniform of authority opening the door with its jangle bells. He looks straight down at the table top, straight down through the table now to bond again with the force that drives him. He takes the deepest of breaths, and compels his eyes up to address this assignment.

"Sas." She has found him easily. She stands cautiously back from the table. "Is that you?"

Time stands still as an empty deserted hornet's nest blowing over a desert dune. Choking on a final dry mouthful of powdery sand, he rises, motioning her to sit.

"Hello Jeira." He coughs deeply, then mutters in a hoarse whisper. "Nice uniform. You do look good. You always have."

"Do you need some water?"

He shakes his head, "I'll be fine."

She smiles. "You look great too, Sas." She loosens her jacket and slides into the bench across from him. "It's been such a long time. How are you?"

He nods. "Acceptable, things are acceptable." He strains to show a brief smile.

"Josh was saying you guys met. You know, maybe I've seen you down on the streets, you never know. Josh says you are involved in this latest movement. Just like back in our valiant knight days." She smiles. "—oh, you know I fly UPAS security." She points up. "We fly air patrol, for security or actually safekeeping on the ground, on the streets where the people are."

"You still carry the sword of righteousness," Staphan speaks slow, glancing up at her. "Josh mentioned something like that." He holds his gaze, then speaks down at the table tapping one palm. "Look Jeira, do you want something? A drink? A Tea?"

"Sure, sorry, we should order. Philli Double Mocha would go fine, smooth on the throat if you want one."

"Yes, I will then, thank you." He flags down the waiter.

"We have a lot to catch up on."

"Yes." He holds up two fingers as he lets the waiter know the order.

"Those sure were great times down by the river. You remember Sas? All those grand plans we had, how we were going to have everyone living in happy villages. Everyone would follow the code of honor," Jeira says. "No one would be a villain, and if they made a wrong move, we would tell them one of our fables that would make things so clear to them. They would understand—they would have to. Everyone wants to be happy down at heart; some just need to be given a little direction."

"Those were quite the dreams we had."

"Don't you still believe in something like that though?" Jeira says. "Anything?"

"Myself? Well, perhaps, maybe in a way. Yet reality has set in," Sas says. "My reality tells me there are some who would not understand the fable's meaning. Some, or many or likely most, just cannot understand—they are not capable."

"Ah yes, reality." Jeira smiles darkly. "But still, there are things worth striving for…you have to have some code to live by, don't you? There must be something that makes you do what you do, right?"

"Yes, look Jeira, I do follow something to that effect." He coughs as his voice becomes a hoarse whisper again.

"Are you okay, Sas?" Her eyebrows furrow with concern. She reaches across to touch him. He winces, drawing his arm back.

"Just a dry throat," he wheezes, holding his hand to his mouth. "Look Jeira, there is something I really need to tell you."

"Yeah, okay Sas. Maybe wait for our tea, it can be so soothing. Can your question wait a minute?" She rises with a smile. "I just need a moment myself, I'll be back in a flash." She walks towards the restroom.

An emptiness settles over him, one that only patient consolation might oh so gradually help to dissipate. He listens around the room to the conversations. Happy talk about the wonders of life, what else would people speak of? Their Teas arrive, and he sips the warm dancing liquid, letting its promised touch wash as a rivulet over the dry sand of his parched throat.

She comes back, beaming.

"Sas. It really is so good to see you." She lifts her cup in a cheers salute and then to her lips. The conversations from around meld back together into a common background buzz as her voice speaks out one distinct word after another. "So tell me about yourself. What have you been up to these last few years?"

He wraps his hands tightly around his cup, holding it as if to shield his thumping chest. "Oh, not much, really, almost nothing at all. Something of a struggle, actually. But recently, I've been trying to get straightened out." He reaches into his pocket, pulling out his crucifix. He puts it on the table in front of her to show. "Speaking of a code to live by, I want to tell you now I follow SonofMaNirvana, maybe you heard of us? We meditate; seek to improve. And we do have a code of conduct; a very important code. What that involves, Jeira, is making amends for the misdeeds of our past. Direct amends."

"That sounds great, Sas," Jeira says. "That would be just like you."

"Ah, yes, look Jeira, that is kind of why I wanted to talk to you. Like I said, there is something I have to tell you." He takes another gulp of the soothing tea, another deep breath, forcing himself to look up at her and hold a steady gaze on her face. "It's about a gathering you were at. A party." His look drops again.

"A party." She puts her cup down. "What party? We hung around down by the river. You, me and Josh. Partying came later."

"There was a gel tub party. You are right; it was a few years later. Did I ever tell you I have a brother? His name is Paul. I saw you there, at the party, but I was too shy to come over and talk. You looked so much like a woman then and I was such a wimp."

Her smile recedes gradually. "You are a great guy, Sas. We were all unsure of ourselves when we were younger. I wish I had seen you at that party. Maybe we could have talked. But a gel tub party." Her eyebrows furrow slightly. She slowly raises her cup for a sip. "That must have been up on the Hill, then? I was only ever at a couple parties up there, both the summer right after high school," she says carefully.

"You probably don't know, Josh didn't, but that is where I lived, where my family lives. That is from whence I came. Yeah, the party was at a house in our neighborhood." His breathing comes shallow. "And I knew what Paul and his two companions that night were up to. It wasn't the first time. They probably gave you the invitation to the party in the first place. Anyway, I knew, and I did nothing. When you know you can do something and you don't, it is a sin. In this case, a cardinal sin." He stares into his Tea Cup, then forces his eyes up again, this time looking directly into her eyes. "I am sorry, Jeira, so sorry. That I did nothing. I could have acted and I did nothing. Truly, from my heart, I express my deepest regret."

She looks back and forth into his eyes, searching for the same memory. It couldn't be *that* party. The last party she ever went to on the Hill. But she hears the voices around the gel tub, the three young men who approached her, Paul, yes, that was one of them. The laughs becoming lucid giggles, then the ride down the hill. She gasps lightly, putting her hand to mouth, as her face drops. She calls on all her resources now, all the techniques the councillor has helped her learn, at this moment to hold her sobs within. This is not the time, and for sure not the place. How can this be, one moment joyful to have reengaged with her childhood crush. And the next moment this…

"I studied criminology for a few years. There are a lot of reasons for deviant behavior, especially among young men." She focuses on the passages that best described it to her from the textbooks. "If they were repeat offenders, they are much more likely to have been detained and become engaged in our legal system."

She looks at the table in front of him.

"My brother has engaged in many acts of what you call deviant behavior. All his life from as far back as I know. It's just not really any kind of deviation for him, it's the way he is and the way he will always be," Sas says. "It is part of his nature and he is extremely clever—focused on not being caught. God is perfect only by having the mistaken pieces of his creation cleaned up by other pieces. Our legal system is not cleaning up this deviant."

"Oh God, Sas, look I have done everything I could to deal with the situation and to forget about it. It was not your fault. I don't blame you." She can't keep the tears from rolling down her face as her voice trails off. "Not at all…"

A long moment of silence follows as they each look into their tea cups.

"Well, I will again express my deepest apology, Jeira, yet words without action remain shallow and meaningless, even if they are now voiced. As I mentioned, my amends must be direct." He takes a deep breath. "My brother has no concept of honor. All I can tell you is, I am going to make it up to you now, through deeds. It is what I must do to make retribution, to accompany my pitiful voice of regret." Staphan's head buzzes, like flies around an open wound. "I promise," he whispers. "Jeira, I am so sorry our get together couldn't have been more pleasant; you are so fair, my lady." He rises, grabbing his jacket. "I must return to the Hill now. There is a task I must carry out under a tightening schedule; I must tarry no further."

Jeira glances up to watch him going, the bells jangling at the door, and then her eyes glare fiercely through the tears falling into the depths of her Tea at the trailer court boys. She struggles to focus; she must hold back anything. She pictures herself with hair cut short, with all power to change all things. She escapes as a bird up into the freedom and wonder of the high sky. But she can't hold her eyes down any longer, and they follow the path Sas took as he walked away. At what he was last saying, her heart won't slow and she shivers inside.

Chapter 21

Tuesday Morning, July 10

"There remains another question reverberating about the annals of my youthful mind," says Ed. "As you are my well educated fellows, my elders, I surrender my impasse to your wise review." They follow each other slowly down the stairs leading to the tunnel entrance. "The issue bears itself out thus; what is the practical value of the extremely wealthy within our societal context? What I am asking is; of what use are they?"

"Some say they create jobs," Josh says, speaking down the stairs towards Ed. "That they contribute to the economy with their business skills. That's the main argument in their favor. And of course not so much recently, but in the past they were glamorized as cultural heroes, presented as upper middle class good guy characters in movies, you know, in drama and in the general media."

Josh stops on the steps for a moment, caught up in this thoughts.

"Hey, that glamorizing might bring in the aspiration factor," Josh says. "When people believe they can become wealthy, it keeps them whistling while they work and dreaming of some day. Which keeps our economy as originally designed going and growing. That old adage; keeping up with the Jones. The truth is, your chances of jumping to a higher social class are actually poor. Ask Lana or Staphan. But the wealthy are the ones on the pedestal, worshipped and admired, so they keep having that influence."

They continue down the last few steps.

"One more mythical benefit," Josh says. "The higher taxes they should but most likely don't pay, as in the political deregulation of stock option payments."

"Mythical," Ed says. "As in not real."

"And CEO's," Josh says, "again more so in the past, get or were traded and treated financially like sports heroes. Like another form of hero worship."

"Nobody likes the All Mart kids." Ed turns back to cock his head, eyebrow raised, looking up. "They do no more than inherit; how do they contribute?"

"Good question." Josh follows Ed stepping down at the bottom. "Look, I'll give you my take. The government we vote in can close tax loopholes, and they can increase progressive taxation and whatnot, you know, when you pay a proportionately higher income tax rate on a higher income, but what have governments actually done in the past? Except for Asha, forget about it. The options we have to vote for are usually a selection of the *toorich* themselves. I can tell you what I would like to do and that's sit each of them down where they have to listen, look them straight in the eye and give a little lecture. Ask a few questions like you're asking right now Ed." Josh's voice becomes louder. He feels his fingers bunching, pressing towards solid fists in a most insistent manner. "What I would say is: Look at me. You embarrass me. Get responsible. Do we have to wipe your little butt for you still? Can't you see what you're doing? Are you so stupid you don't see the connection between your gel tub dinner, your caviar buffets and the woman with her children living in the alley? Or do you really, actually just not care? 'Cause that woman and her kids are far away, comfortably hidden. Well, if you don't care, if you are nice and cozy, I am about to drag you out of your little powder puff world and stick your nose right in it and hold you there until you have to take a deep breath."

"Delirious," Ed says.

"Okay, sorry, a little sidetracked," Josh says. "To answer your basic question they don't contribute, they are a net detriment."

They file along in a slow amble after each other to the tunnel entrance.

"Yo," says Eli. "I hear you, brother."

"Delirious. I am left with the impression there is no real value in maintaining positions such as theirs." Ed walks swinging his arms high as if marching in a military regiment commanded by him. "The ones you people refer to as the *toorich.* So then I wonder why not throw it all in with Cauz and simply blow them unto the kingdom on high?"

Josh sighs. "Because they're people I guess. I mean it's not entirely their fault. Research has said for some time now we would all be better off, them included, if things were more equitable. They need to know that, to learn that, so teaching is our task. You don't choose the circumstances of your birth. They just may not know any better. Yet. I never had a chance to give my little lecture to any of them yet. We are on a campaign to educate them, though. Their next lesson is just coming up, eh Jojo?"

Jojo walks out of the tunnel entrance to meet them, a digital clipboard in one hand and a monkey wrench in the other.

"The Parade was number one and this will be lesson number two." Jojo grins. "Do not mess with the power of the flower. Okay, so, we installed the tap last night on the sanitary line. Now I want you guys to help me feed the worms in one at a time and I need to get them into their ready to move out position. First we have to load their tanks full of flower juice. Then we'll feed them into the pipe."

"Are we using PVCmelt?" Josh asks. "Cauz's idea for a backup plan."

"Well Cauz never showed up with any, so I'm tracking some down," Jojo says. "We still need some other Plan B in my opinion."

"Maybe we smash our way into a transition car," Krino says. "Or walk up the east side of the Hill flying our protest banners."

"No. Gotta be an effective plan," Jojo says. "Those were both tried before."

"So say they get this big stink comin' back at them one more time, but on this occasion right up out from their own john," Krino says. "And say they just pay no mind to that one neither. Then they build their plexon shield so we can't fly them no more flowers. Then what we gonna do?"

"That Bullet still has to go through their wall, well, I believe they would keep it running. They can't seal themselves in completely," Jojo says. "They could build a self-contained water and sewer system to cut us off from physical access through their underground pipes."

"We should start thinking about their food provisions—where those come from," Josh suggests. "When they sealed themselves into a castle in the old days, it was food and water and the attack technology of the ones outside the castle that decided how long the siege would go on."

"We gotta keep talking; keep ahead of them with ideas, with backup plans," Jojo says. "We can't let them silence our voice."

They follow Jojo into the tunnel, over to the stack of pipeworm cases. He shows Josh and Krino how to pop the pipeworm tank covers open and attach the sealed feed line to fill each of them from the polymer barrel. He tells them not to worry, the squiggly effect is gone now as the worms are locked on rigid. He then takes Eli and Ed over to the tap, a straight piece of pipe with valves at each end teeing into the sanitary line at an angle. He gives them a demo on how to open the outside valve, and where the bleed line and valve is to drain pressure from the tap into a small sealed tank for the second load. They put boxes in place to stand on, ready to slide in the first worm.

"My delirious, gentlemen," Ed say. "This actually closely resembles loading torpedoes in a submarine."

"Yo," Eli grunts. "Bouquet fish."

"The count is now exactly twenty four hours," Jojo looks up at the countdown clock. "FFM Mag came out at ten AM yesterday, so they have had one day to consider our published demands. You guys read it? Day after tomorrow we make the liquid strike." He grins. "Unless they make a change before then of course. We wait on shela's instruction."

"That's Cauz's deadline too, remember?" Josh muses. "Like he sure is right in synch with shela's schedule. Which seems right, but I just wonder if he isn't taking all his action commands directly from shela?"

No one responds, not a word is spoken.

Krino breaks the silence. "How we gonna know if they make a change? So then we wouldn't even have to worry none about Cauz."

"The accounts posted in the demands list, if you read it, are public domain," Jojo says. "The whole world has read access. We would see if they start making deposits or not. Simple." He looks at Josh. “I don’t know about Cauz. I thought you were looking into that Josh.”

“Doing my best,” Josh says. “Like I say, he’s hard to figure out. I just keep wondering, you know, maybe someone snuck him in there looking as if he is shela’s Plan B. Don’t ask me who.”

Josh and Krino lift the worm they have loaded with liquid, and pass it up to Ed and Eli who slip it into the tap, and wheel the outside valve closed.

“Closed and locked?” Jojo is serious. “Please double check.”

Ed yanks the valve wheel to show it can’t be opened. “Yes sir.” Eli closes the safety cap and snaps it closed. He nods.

Jojo selects a remote control from the array he has laid out.

“Okay, you can open that inside valve,” says Jojo. “Gotta find a place to park these babies.” He looks at the schematic diagram he has hanging against one dirt wall.

“Kinda like uh commando mission,” says Ed.

“Well, maybe it is,” says Josh. “Or maybe more of a social mission to set a boundary. The kinds of limits people have to learn to put in place more often. Maybe that’s how we have to deal with Cauz too.” He wonders about that in silence for a second.

“Existentially delirious. I can’t forget what Staphan was saying.” Ed taps the valve wheel to show it’s completely open, winking at Jojo. “I mean regarding his father. His dad doesn’t sound any happier than us or anyone else. He’s really not having all that great of a time.”

“Happiness is pretty subjective.” Josh tunes in again. “We know once people have their basic needs met, there is no free trip to greater happiness. Research clearly shows you don’t get any happier as you get richer. Except when you make that quantum leap from not having to having the basic needs.” He pops the tank lid on the next worm, unscrews the cap and steps back to let Krino connect the feed line. He speaks to them all. “The question just might be what those basic needs truly are. Lana mentioned food, clothing and shelter, now that’s just to survive, but you can still be even happier when you live healthy and get the work education brings. So if we want to have a civilized world, we have to include education and health. And a truly free press that reveals what actually is true. So when you allow each citizen access to all the education they aspire to, and make them aware of what is actually happening in their community like Asha was doing and you supply them all with equal health care, you not only increase human capital, I mean that's good economically too, you also increase your net community happiness. So if we use the wealth of the *toorich* that's not making them any happier anyway, and supply the many with colleges and clinics, that's where you net the most happiness. Simple investment strategy."

"Yeah," says Eli. "'Specially kids need that. What Asha give me. I got happy real quick."

"That's del-le-le-lirious." Ed steps back and forth on opposing edges of his box, lifting opposite sides up from the ground to rock his box with precarious balance. "'Cause our Staphan himself does not strike me as the chipper type. Like wouldn't he be all lined up like the All Mart kids? Won't he inherit his father's assets? I suppose someone like him might pass it around to all the right places and make a lot of others happy. Maybe that would put a smile on his face too."

"Yeah, it should." Josh screws the cap back into the next worm and pops the lid closed. "But I believe it's his brother, Paul, that's lined up to inherit. The business strings, anyway."

"Maybe Paul will have one of Lana's BMG's," says Jojo, picking up the next remote control.

"I have my doubts there, the way Staphan was talking." Josh grabs his end of the second worm, ready for someone to grab the other. "Lana says very few have a Bill Gaetz change just like that. She says most of them if they have one at all, long chance there, have a long slow educational type of awakening."

"Do you speak of my brother and myself?" Staphan comes walking through the tunnel towards them. "In my absence?"

"Oh, hey Sas. Look, grab that end of the worm, will ya?" Josh waits for Staphan's help. "Yes we were. No secrets, man. Like we wonder if you are happy and we wonder about your brother Paul."

"Happiness is irrelevant," Staphan says grunting lightly as he lifts his end. "My brother is a serious abomination. Don't expect anything good from him. He needs special treatment in this operation" *Very special, They confirm now.*

"Did you meet with Jeira?" Josh asks as they lift the second pipeworm up to Eli and Ed and Josh turns to pull the lid off the next worm case, unwrapping the paper.

"Yes, Joshua. I am forever in gratitude for your introduction. Or reintroduction," Staphan says. "You see it cannot be happiness that one such as I am allowed to pursue. Maybe others have such grace. When I spoke with your sister about events from the past, it is an inner level of contentment that came my way. I must seek out the truly righteous, I must carry out actions that are righteous, no matter what the cost. That is what allows one a truly fulfilling life. Happiness is a frivolous state of mind."

"D-d-d-delirious. Is she a babe? That would be righteous."

Staphan stares up at Ed. "She is an attractive woman, yet outward appearance is completely superficial. She deserves respect. She is a child of God, and she deserves respect."

"Yes sir, yes sir, three bags full," Ed says, rocking his box wildly. He gradually loses his momentum and comes to a swaying stop. "No, look, I'm sorry Staphan, you are right. Women deserve respect. Asha was the best president we ever had, my mom said so. My mom was the best. You are right."

Staphan turns to the others. "Just to inform you, my father slept poorly last evening. The feedback wire shows disturbing nightmares to have been his close companions. He now seems unable to erase the dream of the mother with her children in the alley. That is to say, the dream is becoming recurring."

"Maybe your father will up and change his mind," says Krino, taking his turn at unpacking another worm. "Maybe on time for our deadline. That would be good for us and from what I'm hearing now, good for him too."

"Yeah, maybe he won't need all those predicted trips in VirtuALL." Josh stands back from the work area, smiling brightly at Staphan. "Maybe that one look was enough. Natural BMG's can actually happen based on what seem like very small events, that's what Lana was saying."

"We will see," says Staphan. "I will return to the *master's* house again this eve, though I fear they are becoming more and more suspicious of my intentions."

Chapter 22

Tuesday Early Evening, July 10

"We never once meet in the same place," says Josh, checking screen. "We're at random select location E8 now. I just can't believe it's totally random, though, there's gotta be some strategy involved."

"She's for sure one smart cookie on pickin' places," says Krino. "This here looks like one of those hip hop open-air joints. We just above the show house."

Josh and Krino lean, elbows on a fancy tile covered wall along the edge of a newly closed twelfth story rooftop cafe, watching the glow on the distant horizon where the sun has recently lost itself behind urban outlines. The air is fresh, almost crisp, as the heat begins to dissipate and a new night settles in. A flock of sparrows flutters about among the remains of table umbrella stands and a scattering of worn chairs and bar stools, looping and swirling around each other, twittering.

"Peace and love brother," Krino says.

"Birds chirping," Josh says. "Evening sky."

"Say you was living out on the plains of Africa, you right close in touch with nature," Krino says. "Cause you gots to be. That is how you survive. You are a hominid, minus a lot of the prefrontal cortex we got us now but still you got some grey matter, and that hominid inside of you and me at this moment, that is the one that smells this fresh air and watches that sun go down and has a moment of peace. Deep, really deep inner peace. 'Cause we never got eaten that day, so we quite content for a minute. You feel it? You know what I am sayin'?"

Josh takes a careful breath and looks at Krino, nodding.

"So like I was saying, you can see the hominid within in children. Cause the brain of a child is growing, just as the brain of homo sapiens sapiens grew over the millennia. You take a two year old, what are they best known for? Temper tantrum, man. Complete loss of control rage and anger, coming out everywhere. That is because they have a brain that is grown about as much as Lucy way back then. Emotion is right there, with nothing to control it yet."

Josh swallows. "And you are telling me that two year old, or that hominid, is still inside of me. Right now. Anger and all."

"Well, that is a part of your brain, it does not go away, just had newer parts that override the emotion now. So, yes, that is what I am sayin', my man."

Josh sighs. "We better go down—time's getting close."

They push away from the wall, Josh tracing one finger along the tiles, hesitant to let go of the tranquility. But he turns to follow his friend.

"Yeah."

They pass through the rooftop access door and step lightly down a set of stairs in the front corner of the old show theatre, looking out over the people as they descend. The crowd is tense and on edge tonight, extra quiet and slightly nervous, seeking out confirmation, consolation. At this third meeting after the excitement of Bouquet Day, they strive to know the risks they take are having some kind of impact. Sauntering down gradually sloping aisle, the friends step into a row to find a pair of soft cushy theatre seats. The lights are dimming as the evening meeting begins. Mother7 sits in a virtual chair, soft lit, waiting with enduring serenity on the wings of the stage area beside the presentation equipment. As if in deep thought.

"You help set up for tonight?" Joshua feels a light grin forming. "Help Xia?"

"Oh yeah, man, I tell you she was happy with the electric connection for this place," Krino says. "I have been helping her. And she been helping me too. We are cooperating." He looks directly at Josh. "You remember I told you DNA is all written in its own language, using one four letter chemical alphabet. Interesting truth is the whole digital world is written in one two-letter alphabet—binary. Sorta like the languages of male and female. If they are bilingual, they communicate. Me and this woman are connecting, man. Like one bio-digital team. I can tell you a couple things now I never knew before."

"Excellent. So, tell me this; is it possible to actually translate back and forth between the four digit language and the two digit binary? Like in any common day situation."

"What? Yeah, okay, I see." Krino strokes his chin. "Hypothetically that is possible. You need a bio-programmer—one who knows both languages at code level. Xia says we got no common upper level macro language yet."

"Okay, so sticking with the hypothetical, say some programmer plants a virus in shela with the intent of filtering out anything negative about say someone like Cauz. So his profile comes through clean as a whistle for her, no matter what the truth. That would still be within shela, so that would still be binary based. Now say there's also some kind of bio-virus planted in Cauz enhancing his aggressive tendencies? That would have to be the four-letter bio based platform 'cause he's a person. So you say, with a bio-programmer involved, these two hypothetical viruses could be working in concert with each other?"

Krino thinks for a moment and shrugs. "Hypothetically."

"Yeah, right. Okay, well tell me this one thing neither of us knew before. Shela's current security status. Tell me more about that."

"Yeah, I can tell you more on that one." Krino brightens. "Xi says a considerable number of viruses now have level 2, maybe level 3 intelligence. They discern situations, especially if the virus is at least partially hereditary. You know, four letter language and similar to the way DNA works. But we are still talking binary-based code. It gets messy, man. She says a level 3 might have some influence on a more complex human-type program. Take Mother7. A level 3 maybe reads her mood pattern, and then attempts some influence. Say some particular occasion come up. Level 3 maybe slide into her to cause a different feeling for a few minutes; say an all okay feeling about say someone like Cauz." Krino shrugs. "Or it might wait for a certain situation, and then bring up or recall a previously defined subconscious option. More and more like biology, this digital world. Take any old situation. A level 3 could recommend she do something a little different than she would normally. You know, like when a thought comes from the back of your mind or my mind. But even more likely for a woman, 'cause it's a lot more similar to an intuition."

"Shit. She said all that?"

"She is one smart woman."

The lights dim and they lower their voices; the somber crowd becomes attentive.

"I have to ask her directly then," Josh whispers.

"Who, Xia?"

"No, shela."

Mother7 has come to her feet, not shining quite as bright as usual or is Josh seeing things? She moves to the center of the stage floor, face down almost as if deciding on the strategy of her words.

"The time for our second action is rapidly approaching." Mother7 looks up from the circle center with her enduring eyes. "The pipeworms you saw demonstrated are standing by at this moment, I am told, in place at specific underground pipe junctions. Ready to be routed to visit the least cooperative Golden Glow households. We have seen some positive movement in the accounts, however slight, so the worms are mobile to accommodate any decisive change up to the last minute. Our countdown now stands at seventeen hours plus."

"I have a question for shela." Joshua stands up abruptly.

Mother7 pauses, her eyes penetrating deep into Josh's being. "Yes?" He feels a shiver rise up from his toes.

"There is at least one among us who has a full military option in place, one who is also counting down the hours. Are you aware?" He catches his breath. "He plans to express his wrath as has been done in the past, through acts of traditional war-like aggression—attack first, negotiate later." Joshua gets a feeling almost like he used to when he was pleading with his own mother. "Will you do something about this?"

Mother7's face turns to a look of concern, of deep compassion. She speaks in slow clear words. "We understand your unease, we do. Perhaps we need to more clearly define our role. We have done some profile filtering of extremes, but no person is pure. Each time one of you shares here, or in other contexts, you add to us. We are but a reflection of you, all of you. We are not your leader, independent of your deepest desires, rather we are an expression of your combined consciences. So we entreat you, you must ask yourself, are you aware? Does this manner of expressing dissatisfaction linger on within you?"

"Oh, I didn't..." Joshua fumbles back to sit, not knowing how to continue. He feels his ever-present bunched up fingers, forcing them to relax again. He searches his mind frantically, wondering what there is to do now. "Shit," he whispers under his breath.

"Relax man," Krino says. "It's cool."

"I don't think so, Krino. Not cool at all." He turns to face his friend, eyes darting back and forth. He takes a deep breath, looking at the floor for a moment. "I know, at least I think I do. Look, I have to go talk to him again. I have to go back to Cauz's place."

"Not now, dawg," Krino says. "Sit tight for a minute."

A flock of sparrows, perhaps those from the roof, bursts through an un-boarded window at that moment, twittering its way in a loop around the high ceiling. Joshua's eyes and ears follow the natural commotion as the flock searches for a way back out, depending totally on their senses in a suddenly confusing situation.

"Well what if...yeah, I suppose you're right. I guess I have a few more hours to try to figure out what else I can say to him." *Or myself.* Her answer, though profound, gave him no answer. If she is influenced by the virus, he can't rely on shela as a source. He's got to deal with this on his own. But is that not what he feels in his own clenching fists? He settles his head down into both hands, forcing himself to listen.

"As expected we continue to receive mixed responses from the Hill. We are now observing a rapid attempt to deploy a virtual Plexon-Bubble over the entire Citadel community," Mother7 says to the crowd. "Transmitters have been erected at the four pillar stations today, and we have detected a test band transmission this afternoon. They have also begun to fill in the hundred meter substations along the wall. They work around the clock as we speak." She walks back and forth now, hands folded behind her back. "But they do have a dilemma, one that is not new to them. That is; where will they draw the classification line between the included and the excluded? The philosophical line that divides." She pauses.

"Man, just like biology," Krino says softly to Josh. "You see, you got your species, but then you got your sub-species. Take canis lupus, now that's a wolf at the species level. But Zaca here is also canis lupus, but she's my familiaris subspecies."

"What? Oh yeah," Josh snaps back into focus. "Things have always been that way with people too, no question. Culturally. Where do you draw a precise line between class divisions?"

"And then you look at familiaris, look at all the dog breeds we have…but people did that, they do that with domestic animals, making some nice friendly lap pooches and some aggressive attack animals. Slight genetic variations."

"Yeah right."

Mother 7 continues. "We all know the physical line that divides, the barrier wall around Citadel Hill. But that wall is not a complete enclosure. The west and south sides are most easily defined by the top of the ridge. But on the east side, there is a gradual continuum through the middle class zone. They have no clear definition in this instance, as they never have had in the past. This is their underbelly, a weakness that is still to our advantage. We have over the years approached the Hill here, on Asha's assassination anniversary. We will watch development along this soft boundary closely through the night. To see how they choose to locate the virtual shield. Their soft spot may very well be to our benefit."

Their weakness. Our weakness. "I gotta go." Joshua jumps to his feet. "Look Krino, you gotta fill me in on what else she says later. I gotta go have some words with Cauz."

"You sure Josh?" Krino frowns. Josh stares at him with a look of grim determination. "Yeah, okay, talk to you, man."

Joshua doesn't wait for the freight elevator, skipping quickly down the twelve sets of stairs to their bottom and out the door to the street. As he heads off down the sidewalk, the feels the buzz of his tc. Who could it be now?

Chapter 23

Tuesday Evening, July 10

Jeira pulls her hair back, almost yanking as she bundles it into a tight knot. As short as she can. She glares forlornly into the mirror. How can life be so uneven? She throws her hairclips hard into her bag. Everything, all of it, not fair. All this shit around her, all that could have happened but hadn't, all that happened that never should have. Why mother had to pass away so before her time?...why they ended up living in a trailer court in the first place?...why are those others living up on the Hill? And how can some of them do what they do? *Stop, don't go there now* she screams silently.

She steps back and pulls her jacket straight, brushing off a piece of lint. Dress code is one thing she's grateful for right now about UPAS. Precise and meticulous, a way of keeping all in order, all under control. The academic focus of proper attire. She looks in the mirror again, wincing at her weary eyes. Try as she might, this evening her most familiar escapes last but scant minutes. Her mind wanders, and her heart that never pays attention much to focus follows or finds its own path. How life could have been, if only Sas had come talk to her at that party. If only she had seen him first, she knows she would have talked to him. If only, she sighs.

She leans into the mirror again, touching at her eyes. She has been tossing and turning, getting minimum sleep, almost thinking of calling in sick for a shift. She knows she has to be alert as a pilot, attentively alert. She must have the self-discipline to ensure that she is okay to fly. She looks deep into her own eyes one more time and decides, yes; she'll fly tonight at least. She takes a deep breath, letting it out slowly and carefully closes up her bag.

Try gratitude, she tells herself, that attitude of gratitude through which one can change frame of mind with willpower and a little effort. How grateful she should be for what she has. One of the few at her age to be working, and in her case, at a professional job she finds quite fulfilling. In an economic situation where that is now so rare. And that work allows her to live in one of the now so small middle class areas of the city, which the majority would see as a move up if they could attain her lifestyle. Her mother had not had what she has, she is socially mobile in an upward direction, a rare situation she has been told so many times by Joshua. So if she were grateful, and wanting to be of use, should she be helping Josh and his on-the-ground team or focus more on her UPAS work, or what? She knows what Josh is doing fits with their mother's wishes, and in her heart, she knows that she has to do a little extra. So if she has so much, what then? What can she actually do in a world so unfair? What can she do…that would truly feel right? Gotta be something to make things fairer, if not for her life, then maybe for others. On the job or associated.

She positions her hat, with the official tilt to the left side, and she can't help thinking how they played the game of lady and knight, how she and Sas caught each other's eye at times the second summer. Now he is off to defend her honor, but ohmygod, what could that mean? The reality is, he won't be off to slay a dragon, but what will the reality be? She shakes her head as she steps out the door of the women officers' dressing room and walks down the hallway to her launch bay—happily ever after is such a far-flung dream. But if Sas has set off on a metaphoric dragon slaying, maybe she can do some honorable deed as well. To create that happy village or as close as possible. In reality.

Stepping through the door to her launch bay, she pops the helihover hatch, and sensing a new peace in the routine, climbs down into the Firefly and straps into the familiar flight seat. Switching on ground contact, checking controls, she feels an inner relief as she releases into the fresh evening air. She smiles remembering Martine is on ground again—and she's flying truly free, in body and spirit. Activity register has her assigned to first patrol the four in place pillar stations, a route becoming routine as a surveillance check. After comes a new route surveying the substations still being installed between the pillars.

She flies the wall, weaving back and forth, getting a feel for the sway, and a sense of euphoric play for a minute. In and out of

Citadel Hill and the communities surrounding, watching her screen and the crime stats switching high to none and back again. She glares at them, wrinkling her nose. *Not fair.* After a full circuit, circling each pillar, she slows to hover at the substation being erected. Selecting a hover position, she lines up the visual and infrared videos, leaving one record setting on for now. Several yellow blips show on the infrared screen moving in slow motion around the substation—those must be the workers. All as it should be. She can even make out worker movement on the visual screen if she looks close.

"So we secure the work on this station, right Martine?"

"Roger that," Martine says. "That's what I'm told, girl."

"And we know what they are building, right?"

"Yes ma'am."

Jeira settles into her reports activity for the evening. Peace has almost returned, and she hums as she focuses on work details. As she brings up her shift report, out of the corner of her eye, she sees two extra yellow blips enter the screen. Pedestrians outside the wall, should be nothing, she focuses again. But something catches her thoughts about the way they moved. She turns her eyes back to watch the blips approach the substation workers. They don't walk like regular down the street, instead moving in spurts, as if from behind one building to the next.

"You see what I am seeing Martine?"

"What? Oh yeah, Jeira, hmmm."

Her full attention turns to them. They reach the last building where they can remain concealed. Then, they both spring out in full view of the workers and move no further. Their icons remain stationary for a moment, as if they're standing there, doing something yet nothing appears to change.

"See that Martine?"

"You know girl, maybe. Maybe not."

Then it is the workers who begin to move. Fast, scrambling, rapidly in the direction away from the substation. Like Parade Day all over. "I can't believe this," Jeira says under her breath. "That has to be them again." The two extra yellow blips turn back and move rapidly away from the substation straight down an alley. Follow them—call in a ground unit goes through her head. Unless they enter a building of course, then they would not be visible. If they had been inside buildings all the time, they would not have been visible at all.

She reaches out to control screen, hesitates, then switches off her one camera feed to ground.

"Martine. Maybe not?"

"I don't see anything at all."

"Me neither. I believe we may have some kind of a visual malfunction. I'll have to log that."

As Jeira turns back to her screen reports, she adds to her task list a note at the bottom that she will need to call in an onboard system malfunction report when she gets time to fill it out. Tonight, if possible, but who knows what other assignments might come up. As she calmly enters data, her mind wanders again and she wonders where Josh is tonight. She'll have to remember to call him after shift in the morning.

Chapter 24

Tuesday Evening, July 10

Josh steps over a stack of pizza boxes, edging sideways behind them over to the window to peer out. His eyes follow the steep slope skyward to meet the mega-houses lined up along the ridge top. Who can a person trust? Oneself even? The first call he got on the way over was Lana, and they talked about people and trust and about shela. But if everyone makes up part of shela, and shela had been tainted, then what? And then the second call. *Disgusting display*...he glances over at Cauz's back now turned towards him...*unnecessary wealth. Such a primal ring that sounds.* He feels his hand bump into cold steel, and his finger carefully tracing out the trigger guard of the SMAW. He looks across at the lineup of rocket children and their attendant paint can beside, waiting for any child's possible re-christening. The LC screen hanging up on the wall now speaks out FFM's latest Golden Glow; then rolls over to a regular broadcast.

He jerks his finger away.

Cauz turns back from the door, a fresh pizza and super size bottle of Fizz in hand. He gently pushes the pizza box across the table, displacing the last one that tumbles off the other edge into the disposal heap on the floor, set to be carefully stacked. He pulls the lid up to grab a slice and expertly thumbs the pop-top release on the Fizz. As he pours himself a glass, he gives Josh a sideways look, and at Josh's slight nod, fills a second.

"You don't mind if I have a chair?" Josh moves towards one of the empty seats at the table. "You not gonna sit to eat?"

He can feel one of Cauz's glares burning holes through him for a second.

"How'd you get to be so pissed, Cauz?" Josh asks, sipping his Fizz. "Like where'd it all come from?" He reaches for a Tofurroni slice himself.

"Family," Cauz replies between caustic bites. "My dear mother was a lost cause. First and most important; she never heard a word I said. No matter how many times I told her, she didn't hear me. And a hundred other things she never noticed."

"What were you telling her?" Josh asks, intrigued. "That she didn't hear."

"The truth, man, just the plain honest truth. What comes out of any child. Take this one gripe she had, all she ever talked about was how the Joshmans were better off than us and the Christoffs were worst off. So I'd say why don't we go help out the Christoffs. That would be an improvement, mother. She couldn't grasp the concept. She didn't hear me at all. All she wanted to do was catch up with the Joshmans." Cauz snorts. "I mean look around you, you see it. She couldn't, she wouldn't, I dunno. She's just like most people, blind to reality, and it just pisses me off. So in symbolic protest, I now dine on my feet."

"What's table etiquette got to do with the truth?"

"At the table, she demanded supreme commander status right from the start. I learned to keep my eyes down, my chin in. I had a state of respect beaten into me before I could talk. Don't cry. Don't be angry. Stuff those tears and rage. Smile when I tell you to. When I learned a few words and questioned procedure, I had it verbally drilled into my head it was that way because *she said so*. Eating at the table was my first tour of duty. Now I eat standing, or sitting here or there, anywhere but at the table. Now when I let my rage out, I decide in what direction. And you know what, it's very freeing. Kinda like back when you could still get on a commercial airliner and fly away to some far off place."

"Right—I was luckier I guess." Josh looks at him. "So you have trouble with shela being female."

"Don't trust women. Not one bit."

"She's the true feminine in all people. Their good sides combined; their spirit—the anima in boys. Everyone has some good in them. You had a pretty good idea there, to help out the Christoffs, you know, that kind of stuff. And your mom, despite all her shortcomings, maybe the discipline you learned from her is useful now. If we combine all that good, then we have our shela. We have to respect her, 'cause she's our conscience all in one. I try to believe she knows better than my own unexpressed rage. Which believe you me I certainly do have."

"Respect. Oh, yeah, respect. Conform, or else. I slid into the Marines just fine, at first." Cauz gulps down his Fizz. "Short time later, I wasn't sitting at their mess hall table any more either. When I bust free of them, I bust free of *her* too. Discipline, huh."

"I know what that's like, I mean breaking free of the Forces. I was an Air Force Joe for just under a year. Served a purpose, though. Helped me learn about the opposite of what I believe in. Maybe your family background is serving a purpose here too. Maybe that rage energy keeps driving you when you look up the ridge."

"Passive aggressive," Cauz says. "That's my psych profile in two words."

"I know what you mean there." Josh brings one hand to this chest and the other clenches into a fist. "I can't do anything except store up this rage. On the inside. Maybe like you say, I just gotta point it the right direction when it comes out."

"It's all dysfunctional," Cauz says. "Families. The military. People on the streets."

"Yeah, people piss me off too. What they do, what they don't do." Josh looks at the bright lights of the houses up above. "And then there's these guys right in front of us, the *toorich*."

"Yes sir, dude." Cauz squints up at his long time targets. "They are the ones who deserve to be raged at the most. They want to have the world running their way because *they say so*." He sneers. "Well, I say no, not any longer."

"Did you slip by shela somehow Cauz?"

"Did you sneak in around shela somehow Josh?"

Josh smiles at first, and then shivers inside as his smile fades. "I don't know any more. I know a part of me is so pissed I want to pick up your little rocket launcher right now. I want to see blood, dripping down from that ridge. Knomley type blood. Then this other part of me holds that anger back. Like it always has. Says it's not right. Like shela says. She says violence is not the way. But that pissed part of me just doesn't give a rat's ass. Justice would be served with the pull of one trigger." Josh looks down at his fists, pleading to them softly.

"Brother!" Cauz picks up the SMAW, grinning Josh's way. "I'll give you a how-to demo, no problem. Look, you set it on your shoulder like this, just put this brace here in front to take the kickback," He holds the weapon out to Josh. "Here, give it a try."

Josh squints side to side into Cauz's eyes. Raising one trembling hand, palm facing out towards Cauz, he barely shakes his head and sits down, looking away. He rocks up on the back two legs of his chair. Staring out the window, he picks up his glass, and lets the cooling Fizz release their claimed bubbles of ecstasy on their slow way down his throat. Ecstasy, so the Fizz ads say. Doesn't feel all that ecstatic. The world holds such a glut of mistruths.

"So what actually is the truth, Cauz?" He asks softly.

Cauz has gently returned the SMAW to its place on the table. He wipes off his hands with WipyClean tissues, throwing them onto a refuse can up against the wall. He picks up his dried up apple, closely examining its mummified shiny skin as he rotates it in one hand. "Newton found truth in an apple. Gravity pulls the apple down, straight and true each and every time. My straight and true comes from my insides." Cauz taps the centre of his chest. "My conscience. Most truth sits hidden pretty deep. My dear mother had hers buried super deep, surrounded by so many walls..." He scowls, then grins. "But hey, when it comes to walls, you can blast your way through." He picks up the SMAW again, carefully raising it to one shoulder and lining his eye up with the scope. "Basic crosshairs. Watch. Here's the safety-lock and release. Push it forward, that's release." He clicks the slide-latch ahead. "When you have a child loaded, and those crosshairs lined up, you just squeeeeze the trigger like any standard issue firearm." He breathes out an aura of peace as he speaks. Josh watches out of the corner of his eye. "These aren't any high tech heat-seekers or nothing. The child launches straight where you point her. Taking down those disgusting displays that should never have been built. Now, for me, that is an apple that falls pretty straight and true. A fulfillment of the truth."

Josh looks at him, taking a deep breath. "I'm gonna tell you one truth, Cauz. I got two calls on my way here. I talked with a woman I'm getting to know. That was fine. But you remember the first meeting with shela, how she said she was gonna do some spot checks?"

Cauz shrugs, looking off to the side.

"Well, I walked over here pretty sure of what I was gonna talk to you about and then shela gives me a spot check call on the way over. Asked for a full reverse feed through my tc."

Cauz looks directly at him now, his eyes questioning.

"I thought about what I know, what I don't, what I suspect." He looks directly back. "I did a quick internal risk assessment. My own intentions might be okay, but my insides are a jumble at any given moment. That's the honest truth. I might be in the same situation and do the opposite, depending on how I'm feeling at that particular time. Like maybe really pissed. I could have just hit the off switch on my tc and maybe I should have. Maybe I should right now." He looks long and hard at Cauz. After a moment he goes on. "Anyway, I decided to let her have it all. She's got an updated profile on me now and I don't know if that was the best thing to do." He taps the centre of his chest as Cauz had. "But I think so."

Cauz's look holds solid, unwavering.

Josh glances away, over at the LC screen, feeling his eyes suddenly drooping, his attention growing fuzzy. "Eleven hours and thirteen minutes."

"Yeeup! That is how much time they got. Officially."

Josh rubs his eyes, struggling to keep his attention in focus. "I tell you what, Cauz, I will make a deal with you."

"Yeah, what?"

Josh pulls his tc from his pocket and puts it in front of him on the table. He looks at Cauz, picks it up and holds it out, finger on the master power switch. He clicks it to off.

"I am now incommunicado, out of the picture, not a thing I can do for or against shela. I want you to confirm absolutely you are doing the same."

Cauz looks at Josh, one eyebrow raised ever so slightly.

"These morons got eleven hours and," he squints at the screen, "twelve minutes."

"You committed to that? Absolutely, no question? Until tomorrow?"

"Soldier's honor." Cauz raises one hand in a salute. "Commitment confirmed."

Josh looks straight at his host. "Look Cauz, I'm fading fast but I usually wake up with a clear head. Those pizza boxes are starting to look comfortable. You don't mind if I catch some shut-eye?"

"You go ahead, partner." Cauz shrugs, waving his finger out the window, "I'll stand watch tonight."

"Watch only?"

"Watch only."

Josh picks a place, sliding thin cardboard boxes into a line for a mattress with extras in a pillow pile. Propaganda, cultural tradition, political lies. He needs sleep more than anything. He nods off, seeking answers in the depths of the universe.

Chapter 25

Tuesday Evening, July 10

"After you babe."

The dog whines, looking up hopefully. But it's Xia who steps smiling brightly through the door and lightly down the first step. Krino follows and then Zaca trails in behind, tail drooping.

"You listen, Kri, level 4 have major influence on situation," Xia says. "Much variation from historical virus that systematically destroy functionality. Instead, level 4 systematically make change in desired outcome. Not destroy but modify. Very difficult to detect."

Man and dog follow the woman down the stairs.

"Hey Xi, what you say is kinda like what we are doin' here," Krino says. "We are systematically bringin' change to the attitude of the *toorich*. Not even biological any more. We're stepping into the cultural."

"Level 5 maybe." Xia's smile widens. "Past biological. Past digital."

"When we become totally one." Krino touches her lightly on the back as they reach the bottom of the stairs. The tunnel entrance looms open and they move towards it.

Xia drops to a whisper. "Maybe."

They walk across the open area to step into the tunnel, now well organized with pipeworm cases neatly stacked in a pile and the polymer barrel rolled over into a corner beside the table of remotes. The smell of wet earth and traces of mechanical oil linger in the air.

"Hey guys. I heard you coming in." Jojo looks up from the floor in front of the table. He lies on a pile of pipeworm cases softened by a thin mattress, hands folded behind his head. "What's happening?"

Krino and Xia look at each other.

"We have us some concerns about Josh," Krino says. "I just tried to call him and a couple times before that tonight. The man shows no response like his tc got shut down. It is after midnight now, so we gettin' pretty close to the end of our count down."

Jojo's eyes narrow. "He's still checking out Cauz?" He tosses his blanket off, rolling over on his side to push himself up to sit.

"That would be one good assumption," says Krino. "Last time my tc had a transmission of his tc's coordinates, Cauz's was the place."

Jojo comes to his feet now. Living on site as both security man and working on details of the pipeworm option, he has spent time making his underground life a little more comfortable. A small water line now runs from the large excavated one to an access tap—with two leads splitting off to a makeshift shower stall in the back and a drinking water tap next to his mattress. A cooler also sits beside the bed and a refuse barrel stands across the cavern with the remains of meals mixed in with construction debris.

"You know, I was just lying here thinking about that guy named Cauz. He is certainly a wild card in our operation." Jojo walks over to the pipeline schematics hanging on the wall. "This is how our underground situation looks now. We are in position and ready to advance." He points to the color sticky-tags on the drawings. "We've got PVC melt loaded as a backup option in half a dozen worms. That's officially now our pipeworm Plan B. We can melt down their pipes if we can't release any more flower juice to surface. Those are the ones marked red, they carry both PVC melt and flower juice."

He walks back to the other two. "But we can't stop someone like Cauz from doing something crazy. I mean really, how do you actually get through to or change the actions of someone like that?" Jojo shrugs.

"Complex virus," says Xia. "Build intelligence. Level 4 minimum."

"What?"

"We been talking over the field of digital viruses," Krino says. "The latest intelligent versions may not be *viruses* any more—what are they called now Xi—*persistent outcome influences, POIs*. They can be used to influence biology or even culture—like us. They persistently attempt to influence an outcome."

"Well hey I've been thinking." Jojo looks directly at both of them. "I don't know how intelligent this is but maybe we should do something kind of crazy too." He walks over to the table, looking over the array of neatly arranged worm controls.

"Like what you thinkin'?" Krino asks.

"Like strike early," Jojo says, looking up. "One thing out of that would be to show Cauz some results. To give him good reason to hold back on his insane plan and hope he sees it's the plan that's insane and not him."

Krino looks to Xia. "This guy is designing Level 4. Or what?" He then scratches Zaca behind the ear. She whines softly. "But that would be banging up against the shela-design ourselves," he says softly.

"Or helping her plan out in the broader sense." Jojo fingers one of the remotes. "Which should be our only intent."

Krino pulls his tc, flipping out small screen. A soft beep sounds as he touches a contact. "Josh still not responding. At all."

"Okay, listen to this. I am responsible for having the pipeworm delivery option in place. That means it has to be functional. Now, to ensure functionality, I should be running field tests." Jojo looks at the other two. "On this liquid release and the PVC pipe melt. I mean, look what happened at the parade. We have to run a test and run it now. To ensure a failsafe system when we really need it."

"Debug beta version," Xia says. "Always necessary."

All three look directly at each other.

Krino shakes his head slightly, a shimmer of doubt shining in his eyes. "Test it how?" His eyes shift back and forth.

"I've been analyzing that. Let me show you." Jojo moves back to the pipeline drawings. "You see for example where these residence lines T into their main street lines? Those are where the fluid flows out of the houses along this part of this ridge. Now that would be directly above Cauz, the one's he's got to be looking at. Within those blocks of houses, there are three that place in the top twenty according to the Golden Glow. Cauz has to be following Golden Glow, so if I were him, I would be targeting those three first. So he's gotta notice if there's any change at all in the status of those three households."

"What is test?" Xia asks. "What are indicators of success?"

"Well, for these three cases I'd say we give 'em both barrels. First, we advance the worms from the street lines past each T and come up the line right into each house. Then we move the worms right up below the main ensuite bathrooms. This time of night may involve some visits to the facilities, so if we're lucky we might catch one of them sitting right on the john. We push our worm blow line through and squirt our loads of liquid straight up their butts if they're there. We hope to interrupt their thoughts at the most delicate of moments."

"Yo." Krino nods. "Yes sir, that would be just fine."

"Or if no one's on the pot, we will basically be fumigating their houses starting with the master bedrooms. Then, on the way back out, still under each house, we dump a load of PVC melt behind the worm and get it back out past the T into the main street lines. The residential lines right below each house will develop major leak problems in a very short time so even if they were on the john and they flushed several times, our flower power juice is not going to leave their property. Not for quite some time. Neither will any of their own shittyness." Jojo looks at Xia. "So indications of success, are that we have released all fluids. We should be able to retrieve our worms with no issues. And we should've caught their attention. Really caught it. In the longer term, or the shorter the better for them, we measure success on how they respond, like what shows up in Golden Glow. Like I said, Cauz has to be monitoring Golden Glow."

"We are tryin' to educate them," Krino says. "About themselves."

"Make change in desired outcome," Xia says. "Modify, but not destroy."

"You're right, Xi'." Krino nods. "Make influence."

"Along with all that, I know, I know, that is our plan," Jojo says, nodding his head. "But from what I can tell about Cauz's intentions for them, we would actually be doing them a favor. A big favor."

"When would we be ready, Jojo?"

"It would just take me a few minutes to move the worms into the appropriate main street lines and then past each of those T's. Then I program the sequence of events for each one and, well, they're set to activate under one command. So, not long."

The stare at each other. "Just let me try call my man Joshua one more time," Krino says. "While you set this up."

Chapter 26

Wednesday Morning, July 11

"Hey bud, Josh. Wake it up. Check this out."

"Uhh. Wha…what? Strength, honor…hey, did we find the truth?"

"I dunno about the whole truth so help me God, but there's somethin' going on. One thing's true for sure, there's one less Knomley kicking around now. Other one's still on the list…check it out."

Josh rolls off his pizza box bed, banging down on the floor. He's struck by the bright light of morning and the now blaring FFM broadcast filling the room. Stumbling to his feet, he fumbles his way back into the chair he had rocking the night before. Cauz gnaws at a piece of cold pizza, eyes glued to the wall-hung screen.

"Jesus, will you look at that. We gotta rename some of the children now, three no question. My three prime targets on the ridge. Looks like even Mr. P. W. Knomley might be slipping down on the high priority list. Still, can't let him off the hook."

Josh focuses on the screen. As his mind clears, he can feel his finger tracing a path to his tc, that power switch connection with his world. The Golden Glow, no longer a background weather-type report, blares out this morning as a front page news item. A live broadcast commentator remarks in detail on recent abrupt changes, pointing out sharp upward trends in contributions to Daring causes.

"Great, I mean, that is fantastic." Josh smiles, still muzzy. "And what did you say, Knomley's slipping down, one less?"

"Down completely." Cauz grins like a child. "All gone from this world. Not Mr. Patrick Knomley. Another Knomley."

"What do you mean?"

"Watch this."

The commentator switches to anchor desk. "In what may be a coincidental correlation of events, those same three prominent family estates now making major contributions to Daring causes have had a breakdown in their sanitary systems early this morning," the news anchor reports. "City sanitary repair crews have been called in. People in the area are reporting the same strong odor noticed at the recent Parade."

"I won't complain," Cauz says. "Just have to paint new names on three of the children. Did lose the easiest targets though."

"Knomley's house isn't on the ridge, right?"

"Nope, neither, that's part of the other story. For Patrick, it's the good old response you get when you point a gun to a person's head. Immediate attention, okay, sort of delayed and still talking back." Cauz lifts his hands above his head, dancing a little jig. "Good work Mrs. SMAW, way to go kids, we got us some response."

"Neither, Cauz? What exactly are you talking about?"

"Just keep watching; they'll show it again. Who is Paul Knomley anyway?"

"That's Knomley's oldest son, Sas's brother I just found out. Now I hear he avoids the public eye like the plague. We think he was in the back of the Patriot and never got out when the citymen were pissing all over the Knomley Limo. Shela's video clip."

"Got no child for him," Cauz says. "Never knew about him."

"I heard his holdings are split up into numbered companies," Josh says. "So they have trouble tracking him in the Golden Glow too."

FFM switches to Citadel Hill news with repeat clips from cameras pointing at a large iron gate, the entrance drive of a house. A paramedic team there carries a covered stretcher out.

"Listen to this," Cauz says.

"Again, early this morning the body of Mr. Paul Knomley now know to be heir apparent to the majority share of KnomCor, was found in his home. Foul play is strongly suspected as police continue their investigation. This is quite an unexpected event in a neighborhood with a historically low crime rate."

"So Paul Knomley is dead?"

"One less."

"And we're not looking at his house from here," Josh says. "What about Knomley senior?"

"We got a second line child here with his name on it. Like father like son they both live less exposed back from the ridgeline. It's one of those lob shots—you set the SMAW sights a little different for them." Cauz picks up the SMAW from the table, walking over to the window. "Golden Glow shows he's gone maybe halfway but he still hasn't paid up in full." He looks through the sights. "He'd make a great better-shape-up icon. Lob shots are a little less accurate, but hey, no big problem."

"Sas," Josh whispers, puzzle pieces sorting in his head. *Had he decided to be his brother's keeper? To make personal sacrifice for the greater good.* These are no longer medieval times. "What's your plan Cauz? You would kill for the greater cause—what you actually believe in, right? But what if you spend the rest of your life hunted, or waiting in execution line?"

"That would not be my plan." Cauz looks across his array of weapons, prying open a can of paint. He checks the time. "The rest on the list still have two hours and…seventeen minutes."

Josh needs something better, and he thinks hard staring at Cauz. "Look, I gotta connect, there's too much happening." He pulls his tc and, holding it high for Cauz to see, switches the master power back on. He watches Cauz's face, then the screen, picking Krino's contact.

Cauz looks back, scowling, but then he shrugs. "Fine, forget the two hour and whatever wait." He picks up the SMAW and the child marked with Knomley's name.

"Hey Krino." Josh listens. "I needed to sleep, bud…you what?" Josh looks at Cauz. "Well he's lining up on three alternatives right now. He says he can hit houses back of the ridge too. Knomley senior's still on his list. Tell me everything you guys did." He listens, and then replaces his tc.

"Shit."

Krino and Jojo have modified their plans, and now all plans are up in the air. *Sas, man if he did what he might have. God!* His fists clench and relax. Can one kill in a righteous fashion? Honorable execution?

He looks at Cauz.

What would shela say? Would the calm of the others smooth out and neutralize the kill anger he feels, that Cauz feels? So shela would be balanced.

"So Cauz, if Mr. P. W. Knomley *is* finally making some real change," Josh says. "Maybe he's finally had enough combat. One son's deserted, moved down here and now his other son's a casualty. He's not gonna be having a great day."

"Yeah, he's shifting in the GG report but not enough…he's been informed and had his chances." Cauz slides the glass panel of the window opened and smashes the insect netting out of the way. "Those other three saw it our way—they fit our *requests*. Like I said, we still got a child with P. W.'s name and now's the time for a visit."

Josh's got to make his own change of plan. He could throw it all in with Cauz, no, can't do that. He has to do some version of Eli's righteous. Sas, up on the Hill, where would he be? At his father's place faking it to look like he wasn't at Paul's, an alibi, or more likely trying to guide his father on his bottom of the Hill dreams. The cardboard box single mother. That's where he'd be…at the house on Cauz's target list.

"Your mother, Cauz," Josh says loud. "Besides her, what pisses you off the most?"

"People." Cauz glares, putting it bluntly.

"Which people?"

"There's the ones who take advantage and even sometimes the ones who let themselves be taken advantage of. That's covers pretty well everyone."

"Still pretty vague." Josh stalls.

"They all piss me off." Cauz makes final adjustments to the settings on the SMAW.

"Think though, who you gonna take out, and who you gonna keep? You have to leave someone in the end. So you figure you got the ones who take advantage in your sites right now."

"Yup…they piss me off the most." Cauz positions himself with a view through the broken screen, raising the SMAW to his shoulder and lining his eye up with the sights. "They're the ones with the power to make change. They've got the attitude problem.

I'm gonna help them wake up and smell the coffee. We keep the righteous, the cooperators, the ones who seek the truth."

"Which truth Cauz, look, I know my friend Sas is still up there on the Hill right now," Josh speaks at a quick chatter pace. "His real name would be Staphan Knomley, that's Paul's brother. He's gotta be the one who influenced his father Mr. Patrick Knomley. And I'm telling you the straight and true flat out honest so-help-me-God truth. He's never taken advantage and now I know it's him that's kept his brother Paul from ever doing so again. He's brought about change, *your way*, and now he's up there. He's on our side Cauz. You release that child…we'd be taking out one of our own."

Cauz glares at Josh, face twitching. His finger pressure on the trigger grip eases, and the SMAW droops ever so slightly from his shoulder.

Chapter 27

Wednesday Morning, July 11

The rapid staccato banging on the door sounds excited.

Then again.

Cauz rises from his slump in a chair, setting the SMAW gently back down in its place on the table and then the now unloaded P. W. child. He reaches his arms towards the ceiling in what turns into a full body stretch, before pulling his sidearm and walking over to twist the doorknob. The apartment door rattle snaps at the end of its chain. Looking through the gap, his face forms into a grin as he kicks the door forward and pulls the chain latch from its sliding bracket to swing the door wide. Ed enters as if walking through the cloud entrance to heaven. "Hello my fine people—and can I ask, how are you gentlemen this morning? Deee...lirious." Another young fellow follows close on his heels with not quite so chipper a step.

Josh turns to look at them and his eyes widen a little. "What's that you've got there? And just what have you guys been up to?"

"Pneumatic special issues, you might remember." Ed holds up a green plastic handgun between finger and thumb. "Allocated to us by our common acquaintance Jojo. Similar in a way to the glass-smashers we utilized in a Blades versus the Gulch Boys confrontation. You were on that one Karmen." He turns to his companion who nods. "We invaded their turf with super slings loaded with ball bearings. Smashed a considerable number of windows out, which was simply a distraction tactic. Same idea here, Jojo said, keeps them scrambling around and distracted."

"So you boys have been out on a mission." Cauz says, walking over to shake hands. "You been up the ridge?"

"Hello sir," Ed says. "That is quite an accurate assumption. By the way, Karmen here was Blades. But like Josh said, anyone can change their mind at any time no matter how committed they were. Now he's with us."

Cauz's face twitches.

"*Ciao.*" Karmen raises a hand.

"Yes sir, we approached the wall quite closely last night," Ed nods. He grabs a slice of pizza, looks at Cauz for approval and passes it over to Karmen. He picks up another for himself. "We delivered that less than sweet aroma of our oh-so-special flowers to a couple Plexon-Bubble circuit crews. The flowers in their dreams will be nightmarish for some time into the future. UPAS was up in the air, but we finished our mission without a care." He spins himself in a circle.

"So you guys went on kind of an independent mission," Josh's jaw hangs slightly. "Or did shela send you?"

"Shela sent us if shela voices her direction through others in her organization," Ed says between bites. "And perhaps by pointing us more closely to of our own consciences. That would be shela too, would it not?"

"Well our efforts are supposed to be coordinated," Josh says. "But it's almost like everyone has their own timetable. Or has shela got more things going than any one group of us knows about?"

"More and more are joining us, sir," Ed says. "So that factor alone would entail added difficulties on maintaining a precisely coordinated schedule." He grins. "When there are enough of us on side, then circumstances will simple shift before our very eyes. Whatever the time table."

"Like critical mass," Josh says softly. "And what comes after…"

"Our own conscience, now that makes a whole lot of sense." Cauz joins in. "Mine tells me if I could just get close enough to Knomley P. Mister." He brandishes his pistol. "Or any one of those top list guys, well then there'd be some straight talking one conscience face to another. I could see an abrupt about face happening. Or else. A couple short ones behind the ear would put an end to all our troubles."

Josh looks directly at Cauz.

"Like El Salvador years ago or any of a hundred other places," Josh says. "Salvo tells us over and over there was always a replacement for who gets it behind the ear." He then emphasizes his point. "And for the real cause, nothing changes."

"Well, be that as it may," Cauz looks back at him. "The only way I can get close would be on the wings of one of SMAW's children. No other way we're in range—and that'd be a quick one way visit."

"Collateral damage, Cauz," Josh says. "Friendly fire casualties."

"You might consider loading your children with liquid, sir," Ed says. "Allow the toddlers to in a way urinate on the doorstep of someone like Mr. P. W. Knomley."

"Yeah," Cauz says, kind of hearing. "An Ex-Blade would say that, huh."

"Hey, check it." Ed points at the screen. "Look, look Karmen, see what I said. Like I informed you, no more FFT. Now it's FFM. Delirious."

"So..." Karmen says. "What you sayin'?"

"Well, what used to be a spotlight on simply the wealthiest of the wealthy has now expanded to include all or quite a few more of the wealthy," Ed says eloquently. "What used to be a narrow beam of light focused on the core of the issue has broadened over a much wider scope. The upper middle class we have today, in socioeconomic terms, has now joined the upper class. The Fortune Five outlook has expanded their view."

A female voice adds sex appeal as the new station logo dances across the screen, a stylized M for million replacing the old T for thousand. "We bring you the top of the hour updates through the new voice of Fortune Five Million."

"Yeah, okay," says Karmen. "Wild."

The commentator takes over. "Thank you Shiva. Now with continued news coverage: this hour we highlight another disruption with Citadel Plexon-Bubble crews…"

"That's gotta be us," Ed dances lightly around Karmen, punching him repeatedly in the shoulder.

"...an update on the radically changing Golden Glow standings, but first more on the mysterious death of Paul Knomley."

"In the top story of the hour, Urban Police now believe they have found the weapon used in the homicide of Mr. Knomley's eldest son Paul Knomley. Mr. Knomley Junior's death appears to have been carried out in what can now be described by the crime scene investigators using a new term. A *ritualistic act*, which some experts now suggest to be associated with one of the city's underground cults...

"What is this ritual thing?" Josh says. "Like what was the weapon?"

"Definitely not a whip wire they said," Cauz informs. "Some kind of knife. A long thin blade—he was stabbed deep and only once. Maybe one of those extendo-bayonets."

Josh feels a shiver run full length up and down his spine. Could Paul have been actually run through with...a sword? Like they played out all those years ago down by the river—crotch to eyeball. The act of honorable execution reserved in medieval times for those who could not grasp honor. Like putting a modern child-biting dog to sleep with a needle.

"...and our next story, whether by coincidence or not, Mr. Patrick W. Knomley has become the latest leader in the developing contest for the Golden Glow award. Analysts speculate on cause and effect, while the FFM top hundred fortunes register appear to be jostling for position in a heated race for top contributor. A new definition of success cultural experts suggest."

"Holy crap," Josh turns to Cauz. "Looks like Mr. P. W. Knomley has become a very generous man."

"...and at 3:15 AM, crews working around the clock to install the Plexon-Bubble substations were sprayed with a liquid similar in smell to the Parade last Saturday. Foremen estimate a minimum of twenty four hours before crews can begin work again."

"Success!" Ed staccatos his feet in a tight circle.

Cauz stares at the flickering numbers changing statuses in the Golden Glow report. He glares at his three just renamed rocket children. Scowling, he throws the paintbrush against the wall.

"How do you stick to any attack plan? I don't even have locations on those next houses on the list."

"Right." Josh has the strangest feeling that something else has shifted, gone missing, something personal. Like he's lost a lifetime companion. He can't put his finger on it...he feels so relaxed, mystically at peace. His hands—could it be? He carefully raises his fingers up before his eyes, wiggling them and flipping his hands in and out, staring. Strangely tranquil, he drops his arms to his sides. He flexes his hands, bunching them into fists, but the fists won't hold.

The fists won't hold!

"Maybe your gun to the head tactic worked, Cauz." Josh speaks in a calm voice that he can hardly recognize as his own. "Or helped anyway."

"Now you say." Cauz glances his way.

"Look at the scoreboard, my friend," Josh says. "The many contribute...meeting our requests." He shrugs, putting one calm hand on Cauz's shoulder. "With things going the way they are now, well Cauz, you could think that maybe we've won."

Cauz ambles away over towards the window, looking out and up. "Whatever." He shakes his head, looking back at Josh, then Ed and then more closely at Karmen. "Yeah, well, could be."

Josh's tc rings. He looks to see Jeira's contact displayed, wondering why she would be calling now. He walks out of Cauz's apartment and down the hall as he answers.

Chapter 28

Wednesday Morning, July 11

"Hey sis. What's up? Where are you?"

"At home Josh. I just came off shift." Jeira has her uniform hung, replaced with casual lounge clothes. Curled up in the corner of the couch, cat purring beside her, she rests as trained to after a nightshift. She shakes her head. "Oh Joshua, what are you guys up to now?"

"Like what?" Josh says.

He meanders down Cauz's building hallway.

"Come on Josh, don't play that innocent act anymore. I know it's you guys. Just like Parade day, that's like what."

"Hey Jeir," Josh says. "Tell me what you can."

"What a bizarre shift tonight Josh," Jeira says." Again. First off, the circuit stations. We were scheduled on a secure with surveillance for a three quarter virtual Plexon-Bubble test at three AM sharp. I had my cameras trained on my assigned station, and I saw something and I just know it's you guys. Because all of a sudden the workmen down there start taking off in all directions. Just like the crowds on Parade day. Now you tell me."

"Would be a second hand story from my end, Jeira," Josh says cautiously. "I could tell you what I know if you actually want. But you know we should keep you free of career damaging knowledge."

Josh leans against the elevator door.

"You are right, we reveal only so much. So I can tell you I have my surveillance cameras recording, but then my entire recording system malfunctions. Like as if someone shut it off...can you believe it? Which means, Josh, that there is no record of what I saw—that's what happened officially."

"I hear you, Jeira," Josh says. "Cool."

"And then Martine tells me the virtual Plexon-Bubble test never happened at all."

"Very interesting as well. We keep our language selective, as always, right?"

"Yes brother," Jeira sighs. "That we do."

"Look, another thing then, have you heard about Paul Knomley? They're showing it all over on FFT."

Jeira uncurls herself, stretching her legs out until she's sitting on the edge of the couch. She brings her fingers to her mouth, heart pounding.

"Hold on a minute." She controls the tone of her voice. "View on." She keeps it up, taking on a work voice speaking to her UPAS screen. "Yes Josh, that name came out in a homicide report late last night." Her heart races, and her hand drops to her throat, but she holds the tone. "Martine couldn't believe that one—that kind of V code never occurs on the Hill."

"Paul Knomley was Sas' brother," Josh says. "We never met him."

"Oh..." She shivers head to toe. Forcing her voice steady, she speaks surprised. "Really?"

"Lana says that'll be significant."

"Who's Lana?"

"A teacher...a woman." Josh hesitates. "Hey, how about the Golden Glow, Jeira, have you seen that today? It's working sister! We're getting back what Asha gave us. Mom would be so happy."

"Okay, I'm looking at Golden Glow now." Jeira switches screens. "Is that the Mr. Patrick Knomley of KnomCor? Wow, is he ever making an adjustment. So you say Paul Knomley was his son—could he be reacting?" She takes a deep breath and speaks in a softer voice. "Or is it you guys and your stink bomb campaign…"

"We don't exactly know either, Jeir. But check out the report—it's not just him. The *toorich* are almost all shifting, like wealth has a new meaning. What Asha talked about all those years back."

"President Asha," Jeira says under her breath.

"Anyway I can tell you a little more about Knomley Senior situation from this end," Josh says. "He might be having a bad day in a way, but his future is looking a whole lot brighter. He's no longer in a guy here's sites as a target list; which is to say his chances of survival have improved significantly. Mr. Knomley is now, due to the actions he's taken, much safer than Paul was...you know what I mean."

"Okay okay, Josh, I get it, I get it, don't say any more. It's hard enough playing law enforcer and listening to my brother and his buddies' action plan."

"No, listen Jeira; we have to talk about one more thing. About Paul. I mean, listen, what if it was Sas?"

"Enough already."

"Think about it," Josh says, leaning into his tc. "The code of honor, the oaths we swore to."

Jeira gasps lightly. "I just met up with Sas after shift two nights ago. He did seem disturbed, but…his own brother." She can picture Sas' face leaving the teashop. "Oh God…," she whispers.

"Remember back down by the river. You, me and Sas," Josh says. "You know, when we talked about honorable blade freedom. You're UPAS, I mean check the weapon on the Paul case last night." Josh pauses, then goes on. "Maybe Sas set his brother free. You know, from himself. From his own inability to understand. Paul would never listen, Sas said, not to us, not to Asha, and so...now he doesn't have to."

Silence rings a long hollow over the tc waves.

"Jeira?"

Josh can hear the cat meow in the background. Jeira strokes the cat's head, feeling the warm wetness trickle down her cheeks. "There may have been another reason too Josh. He may have done it for another reason…another type of honor...no more on this Josh."

"I know he liked you a lot…he was too shy to say so."

"Let's just say he set Paul free and maybe he set himself free in another way. Not that it makes any sense…we were just kids back then and there is no room for honor in today's world. Or liking anyone…"

"Maybe there is Jeira. Sas always knew things we didn't. Maybe there is."

"Yes, if only we could all be a little more like him. I wish I could be in a way, sometimes I wish for a lot of things…" Her voice dwindles to a wisp. She wipes her face with a tissue. The moment is broken by the soft trill of a Peruvian Planteater. "God, now what? Hang on Josh. Someone's at the door."

Josh finds a place to sit on the top stair, grabbing the railing. He hears his sister's door opening, a short interchange of voices, and then the door closing.

"You won't believe what that was." Jeira moves back to the televiewer. "I got a bouquet of flowers."

"Really?"

"My neighbor from down the slope across the street. Just a minute, I have to take them outside. God, not that smell again."

"Not us, Jeira, I swear."

She walks back across the room, arm over her nose.

"You know Josh, early this morning I'm on my way back to base cage," Jeira says. "Such a weird thing—the last leg of my patrol route and there's all these people are out everywhere, especially on the East slope. All carrying colorful bundles across the street...yes, like bunches of flowers. All in one direction too, uphill. Almost like a wave, like an ocean wave of bouquets crashing up the side of the Hill. Maybe I'm catching part of that wave."

"Yeah, sister," Josh says, hand slipping loosely from the railing. "Maybe...maybe everyone's getting the message."

"Well, who are the *toorich* anyway? I guess I'm one of them in a way," Jeira says. "I mean there's always someone further up the hill that each of us. And someone else further down too."

"Some say it's always been that way sister," Josh says. "But some of us know it doesn't have to be."

"Maybe if we don't take a look around us," Jeira says "Our neighbors will do the looking for us."

"And be sending us a bouquet," Josh says.

"Look, Josh, I'll call you back," Jeira says. "There's someone I know across the street, just up the hill a bit. I have to go deliver some flowers."

End

Curious about Sas and his brother Paul? Read the short story *Brother's Keeper* in *Climate Spirit* or at Our Near Future website.

65135557R00126

Made in the USA
Charleston, SC
22 December 2016